Show Control

A Mystery

by
Keith Snyder

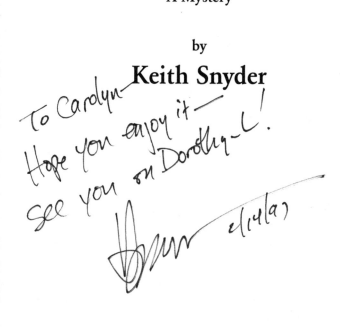

A Write Way Publishing Book

For Kathleen

Write Way Publishing
3806 S. Fraser
Aurora, Colorado 80014

First Edition; 1996

ISBN: 1-885173-11-3

1 2 3 4 5 6 7 8 9 10

Prologue

Freeze.

The woman is motionless bet
ween bright jets of suddenly still flame. He leans closer and notes her position and the time on the frozen clock, glances at the computer screen to verify that its clock reads the same, clicks the mouse, types "end of 4 turns" on the computer keyboard.

Play.
The woman stands for a moment at the front of the stage and then reaches for the collar of her oddly cut costume.
Freeze.
The woman is motionless. He verifies that the clock times are still synchronized, clicks the mouse, types "bitch starts to undress" on the computer keyboard.

Play.
Facing the audience, the woman removes the outer layer of her costume. She now wears only the bottom half of a bikini. A very small black box is clipped to the waistband. Pale pinpoints of light flicker over her bare stomach.
Freeze.
The woman is motionless. He verifies that the clock times are still synchronized, clicks the mouse, types "start of light show—bitch shows tits."
Play.

***
USERNAME: NOTE-ON
PASSWORD: • • • • • • • •
HELLO NOTE-ON
Logon at 16:07:32
You have 1 new mail message.

From: CYBERFINGERS 31-DEC 10:52:47.16
To: NOTE-ON
Subj: gig!
Happy New Year!
I'm doing a run-through of my new thing at the Rust Gar-
den on the fourth. I'm scheduled for ten, so probably ten-
thirty or so. You're on the guest list +1.
Hope to finally meet you.
Roland
-*-

> go forum
MUSE Public Forum
> read new
29805
    RE: News article
    From: MUSE-1   To: ALL
This was on page eight of the L.A. Times today under the
headline, "Performance Artist Dies Onstage."
Pasadena, CA (UPI) - Performance artist Monica Gleason,
27, was pronounced dead on arrival Sunday night after
being fatally wounded by a laser during a performance of
her work, "Light Dance," on the last night of the TechnoArts
conference which is held every December at the Pasadena Convention Center.

Gleason was known in the performance art community for her highly symbolic performance pieces, which incorporated extensive use of electronic synthesizers. An official police spokesman said that suicide is suspected and an investigation is underway.

-*-

29806

　　RE: News article (Re: msg 29805)

　　From: KENQ　　To: MUSE-1

I was at Garrison Sound Labs this morning and some of the techies were trying to figure out what could have gone wrong. She wasn't using anything out of the ordinary, from what they've been able to find out; just a pretty standard stage light setup and some little lasers, all controlled with a Mac.

Did anybody online know Monica Gleason or see the performance?

-*-

29807

　　RE:　News article (Re: msg 29806)

　　From: CYBERFINGERS　To: KENQ

I was at the show and saw the whole thing.. It all happened really quick.. She was at this part in the show where she dances right up close to the laser. She had it hooked up so it homes in on a radio transmitter and she had the transmitter on her so the laser would follow her. Anyway she did this dance where she's got her top off and the laser writes sexual words on her stomach, and she's kind of teasing it, The whole piece was very sexual. Anyway instead of writing words on her, the laser just cuts right through her, and kills her on the spot!. She couldn't get

away from it because of the radio tracking. Pretty awful.
Nobody knew if it was for real at first.

_*_

> bye
NOTE-ON off at 16:04:23
Session time: 2 minutes.
MUSE DISCONNECTED

1

At six-thirty in the morning on January 1, Jason Keltner sat with his friend Paul Reno on the wide, flat-roofed porch of Marengo Manor, the huge, wrecked remains of a turn-of-the-century boarding house, and watched a stream of people and cars flow sluggishly north on Marengo Avenue, toward the Rose Parade route. The locals toted ladders, and people from nearby cities carried collapsed lawn chairs. People from farther than that had arrived on the 31st and hauled Hibachis and mattresses with them. The parade route was on Colorado Boulevard, three short blocks away, and the parade hadn't started yet.

Before Jason lived in the Manor, it had been abandoned, boarded up, de-boarded by industrious high school students, appropriated by homeless people, re-boarded, and finally rented by a bunch of artists, musicians, and college students. Jason had been among the first of the new tenants, and had helped to patch the sagging upstairs ceilings, and hang drywall over the exposed and rotting downstairs timbers, despite a roof that let in water and plumbing that didn't.

The rent was cheap; Jason paid $300 a month for roughly the middle third of the first floor. His friend Robert Goldstein, an actor, rented a drafty upstairs room with no plaster on the east wall for $235.

Behind Paul, through the open front door, two synthesizer keyboards and some smaller rectangular units perched with Jason's little Macintosh computer on a black, L-shaped support system, that loomed like evil Tinkertoys in the corner of the front room. A snaky tangle of colored cables dangled against the wall behind the supports. The open door had a blue bathroom towel pinned up on the inside to block the view from the street. Jason occasionally considered buying mini-blinds, but never got around to it. The back door had an orange towel.

A man humming through a kazoo and wearing cheap, luminous green bracelets, made bug-eyes at them from the sidewalk and went, "googa-googa-googa." Paul bugged his own eyes out, wiggled his fingers in a loose approximation of werewolf claws, and said "heeby-heeby-heeby," in a nasal voice. Paul was built for heebying. He had a malleable face and long, slender limbs.

A yellow Toyota pickup truck with twelve noisy teenagers in the bed, crawled slowly past the Manor in the thick traffic. Six boys in a metallic-blue 1981 Cutlass inched by in the opposite direction and hooted suavely at girls. Some of the girls jeered back at them. Jason angled around to watch additional teenagers pile into the truck bed. The truck looked as though it was on its way to the Puberty Landfill.

Paul stood up and said, "Stuff to do. Happy New Year. Get a haircut, ya goddamn hippie!"

"You're leaving?" said Jason. "Well, happy New Year. Get a job, ya bum."

Paul half-waved and half-saluted, stepped off the porch, and disappeared around a sagging corner of the Manor.

The door behind Jason scraped open and Martin Altamirano came out, yawning. He was short and coffee-colored, with a sleepy expression, and his dark hair shot out in random directions.

He squinted at Jason. "Where's Paul?"

"He had things to do," Jason said.

"Did you guys stay up all night?"

"Yeah."

Behind Martin, the door opened again and Robert Goldstein, six-foot-four and dark-haired, stood in the doorway with three paper-wrapped packages. Robert wiggled his eyebrows meaningfully and said, "Food," in a booming baritone voice.

Martin said, "Gimme." He looked at Jason. "On New Year's morning? Like what kind of things?"

"I don't know," Jason said.

Robert crossed the porch and sat on the edge with his feet down on the dirt where a lawn would have been if the Manor had one. "What do you want," he said. "We have ... lox on a bagel, we have ... pastrami on rye, we have ... lox on a bagel."

"Pastrami," Jason said.

"No, no, I get the pastrami," Martin said. "You can have the raw fish."

"It's not raw fish," Robert said. "It's smoked."

"Oh, smoked fish," Martin said. "Sure. I get the pastrami."

Robert handed out the sandwiches. The tide of parade-goers on the sidewalk swelled and spilled over the curb and into the street, where people in cars honked at it. It had a rhythm.

A middle-aged woman with compressed lips and a green canvas pouch looked at Jason and Robert keenly from the sidewalk, and then crossed the dirt lawn and gave them handbills with "Fugitive Pope" printed on them in bold letters above a grainy picture of the Pope shaking hands with Castro. Jason dropped his on the ground. The woman glared at him.

"I already have that one," he said. Her lips compressed

further and she moved on. Robert tried to fold his handbill into a hat, but couldn't remember how, so he stuffed it into his back pocket. The Fugitive Pope was followed closely by two Secret Vatican Conspiracies and a Save The World's Most Endangered Species: The White Race.

When the actual Rose Parade started on Colorado Boulevard, Jason, Martin, and Robert took their food into the Manor and sat on Jason's sofa, watching the floats and marching bands on TV while a man-and-woman commentator team said stupid things.

Martin got up off the sofa and went toward the back of the Manor. Jason said to Robert, "Is there more coffee?"

"Nope," Robert said. Jason got up and followed Martin into what he called his "pseudo-kitchen."His old green Coleman camp stove sat atop a chipped propane tank between the mini-refrigerator and a cheap dish cabinet that housed the remains of a good set of china. The sleek black Krups coffee and espresso maker sat on the cabinet, next to a rinsed-out tuna can that held matchbooks with colorful restaurant logos on them. There was a real kitchen in the front part of the Manor, but it was out the front door, across the porch, through another door, and across a room, so the tenants almost never used it.

Jason ground four measures of Chocolate Mocha beans in an electric grinder and started coffee brewing. When it began to trickle asthmatically into its pot, he went into the front room. Robert was sitting on a piano bench in front of the compact Macintosh computer that Jason used for music. The Rose Parade was still going on TV, but with the sound off, which made the man-and-woman commentator team seem more intelligent.

The Macintosh screen displayed a fantasy adventure game to which Jason had unthinkingly introduced Robert.

"Did your character get eaten again?" said Jason.

"All my characters get eaten. This one's name is 'Snack.'"

Jason fished in his pocket for a rubber band and pulled his hair back into a ponytail. Robert turned back to the Macintosh, carefully considered his game options, and carefully hit a key. Snack was eaten by a Huge Brown Bat. Robert started another game and named the new character "Morsel."

Jason glanced at the TV screen. The parade was over and the commentators were gone. "Second half's starting," Jason said. Robert got up and they both went out onto the porch, ate more delicatessen food, and watched the ex-parade-goers march south with less energy than they had marched north. Martin came out and joined them.

"Ai shoth—" said Robert thickly. He shook his head and gestured for time out while he swallowed. Then he said, "I thought you had to work today."

"No, yesterday," said Jason. "Month's end."

"What's month's end?"

"Last day of every month I have to read all the big meters so Municipal Water knows how much to charge the cities it supplies water to. Not that they use what I tell them, but I have to do it anyway."

"Why don't they use what you tell them?"

"Because they already know what figures they need to put in their billing."

"Then why do you have to do it anyway?"

"I don't know, Robert," Jason said impatiently. "It's a day job. Day people don't know why they do anything."

"Anybody make resolutions?" Martin asked through his bagel.

"Resolutions?" Robert echoed through his own.

Jason attempted a squinty-eyed bandido. "We dohn need no steenking reso...¿resoluciónes?"

Martin said, "Sounds good to me." When no one answered his question, he said, "So? Anybody make resolutions?"

Robert said, "I resolved to spend more time going on auditions and working on my career."

"That's cool," said Martin. "Jason?"

Jason shook his head. "I don't make resolutions. I figure either you're going to do something or you're not, and talking about it doesn't do much either way."

Robert said, "Do you think Paul makes resolutions?"

"I don't know," said Jason. "I stopped trying to figure him out. Could you pass the cream cheese?"

Robert was staring into space in the general direction of the dead tree in the front yard, so Jason reached past him and took the cream cheese. The other turn-of-the-century houses along Marengo sported big live trees. A big live tree in front of the Manor would have looked like a corsage on a corpse.

"I bet he does," said Robert, finally. "'I resolve to be mysterious and not tell anyone more than half the truth about anything.'"

Jason grinned. "'I resolve to buy more camera equipment and music equipment than anyone I know and not tell anyone where I got the money.'"

Robert grinned back. "'I resolve to claim bizarre sexual adventures with at least a dozen women known to all my friends.'"

Martin looked back and forth at them. "Is Paul really that full of shit?"

"Yes, he is," said Jason. "Yep."

Robert said, "I actually believed him for a little while."

Jason said, "Everyone does, for a little while."

Martin frowned. "So where does he really get the money?"

"I don't know. I never know what I can believe from him, so I just don't believe any of it."

Robert nodded, smiling. "He told me once that he was making a living as an anonymous contact for members of the federal witness relocation program."

"Yeah, right," Jason said. "I remember that. And another time, he said he was doing some programming for the government, but he wasn't allowed to talk about the details. The only computer he's ever owned is so old that he can't even find software for it, so either he's full of it, or the government's even more messed up than we thought. So, what about you, Martin? Any resolutions?"

"Definitely. I resolve to get my butt in gear and get art jobs, save up some money, and get off your couch."

"It's not as though I'm using it," said Jason.

Martin pointed his bagel at Jason. "Now, that's not the point and you know it."

"Yeah, well. You're welcome to stay another few months if you want to."

Robert said, "My valuable opinion, for which there is consistently an overwhelming demand, is that you should resolve to finish your comic book instead of getting lots of art jobs."

Jason said, "The Mega Mole comic book? Yeah, I think so, too."

"Furthermore," said Martin, "I resolve to find a nice, regular, normal, healthy, gorgeous, intelligent, sexy woman who thinks I'm a god."

Robert put his hand on Martin's shoulder sympathetically and said, "I was really with you until the thinking you're a god part."

"Anyway, finding them isn't the hard part," said Martin. "It's keeping them." He laughed.

Robert looked quickly at Jason, who rotated his bagel absently and stared at it.

Martin followed Robert's gaze and then grimaced. "Oops," he said. "I'm sorry."

"It's okay," said Jason.

There was silence.

"I'm sorry," Martin said again. "When's it final?"

"Twenty-sixth of this month."

"How do you feel?"

Jason stopped playing with his bagel and considered the question.

"I don't know," he said, finally. "I'm not feeling a lot these days."

Martin made a warning sound in his throat. "Mmmmmm, that's not good."

"You're probably right." Jason raised his eyebrows. "But that's how it is." He stood up. "More coffee?" Martin and Robert both said yes, so he went into the house.

When he came back out with the pot, Robert was saying, "Oh, I think it's safe to say that the chances of that are so close to zero as to make very little difference."

Jason poured coffee into Robert's out-held mug and said, "No chance of what?"

Martin and Robert glanced at each other, and then Robert said, "Of you changing the channel on the Beat Up Jason Show and finding a girl."

Jason smiled a little.

"True," he said. "Martin? Coffee?"

When Jason was sitting again, he said, "Actually, I met somebody at that electronic music conference."

Martin said, "No way! Who?"

"Her name was Monica Gleason," Jason said.

Martin frowned. "I know I know that name. Why do I know that name?"

"She was in the news," Jason said. "She performed at that electronic music thing I went to."

Martin frowned and then suddenly looked horrified. "Monica, the performance artist Monica? The one who ... her?"

"Yeah."

"I read about her in the paper! You and her were seeing each other?"

Jason sipped his coffee. "No. We spent a little time together. Nothing serious. Just some conversation at the Salt Shaker before her performance on Saturday night. Nothing serious."

"Wow," said Robert. "I'm sorry."

"No reason for you to be sorry," said Jason. "You didn't do it."

Martin ducked his head in anger. "You know, I really wish you would stop doing that."

"What."

"You're purposely avoiding what I really mean when you know better."

"What should I say instead when someone apologizes for somebody being dead? 'Good?'"

"You know," said Martin, "you're really pissing me off. And you're pissing Robert off, too, and if you had more friends, you'd be pissing them off as well."

Jason nodded. "I know." His right hand fluttered. He put it in his lap and picked up his coffee with his left hand. "Just how it goes, I guess."

"We both care about you," said Martin.

"I know you do," said Jason.

"You shouldn't blame yourself," Robert said.

Jason said, "For which? The divorce or Monica being killed?"

"Well, either, but I meant the divorce."

"It's not about blame."

"Then what?" said Martin.

"It's about having half of yourself suddenly torn off and killed," said Jason. "It's exactly about that." He sipped his coffee and then looked around the porch. "Did I forget the sugar? I did." He got up and went into the house. Behind him, he heard Robert say quietly, "Can't argue with that," and Martin say, "Nope."

2

January 2 was a stupid day.

After falling dead asleep in his clothes and shoes midafternoon on New Year's Day, Jason found himself lying in the dark at 2:30 AM, staring at the ceiling and listening to the grating of the automatic garage door in the condos behind the Manor.

At 4:15, he got up, changed his socks, and drove his old Plymouth to Denny's, where he failed to understand the *Los Angeles Times'* stock market pages over pancakes fashioned from some amazing new super-expanding syrup-absorbing foam substance. If a tanker ship carrying fake maple syrup ever cracked open and started harming the environment, Jason would know what to do.

The coffee was awful. There was a small notice in the Metro section for a gathering of the Gleason family. He looked at it for a while.

After reading most of the headlines and all of the comics except for "Apartment 3-G," for which he compensated by reading "Calvin and Hobbes" twice, Jason drove the Plymouth aimlessly around the San Gabriel Valley, humming to fill the void in the dashboard where the radio should have been, and ended up on the Ventura Freeway. In Van Nuys, he switched onto the southbound San Diego Freeway, drove the two and a half hours to San Diego, filled up the tank, and drove back to Pasadena.

His jaw hurt from gnashing the drum parts of the songs he had been humming when he arrived back at the Manor a little after noon. His phone was ringing. He shouldered the back door open and snapped the receiver up before the answering machine on the bookcase could click on.

"Hello?" said the voice on the phone, and Jason's heart and lungs stopped working. When he got them going again, he said, "Hello, Marisa. What's up?"

"Well, I was just calling to see if maybe you'd like to get together tonight with me and have a drink?"

Jason stopped talking and took a breath. Maybe ten seconds passed and then she said, "Hello?"

"Yes," he said, "I'm here. I don't know if that would be a good idea."

"Why not? I think it would be nice if we could be friends. Louis thinks so, too. He's very concerned about you."

There was a buzzy tightening in his chest that always happened when she said "Louis."

"Mr. Benz has never met me."

"He can still be very concerned. He doesn't need to meet someone to be very concerned about them. Besides, I think Mercedes Benzes are nice cars. So look, do you want to have a drink with me or not?"

"I don't know. Every time we get together, you end up hurting me. I mean," he said quickly, "I end up getting hurt. I didn't mean to imply that it was your fault."

"That's a very valid point," she said.

Valid point, Jason thought. *She's still in therapy.* "Well," he said, "maybe we could get together and see what happens."

"Have you been to Giggles? It's kind of hard to find. I'll pick you up. Is six o'clock okay?"

"Fine. Wait, no. How's seven?"

"Okay, seven o'clock. It's a date."

When he hung up, Martin was standing in the doorway to the front room, looking at him.

"Shut up," said Jason.

"What?" protested Martin. Someone on the porch knocked authoritatively on the front door, rattling its loose panes of glass. "What?" Martin asked again, half-turning to the door.

"Nothing."

Shaking his head, Martin peeked behind the blue towel that covered the door's little windows. Then he looked at Jason, shrugged, and opened the door. A red-haired woman in her mid-thirties stood on the doorstep. She was wearing slacks and a blouse with a little black ribbon thing that wanted to be a tie.

"Jason Keltner?" she asked Martin.

Jason said, "That's me."

The woman produced a police shield in a plastic slipcase. "Detective Johns. May I come in?" She had a pleasant alto voice, smooth, with a slight burr to it.

"Sure," said Jason. Martin stepped back and opened the door wider and Jason grabbed a red plastic folding chair that was leaning against the piano and set it up, and she sat down. Behind her, Martin excused himself, gave Jason a "not beautiful, but not bad" look that Jason ignored, eyed her rump pointedly, and went into the pseudo-kitchen.

Jason sat on the piano bench, facing her, put his hands together flat on the surface of the bench between his legs and leaned forward a little. "What can I do for you?"

She folded her hands calmly in her lap. "I'm investigating the death of Monica Gleason. I understand that you knew her. What can you tell me?"

"Not very much," Jason said, shaking his head. "I only knew her for about a day."

"Which day would that be?"

"Um ... Saturday. I met her at a convention and we talked for a while and had some coffee over at the Salt Shaker."

"About what time was that?"

"Oh, I don't know. I'm not good with time. Maybe eleven-thirty or so, until maybe one-thirty. More or less."

"What did you talk about?"

"Electronic music stuff, mostly. She has some ... had some equipment that I'd like to have, so I was asking her a lot of questions about how it worked and how flexible it was, things like that."

Detective Johns looked at the studio in the corner of the front room. "It looks like you have a lot of equipment already."

Jason turned around and looked at it. "I guess so. But it's never enough."

"Are you familiar with the MIDI Show Control protocol?"

"I've read about it."

"Do you know how to run a MIDI stage laser set?"

Jason looked at her with interest. "You've done some homework."

"I always do my homework."

"Really? What is MIDI an acronym for?"

"Do you know how to run a MIDI stage laser set, Mr. Keltner?"

"No, I don't."

She waited and looked at him, and didn't say anything. It was a trick Jason used sometimes to get people to talk to him. He folded his hands in his lap and waited, too.

The silence got uncomfortable, but she still didn't say anything. How smart was it to play mental chicken with a cop? Maybe not very. He let it go for a few more seconds, and then said, "I still don't."

"We could do this downtown," she said.

"Good. You could tell me how to run a MIDI stage laser set on the way."

"Maybe you already know how."

Jason spread his hands, palms up.

She said, "What did you talk about besides her MIDI laser setup?"

"We discussed the lack of subtlety you find in so many cops these days."

Her eyes narrowed. "I *will* take you downtown if I have to, Mr. Keltner," she said. "Would you like that?"

Jason leaned back and said, "Does anybody ever say 'yes' to that?"

"Answer my questions, please."

"Ask me some that aren't veiled implications."

"What did you talk about at the Salt Shaker?"

"Like I said, mostly technical stuff. The things at the conference. There was a lot of new music technology there, and it's not very often you find someone who thinks that's interesting, so we spent most of the time talking about that. We also made a tentative date for tonight. Um ... we talked about religion for a while. She's Baha'i. I mean, was. I never heard of it before, so we talked about that."

"Anything else?"

"We both liked the carrot cake."

She did the waiting trick again and he waited again.

"Nothing else?" she said finally.

"The amazing carrot cake caper doesn't interest you strangely?"

"No."

"Oh."

"What else?"

"She was thinking about blowing off her performance. She was nervous."

"Why?"

"Because people get nervous before they perform."

"What did you say to that?"

"I told her she shouldn't let nervousness prevent her from performing."

"And then she did the performance and died."

"Yes."

"You probably don't feel too good about that."

Jason shrugged, without looking at her. Detective Johns looked patient, pursed her lips thoughtfully, and stood up.

"If you remember anything else, call me at this number," she said, and gave him a business card.

He took it and opened the door. "We're not going downtown?"

"Not this time. But stay where I can find you." Halfway off the porch, she paused, and then turned and said, "By the way: Musical Instrument Digital Interface."

"Very good," Jason said. "A cookie for you."

She didn't smile. Instead, she turned around and left. Martin came into the front room, wide-eyed, and said, "Man, are you out of your mind, talking to a cop like that?"

"I was kind of hoping she would take me downtown."

Martin pointed at him and said, "You better snap out of this soon, dude."

At 4:30, Jason was sitting in the Plymouth outside a blight of condominiums in Chatsworth, watching the Gleason family gathering and wondering what it said about him that he was there.

The guests came and went, and the general noise level ebbed and surged. After a while, a little girl about ten years old ran out of the brown condo and slammed the door behind her. She ran onto the condo greenbelt and sat on one of the swings, looking down.

Jason watched her for a few minutes and then got out of his car and walked over.

"Do you want to be by yourself, or is it okay for me to sit here?" he asked.

She shrugged. "Yeah."

"Yeah it's okay, or yeah you want to be by yourself?"

"Yeah, it's okay."

Jason sat on a swing. Swings had gotten narrower since he'd last sat on one. He crossed his ankles and sat farther back, and had a flash of being scared of going so high on a swing that the chains would go slack and drop him head-down onto the hard distant ground. There was a small, gusty breeze; it was about the right time of the afternoon for the Santa Anas.

"I'm Jason," he said, extending his hand around the chains of the swing.

She shook his hand. "My name is Aileen Elizabeth Gleason."

"Nice to meet you. What's up?"

"Nothing."

"Oh." Why was this little girl able to sit outside by herself and talk to strangers?

"You don't look too happy," he said.

"Do you think my sister committed suicide?" She looked obliquely around the chain between them. "'Cause she didn't."

"Uh," Jason said. "Well."

"She didn't. I want to be like her when I'm a woman. I'm going to run away to Los Angeles when I'm sixteen."

"Uh, I see," Jason said. "Well, you can't have a driver's license here until you're eighteen, and you can't rent an apartment, either. Maybe you could wait until you're eighteen or nineteen."

"Whatever," Aileen said. She started to swing a little. It was probably good that he had had no children with Marisa.

"Want me to push you?" Jason said.

She said, "No," and stopped swinging.

It got cooler, and a short blond woman came into the doorway of the apartment and called for Aileen, and Aileen went in. No one came out and called for Jason. He walked to his car and went home.

3

Giggles was on the ground floor of a corporate building, a big bar with a split-level floor and red vinyl booths. Jason had figured on ferns in wicker hangers, and was disappointed to find that he'd figured correctly. He sat with Marisa in a booth, and a waitress with a name tag that said "Cyndi" gave them plastic-laminated menus. Cyndi wore her hair gathered atop her head in a poofy spill that looked like a lawn sprinkler. All Jason could think of to drink was a rum and Coke, and Marisa ordered a flossy ice cream thing.

"I'm very glad you came," said Marisa. She was dressed smartly in a businessy-skirt outfit with a white blouse that she wore with the collar open. It contrasted nicely with the dark skin of her throat. A pair of large sunglasses with a graduated tint lay folded on the table.

Jason said, "I almost didn't."

"I know. What do you think of the place?"

"Lots of ferns," Jason said.

She leaned forward earnestly and placed her hand on his. Her hand felt small and cool. "I'm hoping we can be friends. Do you think we can?"

He started to answer twice before giving up and saying, "I don't know."

"I understand."

Jason doubted that.

"I think I'm getting a raise at work," she said.

"Ah," he said, in a tone he hoped sounded meaningful.

She looked at him expectantly.

"A raise means more money," he said finally, nodding.

"I think so," she agreed. "I'm thinking of moving to one of the beach communities. I have a new friend with a house on the beach. It's really great."

They'd once gone to the beach with her family and played smashball with a little purple rubber ball. Jason said, "Marisa, I don't think I want to hear about your new friend."

The corner of her mouth quirked up and she looked bored and said, "Okay, whatever."

He stared at his drink. "I'm sorry. I'm still not used to this."

"Well, I think you should just get over it. Louis thinks so, too."

Fuck Louis, thought Jason, and then could see her doing exactly that, except that he'd never met Louis, so he had no face. He closed his eyes, but it didn't help.

When he opened them, she was looking casually off into the corner of the room at nothing.

"So ..." he said, groping, "Have you talked to any of our friends lately?"

"I saw Martin Altamirano at the video store. And Paul Reno and I went to Santa Barbara for a music festival."

"That's nice. No problems because of the divorce?"

"No. Why would there be?"

"No reason. It just seemed like there might be."

"Do you think there's something wrong with that?"

"No," he said, surprised. *Why is she getting defensive?*

"Because I think there's nothing wrong with it."

The chest tightness came faintly. He finished his drink.
She said, "How's work?"
"Okay," he said. "Let's talk about you and Paul."
"I don't think there's anything wrong with it."
The tightness grew. His fingers felt cold. "With what?"
"Like ... going to Santa Barbara and stuff like that."
"Anything you want to tell me?"
"I don't think you are in any state to have a calm conver-
sation."
The tightness went away, and a clear coldness came. He
spoke quietly. "Am I yelling? Am I banging on things?"
Cyndi the sprinkler-head bopped up to the table and said,
"Anything else for you folks?"
"I'm fine," said Marisa.
"Another rum and Coke, please," said Jason.
Cyndi said, "One rum and Coke," and bopped away with
her hair cutely bouncing.
"Okay," Marisa said. "Do you mean am I sleeping with
him or am I in love with him?"
He felt like ice. "Either will do."
Cyndi came perkily back with his drink. He drank it.
Marisa said, "I don't know if I should talk about it."
Jason said, "Yes or no?"
She studied his face. "Well ... okay, yes we slept together."
Everything stopped. The ice receded.
She looked uncertain and toyed with her straw. "So ...
what do you think?"
The restaurant noise faded and there was no sound or
motion anywhere in the world, only a small sensation of trem-
bling or spinning, with Jason at its center, immobile.
He couldn't say anything.
In a few moments, the world started sluggishly again, and

his breath and heartbeat returned simultaneously with the restaurant clatter. He stood up and said, "I think you're a sleaze and I think I'm walking home."

It wasn't a very good parting line. He put ten dollars on the table, turned, and walked the wrong way, nearly into the kitchen, got his bearings, and finally found the front door. On the way out, he saw Marisa talking urgently into one of the pay telephones by the restrooms.

It was cool outside. Giggles was on Buena Vista, which curved somewhere. Jason wasn't sure which side of the curve he was on. He chose a direction and started walking. *Shouldn't have let her drive.*

Yes or no?

... yes we slept together.

Hot spurts of rage and pain tried to break through the nothing, but were immediately damped. *It would be nice to cry.* That he could feel the spurts at all was probably due to the rum-and-Cokes.

... yes we slept together.

He smashed savagely at the door of an empty office building with his forearm. Pain surged up through his arm. *There! I can feel something!*

Well ... okay, yes we slept—

He'd gone the wrong way on Buena Vista. Sitting down heavily on a low brick wall in front of an office building, he looked at the traffic and the Warner Brothers' water tower that poked up over the trees and some three-story buildings. He soon realized that he was looking for Marisa's black Celica, and shook his head; even if she were out searching for him, which seemed unlikely, she'd never find him, because he'd walked the wrong way on Buena Vista.

The unreal picture of Marisa at the pay phone, giving her

attention and support to the *other* guy—to Paul—came to him. She wasn't supposed to feel that way about someone else.

His arm throbbed where he'd hit it, the pain less welcome.

He stood up and started walking. He could find an automated teller machine, take out three hundred dollars, and another three hundred in another day, and not go home for a couple of weeks.

He jammed his hands into his jacket pockets, felt something in the left one, and pulled it out. It was a cheap white business card: *Monica Gleason*, with her Oxnard Avenue address on it. Oxnard was two main streets away.

Something to do.

At the corner of Lankershim Boulevard, he turned and caught sight of his reflection in the glass of a Denny's restaurant, his dark image superimposed over an old couple wearing identical baseball caps and eating their Senior's Specials in the lighted window. He looked like some divorced loser holding a business card. *What a stupid day*, he thought.

It started to hail.

4

Hail never lasts in Los Angeles. Forty minutes later, sodden in the dark rain, Jason stood in front of the Oxnard Gardens Apartments and deduced that Monica Gleason had not lived luxuriously. Though better-maintained than the Manor, it was still a dump, a one-story brown stucco building of twenty-odd units with "security," which Jason cleverly thwarted by trying all the dented metal doorknobs until he found one that turned.

The Oxnard Gardens Apartments had been designed by someone symmetrical, with a swimming pool and a bunch of ugly, stumpy plants in the middle of what was probably called a "courtyard."

Aha, Jason thought, *the "Gardens."*

The rain made conflicting circles in the lighted pool. He walked around the pool and down a short hallway with a burned-out light bulb, to number 15. A swath of yellow plastic police tape glistened on the door. Jason pulled his soggy jacket sleeve over his hand to prevent fingerprints and tried the knob, but he couldn't get a grip through the fabric. He shrugged to pull his cuffs back over his wrists and tried the knob with the backs of his hands. It was locked. He went back down the dingy hallway and around the outside of the building. Monica's scratched plastic window was waist-high from the concrete parking lot. There was no police tape on it. He pressed against it with the heels of his palms and then pushed up, and it slid up into its upper aluminum track, releasing its lower edge from the lower track. *Things learned from living low.*

His conscience yelled somewhere in the distance in his mind, but he ignored it, released the window from its upper track, put it inside the apartment, and climbed in.

A lamp in the parking lot bathed Monica's "furnished" apartment in thin light the color of skim milk. An ugly corner group of two twin beds and a square table monopolized most of the square footage. The beds were enclosed in lumpy fitted coverings of a coarse gold fabric; the table was fake walnut and bore a soldering iron and a half-disassembled Mini-Moog, a little synthesizer dating from sometime around the dawn of man. A compact Macintosh computer, screen dark, sat on a high counter that sprouted from the right-hand wall. Behind it was a kitchenette. In front of it were two mismatched barstools, a jumble of black equipment cases, and a pile of neatly wound patchcords and cables. The occasional muffled swish of cars on wet asphalt, and the tap of rain on the air conditioner next door seemed quieter than complete silence would have. He didn't belong in this apartment, with these things and these sounds. *But hell, here I am.*

Filling the wall opposite the corner group were three home-made block-and-board bookshelves crammed with magazines and paperback books. The magazines had names like *Keyboard, Electronic Musician,* and *AfterTouch.* Mixed in with them were technical manuals and loose spec sheets for synthesizers and MIDI gear.

He walked to the counter, fumbled through his jacket sleeve behind the Macintosh for the switch, and switched it on, adding the whir of its electric fan to the sounds in the room and a further bluish cast to the skim milk light. The whir was marred by a soft and repetitive scrape. Jason's Macintosh had once had the same problem, and he'd taken it to a repair shop. He wondered if Monica had been planning to fix hers; probably, a woman who would take apart a Mini-Moog would repair her own cooling fan.

...yes, we slept together.

While he waited for the Macintosh to remember that it was a Macintosh, he put his head sideways and looked at the spines of the books on the bookshelves. *A Brief History of Time* shared a shelf with *Love's Foolish Fury* and *Gödel, Escher, Bach.* On a lower shelf, *The Design of Everyday Things*, one of the only hardcovers, nestled uncomfortably between *The Lathe of Heaven* and a battered *Hollywood Wives.*

He straightened from the bookshelves. *Eclectic.*

When the computer was ready, Jason looked behind it. From one of its rear connectors, a thin cable snaked across the countertop and along the wall to a three-inch plastic box plugged into a wall socket. Another cable ran from the little box to a telephone jack.

He browsed through the computer and discovered that Monica used a program called Vision to make music. Jason used a competing program called Performer. If she hadn't been dead, they could have argued about it. He also found Phone Courier, a program that he used on his own Mac for communicating with other computers over the telephone lines.

He put his index finger to his lips and thought for a minute. Then he started up Phone Courier. When it was running, he changed its configuration, felt around the front of the Mac through his jacket sleeve until he found the small dial that controlled screen brightness, and turned it counter-clockwise. The screen faded to black.

Then he climbed out, pulled the window through its open-ing and hooked it into its tracks, and waited for the eastbound bus, relatively dry under a Plexiglas shelter on the corner.

What had Marisa said to Paul on the phone?

After ten minutes of waiting, he thought of looking for a bus schedule, and found one mounted in the shelter, but couldn't read it, because there wasn't enough light. As he squinted at it, a blue Trans-Am with Trini Lopez blaring from half-open windows stopped at the intersection, and he was able to make out in the light from its headlights that the last bus had run while he had been sitting among the ferns with Marisa. He started walking again, noting the doppler effect on "Lemon Tree" as the Trans-Am roared past.

He shoved his back door open at five-fifty in the morn-ing. Martin wasn't there. He took off his wet clothes and called Municipal Water, asked for the pipeline maintenance crew, told them he was sick, and reminded them that it was the day for taking water samples for taste-and-odor tests. Some-one on the crew would pull the easy duty, fill all fourteen one-quart glass bottles from the first test spigot on the patrol route, make up some reasonable-looking meter readings, and spend the day in the cool dark of the Village Saloon. Jason's readings would come out funny the next day.

He sat on the bed for a long time, staring straight ahead at nothing. Then he put on an old bathrobe, went into the front room, and started Phone Courier on his Macintosh. Then he stood up, got Monica Gleason's business card from his jacket in the bedroom, and set Phone Courier to dial her number.

Nothing happened at first, and he was afraid he hadn't configured her copy of Phone Courier correctly, but then the words, "Connect 2400" appeared on the screen. He tapped a few commands on the keyboard and then went into the pseudo-kitchen and made coffee from whatever grounds were left in the grinder, drank three old-fashioned Coca-Cola glasses full of coffee with milk and sugar, shuffled across the flat gray carpet, lay down on his futon, and fell immediately asleep.

5

He awoke several times during the evening, and finally got up at 8:30, the time he usually went to bed, in order to get up at 4:30 in the morning for work. He'd call in sick again when morning came, and lose another sick day. In the bathroom, he stared at his scruffy reflection in the mirrored plastic medicine cabinet and decided not to brush his teeth because the mint would conflict with the coffee he was going to drink.

In the pseudo-kitchen, he pulled the pot out of the coffeemaker and went carefully outside on bare feet to dump the dark, overboiled coffee on the dirt. Waldo, a dingy gray-and-white cat from the condos, crouched under the tree behind the Manor, eating a dead sandwich from the dumpster and growling. He was having a hard time growling and swallowing at the same time, but the effort was impressive. Jason shook the last drops out of the empty coffeepot and went back inside.

Ten minutes later, on his way into the living room, he glanced at the answering machine. There were four new messages. He sat down in the dark in front of the Macintosh and started looking at the things that Phone Courier had copied from Monica Gleason's Macintosh while he'd been asleep.

Following standard Macintosh convention, things were kept in imaginary folders. Jason looked through them without a directed purpose, moving the mouse and clicking it to look in folders with his right hand and holding his coffee mug with his left. The official rule was No Open Beverages In Jason's Studio, but Martin wasn't around to see it broken. Probably out bowling with nice, normal, gorgeous, intelligent, sexy women.

Monica's Macintosh had a copy of GoGet, a program that automated interaction with MUSE, an international musicians' network that Jason belonged to. He'd have to look further into that.

He opened a folder called "Music," and realized that he had all the data that comprised Monica's music and her stage show. He thought about privacy for a minute before turning on his music gear, but it didn't seem right that no one should hear her art.

Since he and Monica had used different synthesizers, he wouldn't be able to reproduce the same sounds that she had used; he would just have to play her music using sounds from his own equipment. He hoped that she had used informative words like "piano" or "Moog bass" for the musical parts, instead of gossamer New Agey names like "Eternity" or "Celestial Twilight."

It took an hour to configure things so that her music would play back correctly on his system, longer than things usually took him, but he didn't know her software, and had no manual. The first piece he tried was called "Aileen." After half an hour of reconfiguration, he was able to start playback.

"Aileen" was in three movements. The first was upbeat. Jason began adjusting volumes and placements in the stereo field as it played, refining it for his setup. *Stop engineering*, he thought suddenly, *Stop messing with MIDI controllers and just listen to the music. What does the music say?*

The music danced and lilted, and Jason thought of Aileen with a bubble wand, or dragging a kitten around, and Monica being a snotty big sister. The theme restarted itself, and then a swirl of orchestral sounds swept in like wind, clearing away the first movement and ushering in the second.

The theme from the first movement played again, but lower and transposed into a sadder scale. From a string section, dissonant swells, bending in pitch, shifted and jockeyed with a sustaining bowed bass sound that Monica had transposed lower than the lowest note of a real bass. Synthetic flute sounds trilled unsettlingly, answering the theme.

Percussion entered: low drums rolled dully under quick rhythms of sticks hitting sticks. Talking drums responded in confident cadences, breathed for a bar, answered again.

Strengthless under the battery, the orchestra faded and waited, and the percussion continued for eight bars and stopped cold, and Jason was slapped by the sudden silence.

Monica's Unfinished Symphony. Or maybe *Synthony*. There wasn't really a word for it. It seemed wrong to make any sound in the silence where the third movement should have been, so Jason sat and watched the onscreen counter dutifully count off hundreds of silent beats and unused measures. When Martin came in at two o'clock, the reluctant sound of the back door being forced away from its frame seemed an appropriate ending, so Jason stopped playback and the counter ceased counting at measure 3386, beat 3.

Martin poked his head into the front room and said, "Hey."

Jason nodded. He didn't feel like talking.

"Mind if I turn on the light?"

Jason gestured toward the light switch. Martin picked his

way across the room and turned it on.

"Well," Martin said, "it's nice to see you finally working on ... Are you okay?"

Jason said, "Yeah, I'm fine," but it got hung up somewhere on the way out and ended up as an unintelligible gargle. Clearing his throat didn't help much, either. After another try, he got it right. *That was weird.*

Martin was looking at him strangely.

"What?" Jason said.

Still with the strange look, Martin shook his head slightly. "You don't even know you're crying, do you?"

Surprised, Jason reached a hand toward his face, saying, "I'm not—" and then fell silent.

Martin sat down on the couch and didn't say anything. Jason looked at the wetness on his fingertips and raised his eyebrows. After a little while, he said, "You want to go to Shakers?"

"Sure," Martin said. After Jason changed into jeans and a shirt, they went onto the porch, and Martin waited for Jason to lock the front door. Then they walked three blocks, past a gas station, an auto painting business, and the Pasadena train station, to the Salt Shaker Coffee Shop, where they drank average coffee and talked about other things.

As they walked home in the dark, Martin said, "So what's going on?"

"You know," Jason said. "Same thing."

"The divorce."

"Not so much the divorce itself. I keep having this feeling like, 'No, no, this is not the way it's supposed to go.'"

"Like you wish you could change things?"

"No, I don't really wish anything."

"How are you sleeping?"

Jason shrugged.

While they were cutting diagonally through the Mobil gas station, Martin asked again, "How are you sleeping?"

Jason said, "I stay up late and wear myself out so I'll go to sleep right away and not lie there awake."

"So you won't think about it?"

"Yeah."

"Why were you crying when I came in before?"

Jason answered slowly. "I'm not sure. I drove to where Monica's family was gathered."

At the Manor, Jason unlocked the front door, and they went in.

"So you were at this family thing," prompted Martin.

"Yeah. I met her little sister. She was absolutely sure that Monica didn't kill herself."

Martin sat on the couch and Jason sat on the piano bench.

"I mean absolutely. She had no doubt at all. Total belief."

"That's little kids."

"I guess."

"So what was going on when I came in?"

Jason told him about entering Monica's apartment and playing her music.

"All because her little sister said she didn't kill herself," said Martin.

"Yes."

"And maybe because you feel a little responsible for Monica being on stage at all."

Jason shrugged. It felt redundant.

Martin took in a long breath, held it, and released it.

"And maybe because you've been in this blue funk for the last year—"

"Six months."

"Six months, and now you get a little crazy?"

Jason stared at the wall.

Martin said, "Are you sure you didn't leave fingerprints?"

"Pretty sure."

"Can anybody trace your little computer phone trick?"

"I don't know."

"What are you going to do now?"

"I don't know."

"But you're not done with this."

Jason was silent.

Martin said, "Easier than actually dealing with live women."

Jason looked at him.

"Sorry."

"Okay."

Martin said, "But mostly because of the little sister."

"Tell me a better reason," Jason said.

"I'm not the one who needs a better reason, you idiot," Martin said. He looked at the Macintosh. Its onscreen clock read 4:15. "Isn't it time for you to call in sick?"

6

USERNAME: MGLEASON
PASSWORD: ● ● ● ● ● ● ● ●
HELLO MGLEASON
Logon at 06:44:18
You have 2 new mail messages.

#1
From: TINKERTOY 29-DEC 08:01:56
To: MGLEASON
Subj: show

Hi, M!
I don't think I'll be able to get out to Pasadena, but thanks
for the offer anyway. I'm interested in hearing how the new
gear works out. Maybe next time! :-)
Break a leg!
-*-

#2
From: MeTaMuSiC 30-DEC 20:15:48
To: MGLEASON
Subj: !!!

Monica, what is your problem??? I've been calling you for
the last three days and keep getting your machine!! Are
you going to talk to me or what!?!?!?!
Call me, okay??
N

_ _*

>bye
NOTE-ON off at 06:46:03
Session time: 2 minutes.
MUSE DISCONNECTED

"Hey," said Jason, as GoGet, finished with the session,
severed the connection between his Macintosh and MUSE.

Martin looked up from the sofa, where he was idly flipping the pages of Jason's music magazines. "What?"

"I think it's a clue."

Martin sat up. "What kind of clue?"

"I don't know. Are there kinds of clues? Come look at
this."

Martin swiveled around on the sofa to see the Macintosh
screen. GoGet was sorting the messages it had just retrieved
from MUSE, and a little picture of a wristwatch on the screen
meant it wasn't quite done yet.

"Wait a minute until the watch goes away," said Jason.
"Monica's copy of GoGet has her MUSE password in it, so I
logged in as her and picked up her unread mail. MUSE doesn't
know the difference." The watch disappeared. He clicked the
mouse to call up the second private mail message and they
both read it.

Martin said, "'N.'"

"Let's find out who that is." Clicking the mouse again, he

called up a list of the MUSE members and sent GoGet searching for the entry for "MeTaMuSiC." After a few seconds, the information was displayed on the screen.

"'N. Platt,'" said Jason.

Martin read the rest of the entry. "'Focus: Sound design and audio for video. Company: Sound Reasoning, Inc., Eight Four Two Four Sunset Blvd., Suite Eighty-Three, Hollywood, C.A.' What's sound design?"

"Just what it sounds like. Making noises for movies, designing sounds for synthesizers. Stuff like that."

"He's in Hollywood. You going to go see him?"

"Or her. Um, I guess so. I hadn't really thought that far. Yeah, I think I will."

"I'll go, too. Robert made me promise I'd keep an eye on you."

"I don't want you to go. Where is Robert?"

"At work. I'm going anyway."

"What's he doing today?"

"The same. Office temp stuff. I'm going."

"He should get a real job," said Jason, standing. "If you're going, you can buy breakfast."

Eighty-four Twenty-four Sunset Boulevard was a twenty-four-hour telephone and mailbox service called Mailbox City. Jason found box number 83, and then he and Martin walked a couple of blocks to a Denny's and ate breakfast.

"This is the only Denny's I've ever been in that has a bar," said Jason.

"This is the only bar I've ever been in that has a Denny's," said Martin.

"Oh yeah," said Jason. "I forgot. Everything is relative. Thank you for pointing out to me the error of my assump-

tion of the absoluteness of the concepts, 'Denny's' and 'bar.'"
He flagged down a passing waiter and said, "Could I have
some coffee, please?"

The waiter said, "Sure," and then, in a louder voice, and
apparently to the room at large, "Would someone please coffee this gentleman?"

Martin looked appraisingly at him. "How you feeling?"

"Weird. Last night I felt focused. Now I don't. I'm still
not going to leave this thing alone, but at the moment, it
doesn't *feel* like an obsession."

"What does it feel like?"

"Feels a lot like a day job."

Martin made a face that said *I don't get it, but whatever.*

Another waiter brought Jason a cup of coffee and went
away.

"Egad," Jason said. "I've been coffee'd."

After a couple of minutes of eating, Martin said, "If you
don't mind my asking, now what?"

"You think I know?" Jason sprinkled Tabasco Sauce and
salt over his hash browns and warily took a bite. He could still
taste them. He ate some anyway.

Martin sipped his coffee. "So what are you going to do
next?"

"Heck, I don't know." His eyes were starting to water from
the Tabasco Sauce. "Hoo," he said, and drank most of his
water. "I don't know. I don't even know what I would have
said to N. Platt had he or she been there. But at least now that
I've rented a mailbox, I have an excuse to be around sometimes. Unlike you."

"Hey," Martin protested, throwing his hands up in deferment of responsibility, "I promised Robert I'd babysit you."

"Martin, of the three of us, who needs the most
babysitting?"

"Robert. Usually. Me, sometimes. These days, you."

A beautiful blonde waitress appeared at their table with two pots of coffee and said, "Hi, guys. Refills?" in a Midwestern twang.

"Martin?" Jason said, "More weird black caustic substance?"

"Decaf, please," Martin said, holding his mug out. Jason smiled pleasantly and covered his with his hand when the waitress gestured with the pot.

"Actress," they both said when she left.

"But she really wants to direct," Jason added.

Martin watched her shapely departure. "She can direct me any time."

Jason shook his head. "Men."

"Ain't we dogs?"

At the register, Jason impatiently waited while Martin got the waitress talking so that he could then listen understandingly to how hard it was to make it in this town.

After Martin struck out, they walked past music stores and clothing stores back to Jason's car, looking at the Hollywood people with their shredded denim and various piercings. After he and Marisa separated, Jason had tried to keep busy at night by occasionally playing keyboards with local rock bands in clubs on Sunset, but he'd never enjoyed it. Short of knitting, he couldn't think of a duller way to spend an evening than playing whole-note chords behind a noisy guitar band while snaky leather-clad weasels perfected their bored expressions. And without exception, the women he'd met had all the warmth and none of the sincerity of a tax audit. *Actually,* he thought, *knitting might be more interesting, and it never makes your ears ring for a week.*

On the way home, Jason said, "You want to go out tonight? I've got two comps at the Rust Garden for some MIDI performance art stuff. Guy on MUSE and I have been failing to connect for the better part of a year, and he's playing tonight."

"Sure," Martin said. "Is there a drink minimum?"

"I don't think so."

"Okay."

"How about we leave around nine-thirty?"

"Oh, that's fine."

A little later, Martin said, "Man, you must feel exhausted," and Jason suddenly did.

At the Manor, Martin went out to get a newspaper from a coin-operated machine on the corner, and Jason went to bed.

7

*A*nyone can be anyone in the Net. Or no one. Or more than one.

He prefers to remain anonymous, a shadow figure, allowing himself to be glimpsed only rarely, and fleetingly, and then only in planned excursions under a name created expressly for the occasion, and permanently discarded immediately thereafter.

A word for him is "lurker," an awkward party guest hunkered down in the datastream, never participating in the conversation, but never leaving.

Anyone can find anything on the Net. Nestled together on Net-connected hard disks are libraries of software: essays and computer games; digital sound recordings and lists of telephone numbers for computer services; engineering data and book reviews; sex pictures and employment opportunities; the archives of thousands of "chats," conversations between people who might be thousands of miles separate, yet who converse in real-time over the Net. All this is available to the computer-owning public for a few dollars a month and a few cents a minute.

For somewhat more money, the computer-owning public can take advantage of online services. Sending a fax without a fax machine is as easy as booking a flight to Rio and ordering traveler's checks and new luggage. After double-checking your available credit, of course.

And other services. Like any community, the Net has its red light *districts: Husbands stay up late while their wives are in bed, and type hotly to unseen virtual bed companions they believe to be slim and female. Their wives dally in the datastream during the day, while their husbands work.*

And other services.

Although he has many accounts on the Net, he does not pay for them, and never receives a bill. The illegality of his presence does not bother him at all; its flexibility and numerous points of entry leave the Net vulnerable, and he goes where he is able. He comes in through the window, and if that doesn't work, he tries the plumbing.

A skulking ghost striking business deals with transparent phantasms, he takes advantage of other services not sanctioned by the Net, services offered by others who also do not pay for their Net accounts.

This day—or maybe night—he calls himself "Raptor" and sends a message to a man, woman, or child called "Pollux," who has done similar work for him previously. He likes that he has dealt with Pollux before. It's better that way.

It isn't long before Pollux responds.

8

The shooting happened while Jason and Robert were sitting in two bent lawn chairs on the porch of the Manor, enjoying the chilly air of early evening and arguing about autonomy. Robert had just said, "But that's circular logic again," and Jason was in the middle of saying, "Yeah? So what?" when a battered gold AMC Javelin with mirror-film on its windows pulled to the curb and slowed directly in front of them. The front passenger window rolled halfway down and a rifle barrel poked out, swaying a little in the odd way that long things do when they're being held at only one end. It took about two seconds for Jason to turn to yell something wordless at Robert and jump half-backward into the open front door just as Robert did the same. The rifle fired at the same instant as they collided in the doorway and fell, still half outside, legs caught in their chairs. Jason raised his head to see outside, but glass shards fell on him, and Robert's head and shoulder blocked his vision. He shoved Robert off and wrenched himself out of the twisted tangle of chair and Robert legs, stood up and moved toward the sidewalk, hooked his foot on a chair, and crashed to the concrete porch. The gold Javelin spun its tires turning left onto Del Mar and disappeared, trailing the sound of a badly tuned engine.

Looking where the Javelin had gone, Jason raised himself carefully off the porch and hobbled into the house. Robert, whitefaced, had the phone against his ear.

"Wha!" said Jason. He wasn't sure what he had meant to say, but that hadn't been it.

Robert enunciated clearly, "I am calling the police. Hello? I, yes, hello? Hello?" He looked at Jason. "I'm on hold."

"Yhah," said Jason. *Comebacks are my game.*

"Hello? Yes, I'm at Marengo and Del Mar, and I was just shot at ... what? What? Del Mar. I was just ... what? Marengo and Del Mar. This guy just drove up and ... what? Robert Goldstein. Goldstein. G-O-L-D-S-T-E-I-N. Yes, Robert. What? Yes, I live here. No, he's gone. Hold on." He covered the phone. "Did you get a license number?"

"No."

Robert uncovered the phone. "No, we didn't. Um, hold on." He covered the phone again. "Do you know what kind of car it was?"

Jason made a gimme-the-phone gesture and Robert handed it over.

"Hello?" he said.

"Who is this?" said a male voice.

"This is Jason Keltner, K-E-L-T-N-E-R. I live here, too. We were both shot at by somebody in a gold AMC Javelin with mirrored windows."

"Did you get the license number?"

"No ..." Jason noticed that he was shaking. An adrenaline rush he hadn't even noticed was wearing off. "No, I didn't get the license number! How many people could there possibly be in the San Gabriel Valley with gold Javelins with silver windows?"

"Yes, sir."

"It's not exactly an everyday automotive fashion choice."

"I understand, sir."

"Sorry. It's not your fault. I don't get shot at often."

"I understand, sir. Two officers are on their way. They will be there within two minutes. Would you like me to remain on the line with you until they get there?"

"No, that won't be necessary. Thank you."

"You're welcome, sir."

Xiaou from one of the upstairs rooms, and Patrice from the attic, came downstairs with surprised and questioning looks on their faces. Xiaou was a student at the Art Center, and Patrice was a secretary who spent most of her salary on rock musicians. They'd heard the shooting. Robert filled them in and they said appropriate things and went back upstairs. Jason made coffee. The cops came, found a bullet hole in the drywall between Jason's front room and the empty apartment behind, found another hole in the flimsy exterior wall of the rear apartment, searched the parking lot for the bullet, found nothing, and questioned Robert and Jason, who gave them the facts and left out the Laurel and Hardy routine in the doorway.

When the cops left, Jason swept the bigger pieces of glass onto a folded piece of newspaper and threw them away while Robert went upstairs for a couple of minutes and then came down with Patrice's Handi-Vac. The glass was from two panes in the door. While Jason vacuumed, Robert leaned against the wall, looked at the bullet hole in the drywall, and brooded.

"Speak," Jason said.

Robert took a minute to answer. "Were you thinking or just acting?"

"When we jumped?"

"Yes."

"Both, I guess."

"What were you thinking?"

"Well," Jason straightened on his knees. "It went something like, 'Car ... Ugly car ... Pointy thing ... Gun ... That's dangerous'—"

Robert's explosive laugh cut him off. "I thought that, too! 'That's dangerous! They shouldn't be waving that around!' Then what?"

"After that it was just, 'Eeaaugghhh!!'"

"Yeah. What did you yell at me?"

"I don't know. I couldn't make words."

He finished vacuuming the broken glass.

"Well," Robert said, "thanks for yelling any thing."

"You're welcome. Sorry I shoved you."

"It's okay. What were you going to do once you got up?"

"I have no idea." He stood up and looked at the door. A month previously, he had replaced three missing panes with cardboard and wide silver duct tape. "They couldn't have shot out the cardboard ones? Now I only have seven glass panes left, and five of those are cracked."

"What happened to the door?" said Martin's voice behind them.

"You tell him," Jason said. "I'm tired of talking about it." He went into the pseudo-kitchen and drank his coffee, listening to Robert explain. Then Martin came in, ashen-faced.

"Hey," Jason said, "you look paler than Robert, and he was here for it."

"Man," Martin said, "did you see the article in the paper I left for you?"

"No, what article?"

Martin talked as he walked through the bathroom into the bedroom. "I didn't want to wake you, and you were still asleep when I left, so I left it on the ... where is it? Oh, here it is."

He emerged from the bathroom with a section of the *Los Angeles Times*. "You covered it up with the blankets. Here, look."

Jason took the paper. It was the front section, folded back to page three. A headline read, "Onstage Death Now Believed Murder." In smaller bold type, it said, "Deadly Laser the Culprit in Bizarre Death." He skimmed over the rest of the article, which took up two six-inch columns, and said nothing more than the headline.

Jason said, "Watson, the game is afoot. Another astounding clue."

"Yeah, let's just hope there's not another astounding shooting at your astounding fool head."

Jason didn't say anything for a minute. Then he said, "I hadn't put that together yet."

"You hadn't put that together yet?" Martin's expression said, *How dumb can you be?* "These are some heavy-duty dudes you're dealing with, man! I'm not going to let you keep this going."

Jason nodded. "Heavy-duty dudes."

"I'm serious. I'm not going to sit by and watch you take a bullet."

"Okay."

"Don't mess around with me on this, Jase! Just let the police do what they're paid to do. You are paid to take water samples, and they are paid to catch bad guys."

"Okay."

The phone rang. Jason said "Okay!" and picked it up.

"Jason." It was Paul Reno.

"Paul."

"I'll talk to you later," Martin said, *sotto voce*, and left.

"How you doing?" said Paul's voice.

Spiffy. "What's up?"

"Listen, I need to talk to you."

"This doesn't count?"

"In person. I don't want to talk to you on the phone. Where can we meet?"

"I don't really have anything to say to you, Paul."

A note of disgust crept into Paul's voice. "Maybe you don't, but I do. Are you going to meet me or not?"

"Nope." Jason hung up and waited. The phone rang. Paul's phone had a redial button.

Jason picked it up.

"What."

"Jason, what are you mad at me for?"

Jason shook his head. There were some things about Paul that you just couldn't make him understand. "Never mind. Are you free now?"

"Right now? Yes."

"The E-Bar. Meet me in half an hour. Wear a red carnation." He hung up again before Paul could answer.

The E-Bar was a little coffeehouse ten minutes from the Manor by foot, down an alley near the Pasadena Train Station, around a corner by the tracks, and into an unmarked red door. The "E" stood for "Espresso." There were usually folding tables and chairs set up in the alley, and a tarot-card reader had taken up residence there recently. On Friday and Saturday nights, it was overrun with wistfully neo-beatnik high school kids smoking clove cigarettes, college students talking football and Kafka, and patiently predatory grownup faux-philosopher/artist/poets who knew Ravi Shankar's discography. There was "entertainment" almost every night.

Jason turned the dark corner in the alley and an amplified whiny sing-song female drone drifted out of the door, accelerated down the alley, and slugged him between the eyes, punching through the cartilage and piercing his brain. "Oh, damn," he groaned. It was Poetry Night. Should have met Paul at The Talking Room instead. The Talking Room never had Poetry Nights.

A hand-scrawled sign on the door claimed "No feet, no torso, no service." He stepped inside and looked around. There were mismatched chairs for about thirty people and enough mismatched chess pieces for two simultaneous games, a counter just inside the door, a big chalkboard with prices on it, a cappuccino machine, a glass-fronted refrigerator with fruit juice and Jolt Cola, a pay phone, a small stage at the back, and an out-of-tune upright piano against one wall. It was crowded. Paul wasn't there yet, of course; if he got there first, he couldn't make an entrance.

The white-faced, black-haired, red-lipped poetess perched on a green barstool on the stage, holding a gray microphone and reading from a yellow spiral notebook. The bulk of her anguish and ennui evidently spent, she concluded her performance with " ... and bleeding leaves kiss my festive face, And fondle my pain, With spiteful thorny tears." The mostly-underaged audience applauded and whistled. Jason refrained from rolling his eyes.

The counterperson was a college-aged girl with black-rimmed glasses and light brown hair bunched in a wide band. When she looked his way, Jason ordered a Café Royale and pointed outside to indicate that he'd be sitting there.

Two of the three outdoor tables for customers were empty. He picked one against the old brick wall at the end of the alley and wiggled each of the two chairs experimentally before sitting and leaving the wobbly one for Paul.

Inside, the Poetry Night MC introduced the next poetess, and then the poetess began to emit her poetry. *Why don't these people ever rhyme or stick to a meter?* Jason thought, suspecting not for the first time that he was just too bluntly built for poetry, though there was one by Robert Frost that seemed to sum up his separation from Marisa. It wasn't about a divorce, though. It was about a haunted house.

The counterperson with the glasses brought him a double-sized mug on a thick saucer, took his four dollars and went away. Jason took a sip. Café Royale was hot chocolate with espresso in it and chocolate syrup drizzled on top.

Paul came around the corner in his leather jacket and black pants and sat down.

"Thanks for meeting me," he said.

Jason lowered his mug halfway and said, "'I dwell in a lonely house I know, that vanished many a summer ago, and left no trace but the cellar walls, and a cellar in which the daylight falls, and the purple-stemmed raspberries grow.'"

Paul looked at him as though he were nuts and said, "Yeah, whatever."

"Don't ask me to recite the next verse, because I don't know it."

"Don't worry, I won't," Paul said dryly. "What was that crap?"

"You know, Paul," Jason said pleasantly, "one very small part of your considerable problem is that besides being an asshole, a fuckup, and a pathological liar, you don't know the difference between that," he said, indicating the amplified voice inside, "and a poem."

Paul stiffened and stood up. "I don't know what your problem is, but I don't need to take this from you."

Jason smashed his mug on the table and, in the same

motion, flew to his feet and slapped Paul hard across the face with the back of his hand. Paul's hand went up and he reeled backward and tried to find his balance. Jason took advantage of Paul's momentum, stepping quickly around the table and shoving him backward into a plant against the wall of the E-Bar.

"What is your fucking problem, Jason?" Paul's voice was unsteady and his fingers kept finding his mouth, searching for damage. There was no blood, but Jason figured the side of his face would be discolored in a little while.

"Well, let's see." Jason pretended to consider. "Here's one big problem: Sometimes I don't pick my friends well and they betray me with my wife."

"Ex-wife."

Jason hit him hard again with his open hand, putting his shoulder behind the blow and his anger into it. Paul staggered against the wall and Jason said, "Yes. Ex-wife."

Paul blinked rapidly, and Jason realized with sudden discomfort that he was trying not to cry. With the discomfort came an almost overpowering revulsion. Paul's tongue flicked into the corner of his mouth. The second blow had drawn a little blood.

"You called me," Jason said. "I didn't call you. We both know what you did, and you and I are no longer friends. If you have something to say to me, say it, but if it's an apology, I swear I'll hurt you badly."

Paul didn't say anything for a few moments.

"Okay," he said after a while. "Let's sit down."

Jason backed up. The noise he'd made had drawn some people into the doorway.

"Go listen to crappy poetry," Jason said. The people murmured and trickled slowly back in.

The counterperson came out with a bundle of rags and a trash bag and started mopping up the Café Royale and putting the ceramic pieces in the bag.

"I'll pay for the mug," Jason said to her.

Paul said, "You won't be playing keys for a couple of days when that hand stiffens up." He was still exploring his mouth with his tongue and fingers.

"I haven't been anyway," Jason said. "But I'm touched by your concern."

Paul sat down again. The counterperson came to the table and offered Jason a clean rag, and he realized that his jeans were covered with Café Royale.

"Thanks," he said, taking the rag and trying to clean his jeans. When they were a little less damp, he sat down and said, "So what did you want to meet me for?"

"Do you mind if I order first?" In Paul's tone was something that strove to sound annoyed, but achieved only petulance. "Cappuccino, please. Jason, would you care for another mug of whatever you were having?"

Jason said, "No, thank you," to the counterperson. When she left, Paul said, "Look, I wanted to talk to you because some things have happened that you might want to know about."

"Such as."

"Do you really want to know, or are you going to go bazerk on me again?"

"Berserk."

"Look. Do you want me to tell you or not?"

It took an effort for Jason to say, "Yes."

"Are you sure?"

"Either tell me or don't, Paul. I have to go out with Martin at nine-thirty, so I don't have a lot of time to dance around and be cute."

"Okay." Paul leaned forward. "I think you might be in danger."

"Really."

"I heard through the grapevine that somebody's out to get you. Somebody dangerous."

"Some heavy-duty dudes?"

"Uh ... yeah."

"Where'd you hear that?"

"Around."

"Don't pull the Mr. Enigmatic act on me, Paul. If you're not going to tell me, say, 'I'm not going to tell you.'"

"Okay, I'm not going to tell you."

"Thanks," Jason said. He took out his wallet, put ten dollars on the table, and pushed his chair back, "You're a pal. I'll have my service put you on the holiday mailing list." He got up and walked up the alley. When he was close to the corner, Paul called, "Jason!"

Jason stopped without turning. He heard Paul's footsteps.

"Jase," Paul said, closer. Jason turned to face him.

"Jason, there's a lot you don't know about me."

"So?"

"And some of what you don't know means I know a lot of people that you'd never want to meet."

"Name six."

"Why are you giving me a hard time? It doesn't matter who they are." When Jason turned away, he said, "Look, I can't tell you who I got the information from because I don't know myself."

"Paul—"

"Will you listen to me? The people I deal with are extremely secretive. If they don't want you to know who they are, you don't know."

"Well, *mil grácias*, Paul, but what do you want me to do, move to Nova Scotia under an assumed name?" Cutting off Paul's reply, he continued, "But hey, thanks for being so specific. Most mysterious warnings you get these days are so vague and unsubstantial."

"Look, just be careful. Jeez."

"Wow," Jason said, "glad you told me that."

He walked out of the alley and around the block, and along the train tracks toward the Manor. Fifteen minutes later, he was in the Plymouth with Martin, going south on the Pasadena Freeway.

9

The Rust Garden was in Hollywood, on an alley parallel with Highland Avenue, near Melrose. It had started life as a small parking lot for a coffeehouse, and was still more parking lot than building. The floor was uneven asphalt with parking spaces still marked in faded paint, and there was no food service.

Jason and Martin parked in front of the coffeehouse and entered through its front door. Inside, four failed-actor types were draped over the circular iron staircase to the loft, speaking opaque dialogue written by a failed-writer type. The clientele was sparse, and no one seemed to be paying attention. Walking toward the back with Martin, Jason waved to the two women behind the counter, and they looked surprised and said, "Hi, Jason!"

Farther back, a man in a long black coat was gesturing with a wooden flute and saying to three people at a table, "So the cops say to me, 'Have you seen anything unusual tonight?'" The people at the table laughed, and Jason clapped him on the shoulder.

"Jason!" the man said. "How you doing? You haven't been around!"

"Hey, David, how you doing?"

"Doing unbelievably. Playing out a lot, man. A lot. Did you hear about Lori?"

"No, what?"

"She got fired, man! They said she was stealing."

Jason frowned. "That's ridiculous."

"No kidding! I'll tell her you said hello. Hey, I heard about your divorce. That's rough. I know."

"Yeah, well. Anyway, we're going to the Garden for some stuff you hate, but nice seeing you."

"Later."

When they parted, Martin said "Do you know everybody here?"

"Not any more," Jason said. "I haven't been around for a long time."

At the back door of the coffeehouse—which was the front door of the Rust Garden—he gave his name to the doorperson, wondered why it always took three searches through the guest list, and walked in behind Martin. The Garden was a little more than half full, which meant there were about twenty-five people sitting in the metal chairs or milling around. A dozen microphones perched on thin stands around the edge of the room, aimed at the audience.

The small stage had been carefully cut on the bottom edge to follow the contour of the pavement. On it, a slender man with glasses pushed up over closely-trimmed black hair, leaned on a wheeled white case that looked like a coffin freezer, intent on the screen of a big Macintosh computer much more powerful than Jason's. Cables snaked everywhere, some of them duct-taped to the pavement and the floor of the stage. A large-screen video monitor sat on a tall rolling stand at the back of the stage.

Jason said, "Roland?"

The man looked away from the screen with an amiably vague expression and said, "Yes?"

Jason extended his hand. "Hi, I'm Jason Keltner, NOTE-ON from MUSE. We finally meet."

Roland's expression became sincerely friendly as he shook Jason's hand. "Yes, finally! What a pleasure to meet you."

"This is my friend, Martin."

"Hi," Martin said. "This is quite a setup you've got here."

Roland looked sourly at the coffin freezer. "Thanks. It's being temperamental right now, I'm afraid."

"Need some help?" Jason said.

"Sure, have a look. I'm stumped."

"Martin, could you save us a table?"

"Okay." Martin found a table near the stage and sat down. Jason stepped up onto the stage and said, "What's wrong with it?" It was strange to be onstage again.

Roland swiveled the screen so Jason could see it better. "I don't know what the problem is. This is a borrowed computer. It was working before, but now I can't open my librarian."

Jason looked at the screen. "You're doing digital audio. Did you optimize the disk before the performance?"

Roland said, "Yes ..." Then realization dawned on his face. "Oh. Oops. I bet I lost a hard disk install." He rolled his eyes. "Duh."

Jason grinned. "That's why you try out your new material here."

"Right, so I can screw up and hardly anybody sees it." He shook his head and sighed. "This is an awful lot to go through for a twenty-minute show. Anyway, thanks."

"Sure."

Roland flipped his glasses down over his face and Jason stepped down and joined Martin at a table near the stage.

"You fixed it?" Martin said.

"No. I don't know how. I just guessed right. He's fixing it now."

"There you go. It's better to be lucky than good."

"I think the saying goes *sometimes* it's better."

Martin was looking around. "There're no women here."

"It's mostly men at these things."

"Why?"

"I don't know. Maybe because most tech types are men."

"Tech types?"

Jason looked around. "Like that guy with the blue plaid shirt."

Martin studied the man. "He looks like those guys in high school who spent all day in the computer lab."

"How come the girls never did that?"

"I don't know."

"Ah," Jason said sagely, "When you have discovered the reason, Grasshopper, you will have discovered the answer."

Martin said, "Sure thing, Master Po, dude."

Jason inclined his head and bowed slightly as the house lights dimmed.

Roland's show was mesmerizing. Constantly entering commands with the mouse, keyboard, and a small, flat bank of sliders, he wove music together with recordings of found sounds: conversations, engine noises, restaurant ambiences, and things Jason couldn't identify. The sounds looped and fragmented, became seeds of new sounds, and grew stranger. Jason was startled to hear his own voice say, "Martin, could you save us a table?" through the speakers, and Martin's voice reply, "Okay."

Martin leaned over and whispered in clear awe, "How'd he do that?"

Jason whispered back, "See those microphones? They've been on the whole time."

Martin shook his head slightly and said, "Whoa."

Their recorded and amplified voices mutated under Roland's control, warbling and wobbling until they were no longer recognizable as natural sounds, becoming indistinguishable components of the bizarre texture of sound generated by the gear in the coffin freezer, metamorphosing under the flicks of Roland's hands on the sliders.

The mélange of sounds grew in a slow crescendo and, although there was nothing that could be called a tempo, the rate of mutation of the layers of sound increased, creating the impression of an *accelerando*. The screen reflected in Roland's glasses as his sound structure built to a thundering climax of unnatural sounds that rattled the Rust Garden's thin walls and burst sharply into a sudden return to the original sounds, which faded and repeated, until the only sound was the swishing hum of Roland's gear through his amplifier.

Martin was the first to applaud, and the room filled with the sounds of stomps and whistles. As the audience moved toward the back of the room and was reabsorbed by the coffeehouse, Jason and Martin walked to the stage. A pudgy man with messy dark hair and smeared glasses had cornered Roland, who was nodding politely and obviously trying to ignore the fact that the pudgy man sprayed a little when he talked. When Roland noticed Jason and Martin, he broke into the stream of technical talk with, "Jason, hi! This is ... I'm sorry, what was your name?"

The man took a moment to answer, as though it took time for him to understand the question. "Virgil."

"Virgil, this is Jason and Martin. Virgil's on MUSE, too."

"Really," Jason said. "What's your username?"

"Oh," Virgil said, and there was another pause. Jason waited. "I'm sure you wouldn't know it," Virgil finally finished.

"Maybe. What is it?"

Another long pause. "BIGVIRG." An impish look stole into his eyes, and after another pause, he said, "I told you you wouldn't know it."

"And you were right," Jason said. "Well, it was nice to meet you." He turned to Roland and said, "Listen, I need to talk to you."

"Okay," Roland said. "Virgil, it was nice to meet you. I'll see you around on MUSE."

Virgil said, "Okay," waited for a moment, and then ambled away.

"Thanks," Roland said in a low voice. "I owe you several."

"No problem. That must happen to you all the time. It happens to me a lot, and my setup is about a tenth as impressive as yours."

Martin said, "What happens?"

Roland said, "Every time I play out, some techie comes up afterward and wants to talk equipment. I can hang with it sometimes, but the equipment's not really the point. I like talking to people afterward; I just don't like to get into endless gear specs."

Martin said, "What was that guy's problem?"

"He's a programmer," Roland said. "Mainframes."

Martin looked blank, so Jason said, "A lot of good programmers I know talk like that. It's as though English is a second language to them, with their first language being code."

"Code?"

Roland said, "What computer programs are written in."

"Oh."

"So," Jason continued, "in extreme cases, you get guys like that, who seem to even think in code, and when they actually have to communicate with human beings, they have to translate back and forth from code to English. Those long silences are kind of time-outs to assemble sentences."

"Exactly," Roland said.

"That's really weird," Martin said.

"I get that way myself when I'm heavily into performing or composing," Jason said, and Roland nodded. "I start thinking like a quarter note and can't talk. 'There are more things under heaven than are dreamt of in your philosophy,' Martin."

"Oh, I'm quite sure of that," Martin said. "That's why I don't *have* a philosophy. Was that *Hamlet* or *Macbeth*? I always get them mixed up."

"Me too, but it's one or the other," Jason said, at the same time as Roland said, "*Hamlet.*"

"It's from *Hamlet*," Jason said.

"How can you confuse *Hamlet* and *Macbeth*?" Roland said.

"I'm a musician and he's an artist," Jason said. "We can confuse anything."

They helped Roland coil his cables and carry his equipment cases to his car. When he left, they went into the coffeehouse and drank cappuccino. Jason picked up an *L.A. Reader* and read Cecil Adams' column to Martin. A three-piece band that had been setting up when they came in started to play. Jason winced and glanced at Martin. Martin was wincing, too. They put money on the table and left hastily.

Down the street where they had parked, there was a car just like Jason's with a smashed rear window. As they approached it, it took Jason a minute to make the jump from *This isn't my car because my car doesn't have a smashed rear window* to *Somebody smashed my window!*

"Oh!" Martin said. Jason's mouth tightened and he walked around the car. It seemed to be just the rear window.

"Great."

"Oh, gosh," Martin said.

Jason unlocked the driver's door and looked inside. There was broken glass all the way to the front floorboard and on top of the dash.

He sighed heavily and straightened up.

"Should we call the cops?" Martin said, still wide-eyed.

"I don't see why," Jason said, walking to the back of the car. "I don't think anything's missing. It'll take them an hour to get here, if they come at all, and what are they going to do?"

"I guess," Martin said. Jason unlocked the trunk and thumped it sharply with the side of his fist just above the lock. A few pieces of loose glass fell out of the rear window frame and the trunk opened a few inches. Jason propped it open with a stick that he kept next to the bumper jack, and took a thick gray blanket out, removed the stick, and closed the trunk. He brushed most of the glass off the front seat with a newspaper section from the back, and then unfolded the blanket and refolded it to fit the front seat, and they got into the car.

"That's a shame," Martin said, twisting to see the rear window. "Are you insured?"

"Yeah, but only liability." Jason started the car and looked behind him for traffic.

"That's really a shame. Why would somebody do that?"

Jason had no answer, so he didn't say anything and pulled onto Highland. For the next few blocks, Martin started to say something and then didn't, three times.

"What?" Jason finally demanded, exasperated.

"I don't know if I should say, because it might be nothing."

"Yes?"

"Well ... do you think this could be related to your poking around about Monica Gleason?"

"I don't think so."

"Why not? Maybe N. Platt found out you were after him."

Jason pondered. "Or her. Well, I guess it could be."

"I think maybe you should go see that lady cop."

"Detective Johns."

"Right, her."

On the Pasadena Freeway, Jason said, "Martin?"

"Yeah?"

"How come Detective Johns is a lady cop, and not just a cop?"

Martin looked surprised. "Uh, I don't mean anything by that. It's just how I talk."

Jason nodded.

"You think it's wrong?"

"I don't think anything. I was just wondering."

In his peripheral vision, Jason could see Martin inspecting him.

"Yes?"

"How are you feeling?"

"Fine. How are you?"

Martin didn't answer. They were silent all the way back to the Manor.

10

USERNAME: NOTE-ON
PASSWORD: • • • • • • • •
HELLO NOTE-ON
Logon at 6-JAN 08:32:38
You have 2 new mail messages.

#1
From: CYBERFINGERS 5-JAN 03:22:17.59
To: NOTE-ON
Subj: gig!

I enjoyed meeting you last night. Thanks for the help! I'll let
you know when I'm playing again.
Take it easy,
Roland
-*-

#2
From: PREDATOR   5-JAN 04:12:33.00
To: NOTE-ON
Subj: bang bang your dead!!!
hi jason keltner. i no you but you dont no me. next time i

wont miss you. did you like what i did to your car.
hahahahahaha
_-*-_
MAIL> send
To: MeTaMuSiC
From: NOTE-ON
Subj: Hello
Enter your message below. When finished, enter ^Z.

What happened to Monica Gleason?
^Z
Message sent.

MAIL> bye
NOTE-ON off at 08:33:12
Session time: 2 minutes.
MUSE DISCONNECTED

The phone rang at 6:30 in the morning. Jason got up from the computer table and picked it up.

"Unh," he said in a sleepy voice. He was awake, but he wanted whoever it was to feel guilty for calling at 6:30 in the morning.

A female voice said, "May I speak to Jason Keltner, please?"

He dropped the sleepy voice. "Yeah, this is Jason."

"Mr. Keltner, this is Detective Johns. I called you several times yesterday, but your answering machine is not accepting messages."

"Really?" He leaned over and looked at it. The little message indicator was flashing furiously. "No wonder. It's full."

"I understand you were involved in a shooting yesterday."

"Yes."

"Why?"

"Why was I involved in a shooting?"

"Yes."

"Uh, because it's hard to stab somebody from a car thirty feet away?"

"Why else?"

"Because my position in the spacetime continuum intersected with the trajectory of a bunch of bullets?"

"Why else?"

"Because of my widespread reputation for making funny noises when wounded?"

"Why else?"

"Because ... ignorant of the contract that had been put out on my folding chair by an international consortium of rocker-recliners, I accidentally wandered into the middle of a Chair Mafia hit?"

"Why else?"

Jason said, "Detective Johns, these witty gems don't spontaneously generate from a void. You have to give me better straight lines than 'Why else.'"

"Okay, how about this? You were involved in a shooting because you've been poking around in the Monica Gleason investigation and somebody got mad at you and decided that it would be better if you were dead."

Jason leaned against the bookcase and cocked the telephone against his shoulder. "Sounds pretty mundane. I found the mafia chair theory much more entertaining."

"Or maybe somebody knows you killed Monica Gleason and wants revenge."

"If you really thought that, I wouldn't be comfy at home, exchanging sparkling banter with you over the phone, dumbfounded and agog that some people still don't know not to call musicians before noon."

"Your slothfulness is not my problem, Mr. Keltner. I have a job to do."

"'Neither sleet nor snow nor darkest night,'" Jason said. "'Slothfulness,' Detective Johns?"

"'Agog,' Mr. Keltner?"

"Great word," Jason said. "I also like 'shrub.'"

"I believe the shooting happened because you've been poking your nose where it doesn't belong."

"Could be. Know what I believe?"

"What." The tone was flat, not at all that of someone gripped by suspense.

"I believe you're jealous that somebody shot at me and not at you, because that means that I'm on to something and you're not."

There was no answer, so Jason said, "The problem is, I don't know what I'm on to. But I might be very pleased to tell you what I've been up to because maybe one of us, and I'm not saying which one, has no idea what he or she is involved in, but suspects that whatever it is could severely limit his or her long-term plans for metabolism."

"Go on."

"If you come over to my place, I'll have fresh coffee for you and two things to show you that just happened."

"Fifteen minutes," Detective Johns said, and hung up.

Jason hung up the phone, said, "Terse, competent, professional," in a deep voice to the empty room, and went and made coffee.

"Nice how you told me this 'just happened.'"

Detective Johns was wearing a blue blouse with the same little black stringy limp bow thing or its sister and sitting in front of Jason's Macintosh, reading the e-mail message from

PREDATOR. Her coffee was in a cream-colored china cup on a matching saucer on the floor. Jason was wearing blue jeans and a T-shirt that said CREATIVE MUSICIANS COALITION. He said, "Um, it did."

She turned and looked at him levelly. "Really."

"Really."

Still looking at him, she tapped the screen with one nail. "This says January fifth, at three-twelve in the morning."

"Oh," Jason said, "That's when the message was sent, not when I received it. Also, that's Eastern time. The big computer where this all happens is on the east coast." She didn't respond. "Either that or I went to the trouble of lying and inviting a detective over, but goofy me, I forgot to change the dates on the screen. Oh, that wacky, bumbling, investigation-side-tracking Jase."

She maintained the level look. Jason said, "I confess. It was me. I did it in the study with the candlestick."

She turned slightly so that she was facing him more directly. The look didn't falter. Jason said, "If you're planning to continue affixing me with your steely gaze, you have to intone something gravely."

"Mr. Keltner—"

"If you have no portents of doom to intone gravely, some will be appointed for you. Do you wish to give up the right to intone portents of doom?"

She said, "Mr. Keltner," again, and then bit down on it and didn't continue. She sat and looked at her fingertips silently for a minute. Then she said, "You are going to be this kind of a pain in the ass every time you feel accused, aren't you?"

"You're much smarter than my ex-wife."

She pursed her lips and nodded. The look and the nod said *fifteen years to retirement.* "What's he talking about with your car?"

"Or she. That's the second thing I wanted to show you. Come outside."

He showed her the Plymouth.

"Did you make a police report?"

"No."

"Why not?"

"For a broken window in Hollywood?"

"Tell me what happened."

Jason told her about the evening, trying not to leave anything out. When he finished, she said, "What about this Roland guy?"

Jason shook his head. "No, I really don't think so. When you move your own electronics around for a living all the time, you get extra sensitive about other people's things. And besides, Martin and I were with him pretty much the whole time."

"How about this Virgil character?"

"I thought of that, but isn't our, uh, perpetrator somebody who targeted me specifically, both with the shooting and with the window smashing? So it couldn't have been somebody I met just last night."

"What about this Martin guy? Would he have any reason to want to bother you?"

Jason smiled. "Martin's about as vindictive as a Fig Newton. We've been friends for a long time, and he's crashing on my couch these days."

"Can you think of anyone who would want to harass you?"

"I've been trying to, but I can't think of anybody. I suppose there are plenty of people who don't like me, despite my sweet disposition and radiant countenance, but as far as I know, I've never made any serious enemies."

Detective Johns leaned against the staircase handrail and almost lost her balance when it wobbled. She moved a few feet to her left and leaned against the flimsy siding that contained the storage area under the staircase. "Well, you've managed to make a serious enemy now. What exactly have you been getting into?"

"I went to Monica Gleason's wake and met her little sister."

"That's all?"

"Yes."

"You're sure that's all."

"Yes."

The level look came back. "Mr. Keltner, people are not shot at for attending wakes."

Jason pursed his lips and drew his breath in. "Have you ever been divorced?"

She looked taken aback."Why?"

"Have you?"

"I don't think it's relevant."

"If you have been, do you remember how exhausted and numb you were?"

She pursed her lips.

"Remember how you did maybe one or two things that just weren't the kind of thing you do?"

She studied him for a long time. He didn't see any change in her face to indicate that she had reached a conclusion. "All right. Tell me what else you did."

Jason took a deep breath and told her about entering Monica Gleason's apartment through the window. He didn't tell her about taking the data from Monica's computer. Then he stopped talking and waited for her reaction.

She eventually said, "Breaking and entering and interfering in a homicide investigation." She nodded. The set look was back. "We have been a busy boy, haven't we, Mr. Keltner?"

Jason couldn't think of anything to say, so he just looked around the parking lot uncomfortably. Waldo, the gray and white cat, was half-hidden in the tall weeds near the staircase, half asleep. Somebody from the condos came out with a brief-case and got into a dark green Saab, started the engine, and left for work. Waldo's tail flicked and he pounced on something a few inches in front of him and then backed off an inch and stared at it intently. He repeated the pounce, back off, stare sequence several times as whatever it was moved across the patch of weeds. Jason ran out of things to look at, so he looked at Detective Johns.

"So?" he said. "Are you taking me downtown?"

"No."

"Why not?"

"You're not a suspect. I'm only here because your getting shot at might mean you're involved in some way. We checked you out, just like everybody else. You don't fit the profile or the circumstances."

"Which are?"

"Which are police business and none of yours."

"Oh."

"Let's go back inside and you'll tell me everything you know."

"I did already."

"Then you can tell me again."

"Oh boy," Jason said, "The sound of my own voice!"

11

After he told her all the same things twice more, Detective Johns left him, with a stern warning to stay out of the investigation. Jason spent half an hour sweeping glass out of the Plymouth with a yellow plastic whisk-broom and then spent an hour trying to devise clever ways of covering the opening where the rear window had been. Around 9:00, he gave up and left it open and drove to Hollywood, vigilant for unmarked police cars, because he felt paranoid after his talk with the detective. He didn't see any. He decided to interpret that as meaning that there weren't any.

He pulled into the parking structure for patrons of the Chinese Theatre, told the attendants who sat in folding chairs near the entrance that he was going to see a movie so they'd let him park there, and walked twenty minutes to Mailbox City, where he hung around in front, pretending to read the free *L.A. Reader* that he'd gotten from a yellow newsrack, watching nobody open Box 83.

Four hours later, annoyed as hell, he gave up, got a piece of paper and a pen from the mailbox clerk, wrote, "Who killed Monica Gleason? Contact NOTE-ON on MUSE," and slipped it into Box 83.

The walk back to the Parking Structure did nothing to

reduce his annoyance. He got the Plymouth and went to a newsstand on Cahuenga, bought two paperback copies of *The Art Of War*, and read one while he ate two pieces of pepperoni and mushroom pizza at Numero Uno. He drove home and took a pink Post-It notepad from under the papers on his computer table, wrote "Please look through this and meet me tomorrow at noon" on two Post-Its, and stuck them to the covers of the two books. He put one copy on Martin's pillow on the couch and then went out the front door and back into the house through a neighboring door, and up the wooden stairs to the second floor. A short entryway to the right of the top landing was filled with cardboard boxes of dusty paperbacks. He threaded his way through them and propped the other book against Robert's door.

In his apartment, he hunted through his books until he found his own old copy, went back upstairs and borrowed a yellow Hi-Liter marker from Patrice, and sat on the back stairs, reading and Hi-Liting. After about four hours, he got a pad of paper from inside and walked to The Talking Room.

The Talking Room was newer, classier, and more expensive than the E-Bar, and had real food and didn't have poetry nights, so mostly adults went there. The furniture and trim were wood, and there was always either jazz or classical music playing. This time it was jazz. Jason sat halfway back in the long room and read and Hi-Lited *The Art Of War* over a series of Café Mochas, occasionally writing on the pad. When afternoon ended and it began to get dark outside, he tore the top sheet off the pad, folded it, put it inside the book, paid for the Café Mochas and walked back to the Manor, undressed, and went to sleep.

12

He presses RETURN *and the message is sent through the Net. The message is very short. It is encoded. When decoded, it consists only of a time and a telephone number.*

He looks again at the clock on the computer screen. He has time to eat dinner. Then he will go to a pay telephone and receive his call. Then things will be taken care of.

13

Jason's clock-radio alarm went off at eleven. He got up, showered, and had coffee while he made chicken-flavored Top Ramen the wrong way, without the broth. At noon, there was a knock on the front door and he let Martin and Robert in. They both had their copies of *The Art of War*.

Martin sat on the couch and Robert sat on the floor. Jason sat on the piano bench and said, "Well."

Martin glanced at Robert, held up his book, and said, "We decided to wait to see what you have to say, but I just want to say that whatever it is, you're insane, and we won't let you do it."

Jason looked at Robert. Robert didn't look away, but he didn't say anything, either.

Jason tapped his book against his knee and said, "That's not an option. Robert and I were attacked. I didn't declare war on anybody, but somebody's declared war on me. I don't know yet how to respond, but your options consist of helping me or not helping me. 'Not letting me do it' is not one of your choices."

Martin said, "See—" explosively at the same time as Robert said, "Jason..." They looked at each other and then Martin made an eloquent gesture of deference with his shoulders and palms. Robert said, "Jason, what is it exactly that you're thinking about doing with this book?"

"I'm not sure, exactly."

"Then how about not exactly?"

"Not exactly, I'm going to respond to someone shooting at Robert and me."

Martin's restraint expired and he said, "'Respond?' What does that mean, 'Respond?'"

Robert said, "Martin—"

Jason said, "I don't know yet."

Robert said, "If we don't help you, what will you do?"

"Something less than I would do if you helped me."

"Oh, that's clear," Martin said.

Robert said, "Could you be a little more descriptive?"

Jason tapped his other knee. "No." When he saw Martin gearing up for another explosion, he said, "You think I'm being uncommunicative, but I'm not. Or maybe I am, but the reason is that I don't have anything to communicate. I don't know what exactly I want to do. I just thought that it would be a good idea for us to have a talk about what's been going on and what we're going to do about it."

"What we're going to do about it," Martin said, "is let the cops handle it."

"Nope," said Jason. "Cops think the shooting was a random drive-by. And even if they don't believe that, what do they have to go on? Next time I get shot at by someone in a car, I'll think to get the license plate, but that doesn't do any good for now. The cops aren't going to get anywhere."

Martin said, "Maybe it *was* a random drive-by. It could have been."

Jason nodded and said, "Sure,"and waited.

After some time, Robert said, "So much for the random drive-by."

"Here's what I think," Jason said. "I think whoever shot at

us was not the same person as whoever killed Monica and smashed my car window."

"Why not?" said Martin.

"Think about it. The sequence is wrong. Don't you think that smashing someone's car window should come *before* shooting at them?"

Martin started to say something, but stopped and looked thoughtful.

Robert stared at him, and then nodded slowly and said, "Go on."

Jason put the book down. "That says to me that there may be two different people or groups of people who want to kill or harass me. If Monica's killer is one of them, there's a clear motive; I must be on to something I don't know about. But who's the other person and what's the motive?"

Robert said, "Do you have any theories who the second person might be?"

"None. Any ideas?"

Robert looked into the corner of the room with a glassy expression. Martin looked at his feet. Jason had already been over it so many times that he just sat and waited.

"Maybe," Robert said, without looking away from the corner, "Monica's killer hired a shooter, but good help is hard to find these days and the shooter screwed it up."

"No way," said Martin. "Think about it. Why would he bother to do that and then break the car window?"

Robert said, "Because he was so peeved that the guy with the gun missed."

Martin said, "Peeved?"

"Irked?"

Martin made a doubtful noise.

Robert said, "Okay, let's call the guy with the gun 'Mr. Gun' and Monica's killer 'Mr. Fluffy.'"

Martin said, "Why 'Mr. Fluffy?'"

"We can say that there are only two ways that Mr. Gun and Mr. Fluffy can relate to each other: Either they know each other, or they don't. Let's take each possibility, one at a time."

Jason said, "Okay, so let's say that they don't know each other."

"If they don't know each other ..." Maintaining his cornerward gaze, Robert rocked back and forth slightly. "If they don't know each other, then Mr. Gun is either working for himself or for someone else. Do we have any evidence to support that he was working for himself?"

There was silence.

"Do we have any evidence to support that he was working for someone else?"

Jason said, "Well ..." and then the silence resumed.

Finally, Martin said, "This is probably nothing."

Robert looked away from the corner and looked expectant.

"Well," Martin said, "it's just that, don't you think that someone who was trying to kill you for their own personal reason would try to finish the job, and not just shoot once and run away?"

Robert looked up at nothing and his expression became searching. "Jason, what do you think?"

"Could be." Jason thought about it. "And furthermore, I don't think someone who shoots once, misses, and then runs away sounds very professional. I got the definite impression of only one person in the car. Wouldn't a professional have a driver so he could concentrate, and not have to worry about parking and shooting at the same time? And it's only maybe ten yards from the street to the porch; wouldn't a professional *hit* something at that range?"

"Right," said Robert.

Martin nodded and said, "Makes sense to me."

"Okay," Jason said, "So maybe we're dealing with a low-budget hit man."

Robert looked at the ceiling and said, "Which means that we are dealing now with three people; Mr. Fluffy, Mr. Gun, and Mr. Gun's boss, who we'll call—" He narrowed his eyes and made a dredging-for-the-right-word gesture with the tips of his thumb and forefinger.

"Who we'll call 'Mr. Gun's Boss,'" Martin said. "So we can remember it."

"What do we know about Mr. Gun's Boss?" Robert said.

Martin said, "He's a cheap son-of-a-bitch."

Jason said, "He's a coward. Won't do it himself."

Martin said, "Hey!"

Robert looked at him. Jason didn't say anything.

Martin said, "We're helping you, and we weren't going to do that!" He turned to Robert. "Right?"

Robert's gaze drifted distractedly back toward the corner and he said, "Why would Mr. Gun's Boss want to hire someone to shoot at me and Jason and miss?"

Martin made a disgusted sound and threw his hands up.

Jason said, "Oh yeah! Maybe to scare us."

Martin said, "It's too bad it didn't work."

Robert said, "But if it were just to scare us, we're back down to two people, because now there's no reason someone acting on their own wouldn't just shoot once, miss, and run away."

"Which leaves us just where we were," Jason said.

Robert snapped his fingers. "Hey! Do you think Leonard Bernstein stole that car and shot at us?"

Jason said, "Leonard Bernstein's dead."

Robert raised a forefinger. "Aha! We're not just where we were."

Martin said, "Great. We've eliminated Leonard Bernstein as a suspect."

"Thank God we've got Robert," said Jason. "Let's call him 'Mr. Useful.'"

Martin looked back and forth from Robert to Jason. "So now what?"

Nobody said anything for a few minutes.

"Well," Jason finally said, "I don't think we can really deduce much about the Bad Guys with the little evidence we have. I think maybe we ought to worry instead about the fact that we have no evidence that this stuff isn't going to continue."

Robert pursed his lips and looked pensive.

"Oh, I feel incredibly comforted now," Martin said.

Jason picked up his *The Art of War*. "Did you guys have a chance to look through this?"

"A little," Martin said.

"I've read it before," Robert said.

"Any thoughts?" Jason opened his. "I figure we should assume that we are outnumbered and outskilled."

Robert said, "I agree. Since we don't know anything, we have to assume an enemy exists. And since we don't know anything about the enemy's goals, we have to try to be ready for all the possible situations we can think of."

"Like what?" Jason said.

Martin sat forward on the couch. "If I was someone with resources and manpower, and my enemy wasn't, I'd probably just try to strong-arm him."

Jason said, "And I'd do it soon."

Robert nodded in agreement. "Do you accept the premise that all warfare is based on deception?"

Jason said, "Okay," and Martin shrugged and said, "Sure."

Robert said, "Then since the enemy probably knows we have no resources or manpower, we should do everything we can to bolster both."

Jason said, "We've already bolstered manpower just by allying with each other. We're three instead of one. We oughta have a name."

"First Unarmored Division," Robert said.

Jason grinned and said, "Joint Sheafs of Chaff."

Martin said, "The Screamin' Pink Tigers."

Robert said, "The Fightin' Gastropods."

Jason said, "Let's worry about the name later." He took the folded piece of paper out of his book. "I made a list of some of the basics. There seems to be a lot of emphasis placed on not fighting."

Robert gave him a thumbs-up without saying anything.

Martin said, "I like that. I like the not fighting part."

Jason said, "I think our strategy, whatever it is, should hinge on, ah, thwarting his or her plans, rather than confrontation where we might be expected. In a direct confrontation, we're sunk."

Martin said, "Don't get me wrong; I've got nothing against a clean fight, but I'm not crazy about the idea of suicide. This boy ain't no kamikaze."

Robert said thoughtfully, "Assuming we have time to implement it, I might have an idea."

14

Solomon and Tony were crooks. Before they'd been hired full-time, Tony had hurt people for money, and Solomon had been a concert promoter. Tony was five-eight and 195 pounds, all of it muscle. He wore slacks and a yellow shirt and a blue windbreaker that hung down more on the left than the right. Solomon was an inch taller and slender, with a goatee and even, white teeth. He wore a dark, shiny suit and black shoes with tassels.

They stood in the bleak light of the Manor's porch lightbulb on January sixth, in front of Jason's taped cardboard windows. It was a few minutes before midnight. No light showed through the windows or under the door. Tony said softly, "You sure this the place?" His speech had the cadence and accent of West African pidgin English.

Solomon lifted a folded piece of white paper and showed it to Tony without looking at it. Tony made a show of squinting at the paper. In a moment, he said, "Oh, yeah, that one, uh-huh." He nodded.

Solomon pointed with one slender, manicured finger at the corroded metal numerals nailed over the Manor's front doorbell.

Tony nodded. "Ah, yes, I see."

With his finger still pointing at the number, Solomon looked silently at Tony for a moment, and then pressed the doorbell. Tony looked sagely at the metal numerals and nodded as though reverifying something very important.

No light went on inside. Tony shuffled from foot to foot.

Some women walked by on the sidewalk, speaking Spanish. Tony let his breath out in a disdainful hiss. He glanced at Solomon and said, "Mexicans, man," and shook his head. Solomon ignored him. Tony got closer to the front door and tried to see in. "Maybe the doorbell don't work." He rapped on one of the still-intact panes of glass and called, "Hello, anybody?"

There was no answer, and no light went on.

"What we do if nobody here?"

Solomon stroked his goatee and thought. Then he said, in an accent quite different than Tony's, "We were instructed to intimidate the occupant of this domicile. Now, one can intimidate, or one can intimate. You see the difference?"

Tony nodded vigorously and said, "You're so right."

"A man can intimidate, you see, or he can intimate. I consider that this time is, perhaps, a time for intimation. We should intimate while he is gone, so that we may intimidate when he returns."

Tony nodded furiously. "Yes, yes," he said. Solomon was so smart that Tony didn't even understand what he said most of the time.

Solomon looked around. The women had passed and there was no one on the street or the sidewalks. The Manor was still dark. Solomon tried the knob. It was locked, but the pane of glass next to it had a hole in it that looked big enough to get Tony's hand through. Some of the other panes were closed up with cardboard.

"Tony, reach your hand through that hole and open the door."

Tony's brow furrowed. "Why me?"

Solomon looked irritated. "This a thousand dollar suit, bro! You want me snag it on something?"

Tony grumbled and reached his hand through the hole, fished around on the knob for the lock button, and rotated it with his forefinger. Pulling out, he jerked suddenly and said, "Ah!" Moving more carefully, he withdrew his hand and put his mouth on the cut on the back of his wrist. Solomon clucked sagely and said, "Aspire to be more vigilant, bro." He turned the knob and slowly opened the door, and they stepped into Jason's front room.

There was a couch with a blanket spread over it, an upright piano, and a stand made of black tubing in the corner with some things on it under dust covers. A doorway with no door in it opened farther back into darkness. Solomon closed the door. When Tony's eyes had adjusted to the darkness, he looked at Solomon for a clue about what to do next.

"See what's in there," Solomon whispered. Tony took a short length of one-inch heavy pipe from his left jacket pocket and walked quietly through the doorway into a very short passage with a bookshelf, and into the pseudo-kitchen. The floor creaked under his steps. He stepped gracefully to the perimeter of the room to skirt the noisy floorboards, but the floor creaked there, too.

He went into the bathroom. The door on the opposite wall was ajar, and Tony tried to creep across the linoleum to it, but the floor creaked even more loudly than in the pseudo-kitchen. He listened at the door. There was no sound. Slowly, he pushed the door open and looked into Jason's bedroom. There was nobody in there either, just bare, ugly wooden floor and a futon on a wooden frame.

He closed the door, went back into the front room and said to Solomon, "Nobody here. What we do now?"

"Now we intimate, bro." Solomon pulled back one side of his jacket and withdrew the crowbar that hooked over his waistband and hung down into his left trouser leg. Tony smiled and slapped the pipe into his right palm. Solomon raised one warning finger and said, "But remember, bro, we must definitely be quick and efficient, because noise will draw unwanted attention. Dig?"

"Dig," Tony said. He grinned and slapped his palm with the pipe again. Solomon hefted the crowbar and brought it down violently onto one of the covered things on the black stand. Something shattered like glass; he raised the crowbar again and crashed it down onto something else, which also shattered. Tony flipped the piece of pipe into the air in a little circle, caught it at one end, and smashed the remaining panes of glass in the front door, then pocketed the pipe, gripped the back edge of the piano, rocked it twice, and pulled it over onto the floor. The piano made a huge overturned-piano noise, and Tony chuckled gleefully.

"Okay, bro," Solomon said. His eyes danced with excitement. Let's go!"

The sound of the scrape of a shoe on concrete froze both of them. There was another scrape, and then the sound of a shotgun being cocked. Tony's jaw dropped and he said, "Oh!" Solomon pointed toward the back of the apartment and whispered, "There a door there?"

Tony nodded and pointed.

Solomon said, "Go that way! Hurry!" Tony leaped agilely over the piano and sped through the apartment. The back door wasn't quite shut. He wrenched it open and took one running step outside.

Behind Tony, Solomon saw the square-headed shovel arc down from above the open doorway and hit Tony hard in the face, with a dull clang. Tony's piece of pipe didn't stop as suddenly as Tony did. It flew forward into the windshield of the Plymouth, which was parked nose-in to the door. As Tony hit the hood of the Plymouth, Solomon skidded to a stop and looked around, panicked. From the front room came the sound of another shotgun being cocked. He glanced sideways, into the bathroom. There was an open window in the bedroom, through the open door on the opposite bathroom wall.

Bolting through the bathroom, he took one running step into the bedroom, and the wooden floor under him heaved up at an angle and threw him completely off balance. He windmilled his arms and twisted to regain his step, and his crowbar whipped up into his face and knocked out three teeth. Jason stepped in from the side and followed the crowbar with a round-headed shovel swung hard into Solomon's forehead. Solomon crumpled. Jason dropped the shovel, took an extension cord from the futon, and bound Solomon's hands behind his back, making an extra few loops around the futon frame. Then he got another cord and did the same to Solomon's feet.

Outside, Martin yelled, "Did you get him?"

Jason was grinning hard. "We got him! Did you get yours?"

Martin yelled, "I got him! I got him I got him I got him!"

The floor thumped, and Solomon groaned. Jason pulled the cord tight around Solomon's feet and then shoved him until he rolled off the basement door. The door heaved open and Robert, covered in cobwebs and old dirt and leaves, came up the wooden steps into the room with a disgusted expression, holding his arms away from his sides. He shook himself and said, "Bleaaaggh!"

Jason said, "Pick up the shovel and stay here with this

one." He snatched Solomon's crowbar from the bathroom floor and ran out the back door, where Martin was tying Tony's hands behind his back to his feet. Tony's face was bloody, but he seemed more or less conscious.

Martin said, "It worked!" He tugged once on the knot to verify its security, and stood up.

Jason said, "Yeah, it worked!"

They grinned happily at each other, did a three-part handshake and lightly bumped fists, and looked back down at Tony, who was wincing and starting to focus. From inside the house, Robert's voice said, loudly, "That'll teach ya to mess with the Fightin' Gastropods, Mr. Scrotum!"

15

It took all three of them to carry Tony into the bedroom. They bumped his head against the sink on their way through the bathroom and Martin said, "Sorry." Robert seemed to think that was really funny, and giggled for two minutes.

None of the other tenants seemed to be home, so Jason didn't have to tell them that Robert had gotten carried away rehearsing a scene. He hadn't liked that explanation, anyway.

He left Robert and Martin to watch the two captives, went outside and put the shovels back in the shed, and took down Martin's perch: a long two-by-twelve that stretched above the doorway, suspended by the stair landing and one of the rickety ladders. He gathered up the dozen orange, dirty utility cones that had blocked access to the back of the house and put them in the storage area under the stairs. There was a half-eaten sandwich still on the stair landing. He left it there for Waldo the cat.

Inside, he climbed over the wounded piano and went into the front room. Flipping up the blanket that covered the couch, he got on his hands and knees, reached under the couch, and turned a switch, cutting off the sound effect of a doorknob being turned.

He straightened, went to his keyboard stand, and pulled

up one edge of a dustcover. Under it, broken soda bottles sat on a flat plank. He replaced the dustcover. His keyboards were in their road cases in the trunk of the Plymouth.

He went back through the bathroom into the bedroom. The window had been shut and the mini-blinds closed. Solomon and Tony were on the floor. Martin was bandaging Tony's nose, and Robert was leaning against the wall, still cobwebby from the basement, holding a pitchfork from the storage area and leering wildly around the room. Solomon's mouth was split, and blood covered his chin and neck, and soaked the top of his shirt. There was a wad of wet, reddened gauze in his mouth. His forehead was starting to swell. Tony's nose looked odd, and his face and shirt were covered in blood too.

When Jason came in, Martin said softly, "Hey, man, we didn't think about painkillers."

Jason said, "I've got some Percoset from when I had my wisdom teeth out. I'll get it." He went into the pseudo-kitchen, got a little straw basket down from a shelf above the counter, and rooted through the vitamins and old prescriptions until he found the plastic bottle of Percoset. Rattling the pills absently, he took the bottle into the bedroom with two big glasses of water, and two pink drinking straws with Mickey Mouse's face molded in the plastic.

"There's only six left," he said. "Better just give them one each after they've talked to us, or they'll really be in pain later when there aren't any left."

Robert gestured for Jason to come closer, and, still maintaining the wild expression, whispered, "What if we injured them really badly?"

Jason knelt and looked closely at Solomon for a minute, and then at Tony, and said, "I can't tell how bad they are. Martin, can you?"

Martin said, "They'll live. I saw guys hurt worse than this when I was tending bar up in Turlock."

Solomon said something muffled through the gauze and tried to spit it out. Martin looked at Jason. Jason nodded, and Martin pulled the gauze out. Solomon said, "We kill you, motherfucker."

Robert said, "He's so delirious that he's gotten his pronouns mixed up."

Jason knelt again in front of him and said quietly, "You broke into my home and destroyed my property. If you do not shut up and tell me only what I ask, I may let Big Bob there put that pitchfork against your adam's apple and stomp on it until it comes out the back of your neck. He likes that."

Robert leered and said crazily, "Last time, I got Mr. Pitchfork all the way through this guy's head with just one stomp." He accentuated the last word by jabbing the pitchfork toward Solomon, and then leaned forward and said conspiratorially, in a horrified whisper, "And the guy lived." He leered sideways. "Kind of."

Solomon said, "Not afraid of you."

Robert laughed hollowly with his head back and said, "You will be, in time, Mr. Scrotum."

Jason stood up and said, "Give these guys their Percoset." While Martin did that, Jason said, "Watch them for a while, while we pack the camping gear, Big Bob. You can maim them however you want, but no actual death, is that clear?"

Robert was still doing the Psycho Killer. "Okay, boss," he said. He took a bottle of pale green typewriter correction fluid out of his pocket and leered at it with his eyebrows going. Solomon and Tony stared uncomprehendingly at the bottle. Jason and Martin left the room as Robert slowly unscrewed the cap.

***

"Trapped in a little room with Robert with a bottle of Liquid Paper," Martin said. "A fate worse than death." He hoisted Jason's tent bag into the back seat of the Plymouth and pushed it all the way to the side. Robert was singing something in the house.

Jason put his Coleman cooler on the ground. "I know. He's really getting into it, isn't he?"

"Yeah."

They went back into the house for another load. Carrying the small propane camp stove, Jason stopped just shy of the bathroom door on the way out and stood there, trying to make out what Robert was singing. Martin came up next to him, holding an orange backpack. Jason strained to hear, not quite able to make it out. Robert must have changed position, because it suddenly got a little louder, and Jason recognized it. It was the "Brady Bunch" theme, but Robert was improvising his own words about it being The Story/Of A Man Named Scrotum/Who Was Coughing Up A Very Lovely Spleen. Sudden laughter bubbled up into Jason's chest. He looked quickly at Martin, who had just bitten down on his backpack to stifle his own. Jason clapped his free hand over his mouth and backed into the front room, dropped the little stove on the carpet, dropped headfirst onto the couch, and let it out into the cushions. Martin came in with tears streaming down his face onto the backpack.

Every few minutes, they'd get it under control and then look at each other and lose it again, until finally, exhausted, they sat on the floor against the couch and wiped their eyes with the backs of their hands, their chests still occasionally shuddering with giggles that didn't quite materialize.

"Oh, man," Martin said, when he could talk.

"Jeez," Jason agreed.

They sat for a few more minutes, and then Martin sighed shakily and took a pair of coveralls and an auburn wig and fake moustache out of the backpack and put them on. Then he carried the sleeping bags outside past the open bathroom door, looking away from the door and limping just as he passed it. He did the same thing when he came back in for another load. Then he clomped back and forth a few times.

"Did they see you?" Jason said.

Martin nodded and said, "The skinny one looked."

When all the camping gear was in the car and most of the contents of his refrigerator had been transferred to the cooler, Jason picked up a brown paper bag from the counter, took a deep breath, told himself not to laugh, and went into the bedroom.

Robert was crouched across the room from the captives, holding the pitchfork upright and staring straight into Tony's eyes. Tony wasn't meeting his gaze. Everybody had pale green correction fluid on them. Robert had it on his face and arms in squiggly lines and dots, Tony had little smiley faces from his neck to his hairline, and Solomon's forehead said, in block capital letters, "I'm Mr. Scrotum." Two wallets lay on the futon.

Jason said, "I'll take it from here, Big Bob."

Robert said, "But I didn't get to maim them yet."

Jason said, "You had plenty of time to maim them. You should have thought of that before you started singing and doing arts and crafts. I'll take it from here. You go help with the camping provisions."

Reluctantly, Robert said, "Okay." He handed over the pitchfork, snarled, and left the room.

Jason sat on the futon and looked at Solomon and Tony.

"What are your names?" he said, looking from one to the other.

They didn't answer. He said, "Okay, I'll look for myself," and picked up the first wallet. There was no driver's license. A California ID Card bore the name "Solomon Adewale."

Jason said, "Solomon ... how do you pronounce the last name?"

Solomon said derisively, "Do you know who you are dealing with?"

Jason said, "Yes." He looked through the rest of the wallet. There were no credit cards, just a portrait-studio headshot of a woman in her twenties, and sixteen fifty-dollar bills. He took the fifties out of the wallet, folded them over once, and said to Solomon, "'Live on the enemy.'"

Solomon said, "If you know who you are dealing with, you know that you are going to die."

Jason pocketed the money and picked up the other wallet. There was no identification at all in it, and no credit cards, just a ten-dollar bill and two Trojan condoms. He held up one of the little square packages and said, "Considering the lack of any other ID, how about we just call you Reservoir Tip?"

"Preacher gonna kill you," Tony said.

Solomon said, "Shut up, Tony."

Jason added the ten to the money in his pocket and said, "Yeah right. I'd like to see him try."

"Oh, he'll try, all right," Tony said. Solomon said, "Shut up," again, but Tony wasn't having it. "You better believe he'll try. He'll come for you with the juju, American Boy, and you'll die with your soul gone down to everlasting torment."

Jason said, "Really."

Solomon said, "Tony, you shut your mouth now or you'll be the one gone down to everlasting torment."

Tony said, "You'll see. You'll see," and fell silent.

They weren't going to talk any more, at least not soon

enough. Jason put Tony's condom and his wallet on the futon and started taking things out of the brown bag.

A party of four armed thugs entered the house through the open back door the next morning. They found Tony and Solomon tied up with smiley faces and "I'm Mr. Scrotum" written on them in green correction fluid, drinking Percoset-laced Liquid Nutrition for Invalids from two jumbo hamster bottles, saying that there were four of them, the red-haired one had a limp, Big Bob had a pitchfork, and they were going camping.

16

Robert lay on the floor on a closed sleeping bag, while Martin sat on the cooler in the empty apartment behind Jason's, and peered out between the mini-blind slats that faced the parking lot. Jason watched out a similarly mini-blinded side window. The apartment had been empty since the end of November. It had a leaky roof, and no one had yet wanted to rent it. Someone would probably want it in February or March. The cooler and the sleeping bags had never made it into the Plymouth, which was two blocks away, with a car cover over it.

Jason's Macintosh was set up on the floor, with a thin cable running from its back to a telephone jack along the room's baseboard. Its fan whirred softly. He showed Martin and Robert how to connect to the Net and send messages, and then disconnected everything and put it by the back door in a carrying case. They rotated two-hour watches: one looking out the back window, one looking out the side, and one sleeping.

When the four armed thugs arrived in a black Lincoln, Robert was on back-window watch. He made a soft hissing sound to get Martin's attention and tapped Jason lightly on the back. All three of them watched out the back window as the four thugs helped Solomon and Tony hobble to the Lincoln and get in.

The Lincoln pulled out, and as soon as it was out of sight around the corner of the parking lot, Martin and Robert ran out of the apartment to Martin's little green Honda CVCC, and Jason grabbed the Macintosh and ran to a navy blue Mitsubishi compact with a Hertz sticker on the bumper.

He put the Macintosh on the floor in front of the passenger's seat, got in and started the ignition, picked up a walkie-talkie from the seat, turned it on, and said, "You there?"

Martin's CVCC was already out of its parking space and heading out of the lot. The walkie-talkie crackled and Robert's voice said, "That's a big ten-four, good buddy."

"Good," Jason said. He rolled down his window. "Just don't let them see you talking. Hold the walkie-talkie in your lap and use one click for yes and two for no, like we agreed, okay?"

The walkie-talkie clicked four times. Jason pulled out of the parking space, but didn't exit the lot. "Are you on the road?"

One click.

"Are you behind them?"

One click.

"I'm exiting the lot now. Do I turn right?"

Two clicks.

"Left onto Del Mar."

One click.

He drove partway out of the lot and stopped with the nose butting slightly into the street and looked to his left. The Lincoln was two blocks down, waiting in the left turn lane for a red light to turn green, and the CVCC was a block behind it, stopped at a signal. Jason picked up the walkie-talkie and said, "I'm going to guess he's heading south down Arroyo onto the One Ten freeway. I'll parallel you on Marengo. Give me three clicks if he turns off Arroyo before the One-ten. If you think you might have been spotted, stop following him and let me take over."

Martin's voice, very softly, came over the speaker and said, "Anything else you want to tell us for the third time?" Jason depressed the talk button and said, "Nope." He put the walkie-talkie on the seat, opened the window, and turned left out of the driveway, and then left onto Marengo.

The Lincoln entered the freeway at the end of Arroyo. Jason stayed in the middle lanes, about a quarter of a mile behind Martin and Robert, who stayed in the left lane, four cars behind the Lincoln. At the Dodger Stadium offramp, Jason clicked the talk button several times quickly, and they traded places. At the Exposition exit, they traded again. Just after Exposition, the Lincoln signaled right and moved over into the right lane. The CVCC stayed in the left lane, and Jason sped up a little in the second lane and then moved into the right lane, three cars back from the Lincoln. In his rear view mirror, he saw the CVCC fade back and get out of the fast lane.

The Lincoln exited at Martin Luther King Drive and turned left. Jason stayed behind it. As he turned, he saw the CVCC appear at the top of the off ramp behind him.

He followed the Lincoln for several city blocks, until a red light separated them. While he waited impatiently at the light, the Lincoln turned left into a long, narrow parking lot that stretched the length of two blocks. The solid, windowless buildings on the far side of the parking lot looked as though they'd been warehouses around the turn of the century, but some of them had since been converted to business spaces. The Lincoln stopped in front of one that had been painted pale yellow, and two men got out, with Tony between them. The Lincoln started up again, and disappeared behind the building. A huge sign held above the building by a massive metal post said CHURCH OF THE BELIEVERS in what were probably twenty-foot-high letters. Below that, ten-foot letters said, REV. BILLY A. CRYER, PASTOR.

Jason said, "Gotcha," and glanced in the mirror. The CVCC was a block behind him, stopped at another signal. His light changed. Now what? He was in the middle lane, so turning wasn't an option. He didn't want to go past the Church of the Believers and run the risk of being recognized, but it looked necessary.

As Jason began to accelerate, he looked to his left; he saw the Lincoln come to a stop at the intersection. In the front seat, facing him, was Solomon.

Recognition dawned on Solomon's face and Jason's lungs stopped working. He floored the accelerator as Solomon pointed urgently at him and yelled something at the driver. The Lincoln jackrabbited into the intersection against the light and made it through the cross traffic without being hit. It swung in behind him and started to gain. Jason accelerated toward the red light at the intersection ahead of him and got into the left lane. When the Lincoln moved left to follow him, he wrenched the wheel right and cut across three lanes into a gas station, jolting hard as the car bottomed out on the driveway.

He shot through the gas station diagonally, hit a wire trash can on the sidewalk next to a bus stop, and went off the curb onto the cross-street. He couldn't see the CVCC. The Lincoln had gone around traffic in the left turn lane, and was creeping into the intersection. When there was no cross traffic, it hung a sharp right in front of the stopped cars and sped forward toward Jason, who pressed harder on the already-floored accelerator pedal and said, "Goddamn four-banger" under his breath. The Lincoln gained steadily. The signal ahead was green. The orange speedometer needle in the Mitsubishi vibrated a little at the ninety-miles-per-hour mark, and increased very slowly. The Lincoln was two car lengths back with no cars between them, and someone's torso was sticking out one of the passenger's side windows and pointing something at Jason.

Both cars hit the intersection in the left lane at ninety-five miles per hour. Jason cut into the right lane and hit the Mitsubishi's brakes hard. As the compact began to fishtail clockwise, the Lincoln shot past on his left with its brake lights on. The Mitsubishi's angle to its direction of momentum became sharper and Jason's sense of balance went crazy as he turned in the direction of the skid. The Mitsubishi started to come under control, but then it shuddered and spun out fast in a shriek of friction, coming to rest finally in a driveway, pointed toward the street. Jason blinked in confusion at the burnt rubber smell and the red dashboard lights and tried to get his bearings as the Lincoln backed past him, going fast, and then shifted into low gear while still moving and came at him. He hit the accelerator pedal and nothing happened. Staring stupidly at the dashboard lights, he tried it again. Nothing. What the hell was going on? Dash lights on and no power ... what did that mean?

He couldn't think straight. The Lincoln stopped with squealing tires in front of him, and the two passenger's doors opened. Solomon got out of the front, and a well-dressed, slender man with a triangular face and a handgun got out of the back and ran toward the Mitsubishi. Jason stared at the dashboard. *Lights and no power. Lights and no power.*

The engine had stalled out in the spin! He grabbed the key, still in the ignition, and turned it, and the engine started as the slender man reached the compact, grabbed Jason's throat with one hand through the open window, and brought the handgun up to bear on him with the other. Jason shoved his left arm out the window, got it firmly around the man's neck, yanked him in close to the car, and floored the accelerator. The Mitsubishi's first gear was strong, and his arm slammed backward into the window frame, but he managed to hang on until the compact was in the street, where the man fell away. He made a one-armed right, still foggy from the spinout, and glanced at the rear view mirror. Solomon was back in the front seat, and the slender man was on the ground, crawling with his gun into the Lincoln. It took a few seconds for him to get in, and then the Lincoln lurched into motion. Jason's damaged left arm and shoulder hurt like hell. With the Lincoln behind him, he turned the wheel to the right to enter a side street, but pain lanced through his arm and he flinched and botched the turn, sliding into the curb instead and braking hard to avoid hitting the cars parked in front of him. The Lincoln veered to its right to block him in, and a huge, dirty, brown Mercury Marquis shot out of the side street, swerved around Jason, and rammed the Lincoln broadside so hard that both cars ended up on the other side of the street in front of a donut shop, the Lincoln half atop the hood of the Marquis so that Jason could see its undercarriage. A tall man with tea-colored skin and long brown hair slipped nimbly out of the Marquis' driver's window, bowed deeply to Jason, and ran behind the donut shop. There was movement inside the Lincoln.

Martin's CVCC came around the corner and slowed next to the Mitsubishi. Martin and Robert both looked at him with shocked expressions. Martin had his walkie-talkie to his mouth, and his voice said, "Are you okay, man?" in Jason's lap. Jason nodded, waved them on with his right arm, and got behind them when they passed. Sirens sounded somewhere, and a block later, they pulled over to let two LAPD black and whites speed by in the opposite direction.

17

It was just past twilight, and Jason was sitting on the cooler, boiling Kraft Macaroni on the Coleman stove in the light of his propane lantern. The stove was in the Plymouth's propped-open trunk, and the lantern hung from the latch on the raised trunk lid. Two open blue and orange Macaroni and Cheese boxes stood next to the stove, with their tops torn off and the cheese packets inside.

The Plymouth was parked next to Martin's CVCC on a turnoff from the Angeles Crest Highway that overlooked a small valley. Below, the highway threaded around and between the lower hills, and several minutes elapsed between passing cars. Jason had chosen the spot because he figured the Preacher's thugs would be checking all the local campgrounds, and because it didn't cost anything to stay there in their cars for a night, and because it had a good view of the approaching highway from the Los Angeles direction.

He'd returned the Mitsubishi at one o'clock—the only damage was an almost unnoticeable tilt to the rear bumper, probably from when he'd gone off the curb—and then the three of them had gone shopping with Solomon's eight hundred and Tony's ten dollars. Jason hadn't wanted to walk around in the open in the Pasadena area, so they'd driven fifteen miles to Burbank and shopped at a big indoor mall. A sporting goods store at the mall sold shotguns, but after discussing it over Hot Dogs on Sticks, they had all agreed that since none of them knew how to shoot, a gun would be marginally useful at best.

Instead, they spent a hundred dollars on camping supplies and food, and twenty-five on books: *Chaos* and *Illusions* for Robert, and a stack of thick, oversized comic books for Martin. Jason wasn't in a reading mood, but he bought some music magazines anyway. Then they'd gone to a Salvation Army store and bought some old clothes and a pair of pink plastic sunglasses, and gotten a Clairol hair-coloring kit from a drug store next to the Salvation Army store. They had their car keys copied while they were there, and exchanged them.

After Jason told them about the tall man with the long hair, they talked all afternoon about him, but none of their theories seemed any more likely than the others. When Robert's scenarios began to involve crop circles and the Face on Mars, Jason had called the discussion to an end and they'd driven to the turnoff, which was partially hidden from the highway by a semicircle of large boulders. They'd tucked the cars back behind the boulders; Jason didn't expect anyone to notice them there, but he looked at the highway every so often anyway, in case a car slowed.

The air was chilly. Jason put on the torn purple ski jacket with fluff coming out of it that he wore to the filtration plant when it was cold. Martin and Robert sat in two of Robert's webbed aluminum lawn chairs near the edge of the flat dirt area. The collar of Martin's denim jacket was turned up, and his hands were in its pockets, through which he maintained a wobbly grip on an open comic book. Every few minutes, he took one hand out and turned a page. A saucer next to him held two cigarette butts.

Robert was reading *Chaos*. A shiny new blanket-sided canteen hung on a khaki strap over the quilted black fabric of his nylon jacket.

The soft hiss of the propane lantern was familiar, the same hiss Jason remembered from when his family had gone camping when he was younger. Reading by propane light had always seemed somehow magical, even when he had to shoo away the mosquitoes that were attracted to the gleaming white pages of his book.

For a minute, he felt a kind of nostalgic loss. Jason's parents hadn't ended up happy together, and his father had never liked or understood most of the things Jason had done. Still didn't. But when Jason considered the abuse that he saw around him, he figured a few years of garden-variety wrongness was nothing to mist up about.

And none of it detracted from the magic of reading by gaslight. He sighed softly, turned off the burner, walked to the edge of the turnoff, and drained the macaroni into the brush below, tipping the pot slowly so the macaroni wouldn't fall out with the water.

Without looking up, Martin said, "Dinnertime?"

"Yeah," Jason said. He righted the pot and walked back to the Plymouth. "Why don't you kids set the table?"

Martin and Robert got up from the lawn chairs and ambled over.

"Did you bring plates?" Robert said.

"In the back seat." Jason added milk and butter from the cooler to the pot and stirred in the cheese mix with a knife until most of the lumps were gone. Robert got metal plates, forks, and cups out of the Plymouth, and Jason doled out the macaroni and cheese. They sat in the lawn chairs and poured coffee from Martin's dented silver Thermos.

Martin got up, opened the CVCC's hatchback, and hunted around for a decent radio signal. The reception wasn't very good in the hills, and the little bursts of noise and static made the turnoff seem very far from civilization and normality, even though it was only a fifteen-minute drive to Colorado Boulevard.

"Go back to that," Jason said, as Martin turned the radio dial. Youssou N'Dour and Peter Gabriel were singing "Shakin' the Tree."

Martin tuned it in and sat down in his lawn chair. "How's your arm?"

"Hurts," Jason said, "but it doesn't feel permanently damaged."

They ate their dinner. It got darker and colder. Jason pulled the stove and propane tank out of the trunk, set them up in front of the chairs, and lit both burners for heat. Traffic was more infrequent, the cars swishing by every twenty or thirty minutes.

Nobody said anything for a long time. On the radio, Bob Marley sang "Redemption Song." Then Paul Simon sang "Spirit Voices."

Jason said, "I know you guys want to talk more about all this, but I'm just not up to it. Can we have a meeting in the morning?"

Martin said, "Sure," and Robert said, "We'll do breakfast."

They looked at the hills and the sky, though it was slightly too overcast to see many stars. Somebody sang something in a language Jason didn't know.

After a while longer, Martin said, in a sleepy voice, "Good night," turned off the radio, closed the hatchback, and got into the front of the CVCC.

Jason looked at Robert. He looked asleep. "Robert," Jason

said softly. Robert's head slumped a little and he breathed heavily. Jason sat for an hour and looked up at the sky for meteors, but didn't see any. When his neck hurt from looking up, he went to the Plymouth, got *The Art Of War*, and read it by the softly hissing light of the propane lantern until he fell asleep.

18

Jason woke up when it started to get light. Robert wasn't in his chair any more, and the propane lantern was still going. His eyes felt sandy. He turned off the lantern, stood up and stretched.

It was Saturday morning. The valley was filled with fog, and the turnoff and the little brush that Jason could see were almost gray in the thin morning light. It was cold. Jason puffed his breath out and watched the vapor dissipate. Martin was asleep in his survival bag in the tiny front seat of the CVCC, and Robert was in the back seat of the Plymouth with a yellow blanket wrapped around his head.

Jason walked briskly around the turnoff eight times to get his body going, and then lugged the frigid propane tank over to the Plymouth, hooked the stove up to it, and put a scratched and unevenly-colored rectangular griddle on it.

All the sounds—the scraping clink of the propane tank on the ground, the little metal squeak that the hose connector made when he tightened it, the dull clank of the griddle against the stove's steel rack—were strangely isolated. He opened the cooler—plastic click, small sucking noise, slight drag of weight against dirt— and fished half a stick of butter and six eggs for pancake batter out of the icewater. When the first batch was almost done, Martin got out of the CVCC, rubbed his eyes and yawned, and walked carefully in his socks over the rocky ground to the far end of the turnoff. Jason put the pancakes on a metal plate, covered them with a bowl, and poured more. Martin came back and went to the CVCC and put his shoes on.

The Plymouth rocked and its door opened, and Robert got out, grinned lopsidedly, looked around, and went to the far end of the turnoff where Martin had been. When he came back, he said, "Good morning," in a cheerfully booming announcer voice.

"Morning," Jason said.

"Shut up," Martin said, with his eyes closed.

Robert cocked one eyebrow. "Ah, I see someone's feeling cranky this fine, fine morning. And it is, indeed, a fine, fine morning."

"Robert," Martin began. He opened his eyes very slightly and gestured emptily with one hand. "Never mind."

Jason said, "Get your plates."

They banged their plates against the CVCC's front bumper until most of the macaroni remains fell off, and then shook their coffee cups over the edge of the turnoff while Jason turned off the stove and got a bottle of real maple syrup out of the cooler. Then they all sat and ate.

Martin finished his coffee and poured more from the Thermos. Robert said, in a hushed voice, "Martin never has seconds at home."

Martin said, "Robert, I love you dearly." He put his hand on Robert's arm, looked at him imploringly, and said, "But could you at least wait for my coffee to kick in? Please?"

Robert put his fists on his hips like a superhero and said, "For you, my friend Martin, anything." Then he put his head back and said, "Ha ha ha!" in the same superhero voice, without moving his lips.

"Thanks," Martin said, "I'm so glad I asked."

Jason got up with his plate and silverware and tossed them into the trunk of the Plymouth. "Let's break camp."

Half an hour later, everything was packed into the cars. Jason checked the fluids in the Plymouth and the CVCC, and topped up the CVCC's battery from an antifreeze bottle full of water. Then they left the turnoff and drove forty-five minutes to the Castaic Lake recreation area, where they spent the day sitting on covered benches next to the Lake's forebay, reading and playing chess on Martin's small folding magnetic chess board. Martin and Robert were evenly matched, and they both beat Jason consistently. Jason pointed out features of the huge dam and the hydroelectric plant. The plant was a daily stop on his meter run, and supplied electric power to several cities, just as the reservoir was a source of water for much of southern California.

The pipes that carried water from the Colorado River Aqueduct to the filtration plant where Jason worked were huge. An empty twenty-foot section of pipeline sat on the dirt next to the access road, where it had been left during the plant's construction after failing its stress tests. A high point of Municipal Water's bus tours was when the bus drove through it on the way to the plant.

The recreation area closed at five o'clock. They left with everyone else, and drove aimlessly around Castaic.

Castaic was a truckstop town in a sort of architectural adolescence. New housing developments were popping up on the big flat area west of the Interstate and sprouting on the chunky hills immediately east: long, uniform stretches of pink and yellow houses and orange banners that said, "If you lived here, you'd be home now." One of the men at the filtration plant was thinking about buying one. Jason couldn't imagine.

Most of the businesses on the main strip catered to truck drivers. There was a truck wash, a donut shop, a hot dog shack, a bar, a gas station, and a Seven-Eleven. Jason, Robert, and Martin went to the donut shop after they were finished driving around Castaic, and stayed there for the better part of an hour. Jason recommended the apple fritters. He and Martin each had one, and Robert had two. Then they stopped at the gas station and filled the propane tank, and then drove back to the entrance to the forebay.

Ten feet in from the road, a gate made from three-inch metal pipe painted white blocked the road. Jason got out of the Plymouth, leaving the door open and the motor running. He took a round, flat retractable keychain out of his pocket, and unlocked the padlock that held one end of the gate to another piece of pipe sunk vertically into the ground next to the access road. Then he grabbed the free end of the gate and shoved hard; the gate wobbled around on its pivot and swung into a bracket that held it open. That done, he got back into the Plymouth and pulled it forward twenty feet. The CVCC pulled in behind him, and he got out and closed and locked the gate.

They turned their headlights off and drove past the recreation area, stopping at a chain-link gate, where they repeated the procedure. With the CVCC in his rear view mirror, Jason drove into the plant compound on a dusty access road, around rows of white cabinets in a chain-link pen, and to the far side of a low, squat building, where they stopped the cars and turned off the engines.

The building was to their left. To the right was a low depression flanked by foothills. Two brown meter cabinets, six-foot-high narrow metal boxes, stood in the low area, and there was a loud, constant sound of rushing water.

Jason got out of the Plymouth and his shoes crunched on the gravel. The flatness of sound in the depression enhanced the effect, making every footstep and truck noise seem subtly Western.

Robert must have noticed it too, because after he liberated himself from the CVCC, he squinted his eyes in the dim glow from the yellow parking lights and said in a tough whisper, "Do I look like Jack Palance?"

Jason considered it seriously and then said, "Robert, as much as I know this will crush you, you will never look like Jack Palance."

Martin got out of the CVCC. Robert squinted tighter and whispered, "Need more crags, you think?"

Jason said, "Even if you had crags surgically implanted."

Robert nodded dangerously and whispered, "Hmmm."

Jason said, "The dangerous nod is good, though."

Robert nodded dangerously again. Martin said, "You sure we'll be safe here?"

Jason said, "Pretty sure. Nobody's scheduled to read anything until Monday morning, so unless a meteorite hits nearby and Ooze People from Planet Q steal the dam, no one has any reason to be around. We just have to be sure we're out of this fenced-off area before the boating crowd gets here in the morning. We don't want Jack here to scare them."

Martin looked carefully at Robert and said, "Jack who?"

Robert looked evilly through eyes like knife slits and whispered, "Jack Palance."

Martin said, "Oh, I thought you were doing Clint Eastwood."

"No," Robert said. "*This* is Clint Eastwood." He squinted. Jason thought it looked just like Jack Palance. He shot a quick glance at Martin, who was shooting a quick glance back at him. Martin shrugged.

They spread their sleeping bags near the cars, and then went on foot up a dirt path to the top of the concrete rim of the spillway from the other side of the dam. Water flowed turbulently from the top and spread when it hit the forebay. They sat and looked at the faint moonlight gleaming on the shifting, corrugated surface.

"That's a lot of water," Martin said.

"That's a lot of water," Robert whispered dangerously.

Jason took out what was left of Solomon and Tony's money. There was still almost six hundred dollars left. He counted out eight fifties, put the rest back in his wallet, and handed four each to Robert and Martin.

Martin said, "What's this?"

"Funds," Jason said. "Gas, food, whatever. Night sight goggles, shoe phones."

Robert nodded and jammed his into a back pocket.

Martin said, "Thanks."

Jason said, "Robert, stuff falls out of your back pockets when you walk."

Robert said, "Really?" and dug the money back out and jammed it into a front pocket.

Jason said, "Any new ideas about the guy from the car chase? If there's no new ideas, let's just leave it alone for now and talk about it when we have more information."

Martin said, "Nope, not me."

Robert squinted and whispered, "You mean *any* information."

Jason said, "Should we go over tomorrow's stuff?"

Martin said, "I think we've got it."

Robert whispered, "No need." He shook his head slowly and threateningly. "No need."

"Okay."

They sat up and talked about how acting, music, and art were like and unlike each other. Then they talked about which was best for getting girls. There was no consensus. Then they climbed down and slept in their sleeping bags until Robert's new travel alarm went off at six o'clock Sunday morning.

19

*H*e *presses* ENTER.

The machine, in communication with other machines, performs a series of subtractions, followed by a series of additions.

He causes a string of similar operations to be performed; all consist of a series of subtractions, followed by a series of additions.

When he is finished, numbers that were previously large have been reduced to zero. Previous zeroes have been transformed into figures of six and seven digits.

He'd prepared his luggage earlier.

He disappears.

20

Sunday mornings glittered and shone at the Church of the Believers. The congregation, mostly west African, decked themselves out in their second-finest clothes for the weekly services. Their first-finest were reserved for holiday-specific services. Their second-finest beat most people's first-finest by a long shot.

At nine o'clock, in front of the church, no man was without a fresh shine to his shoes and a patterned vest under his shiny coat. No smear could be found on a spectacle lens; no rough, frayed part on a leather belt. The heads of the men were up and proud; their shoulders were square and straight.

The women swathed themselves in expensive, glistening fabrics that flattered good curves and artfully concealed others. Those women who came with men stayed close to them. Those who didn't come with men stayed close to their families.

Their headwear was crafted from the same fabric that wrapped their bodies, and their makeup was applied skillfully and subtlely, flattering good features and artfully concealing others, so that their faces shone gracefully and radiantly, as though burnished, in coruscating, elegant beauty. They chose their perfumes well, and applied them lightly.

All of them smelled good. God deserved no less.

There were three dirty people on the sidewalk outside the door that admitted the Believers into the Church. One of them was sitting up, a short black woman with flyaway hair, wearing a dark blue running suit with red and white stripes around one arm. She didn't smell good. Her lower half was wrapped in a mass of shredded blankets that looked vaguely pink. She watched the narrow parking lot, looking past the finery, and said, "Can you spare any change, ma'am?" softly. Most of the people gave her a dollar without looking at her. When a man saw the man ahead of him give two dollars, and when he knew that the man knew he knew, he would give four dollars. The woman would say, "Thank you, sir. Can you spare any change, ma'am?"

The second dirty person was asleep on a big flattened cardboard box with a filthy blue blanket around him. He lay in a fetal position with his back to the pretty churchgoers. The hair that stuck out between his collar and his dirty knit cap was salt-and-pepper gray. He didn't move, except to breathe heavily.

The third dirty person was Robert in his Salvation Army clothes, pink sunglasses, three-day beard, and Autumn Mist Blond hair, squatting on a *Nigerian Times* newspaper on the sidewalk and muttering. A faded orange baseball cap that said CAL TRANS was jammed onto Robert's head. He'd pushed one of the sunglass lenses out, and he stared blindly with one eye past the churchgoers. The *Nigerian Times* was from a stack near the door.

"Good Master Mustard-seed," he growled, "I know your patience well; that same cowardly, giant-like ox-beef hath devour'd many a gentleman of your house." A young family approached him. The father steered his wife and children around Robert.

"I promise you your kindred hath made my eyes water ere now!" Robert yelled suddenly. The young mother jumped. "I desire you more acquaintance, good Master Mustard-seed!" As the family passed him, he muttered, "Goddamn Squash. Goddamn Peas-blossom," in the Jack Palance whisper.

Across the street, Jason and Martin sat in Martin's CVCC with a Thermos of coffee and watched Robert. They had removed the license plates from both cars earlier in the morning. The Plymouth was parked with the cover over it, in the parking structure in Hollywood near the Chinese theater.

Jason was wearing Wayfarer sunglasses and had his hair bunched under a blue baseball cap. Martin was wearing aviator sunglasses, brown slacks and a tan Marvel Comics T-shirt with holes in it. On his head was the auburn wig and an ugly green canvas cap with ear flaps.

Martin said, "So that's what five cups of coffee will do to you."

Jason said, "He was supposed to not attract attention."

Martin said, "Maybe we should talk to him about it. But you know," he twisted around to face Jason, "this is Robert we're talking about here."

"You look really stupid," Jason said.

"You look like a DEA agent," Martin said. "I'll take stupid."

Across the street, Robert stood up and assumed a shaky *en pointe* position with his hands stuck out like an Egyptian tomb painting.

Jason muttered, "Goddammit, Robert." When Robert seemed to be looking toward the CVCC, Jason threw his hands up.

Robert mimicked the gesture, putting his whole body into it. Jason drew one forefinger sharply across his throat, and Robert went off on a whole new routine, apparently arguing with someone invisible.

"Well, hell," Jason said.

The flock of churchgoers outside the building had begun

to thin. After a few minutes, the ones mingling on the sidewalk looked at their watches and entered the church. Robert got up and paced back and forth in front of the church, and then sat down next to the door, crosslegged, and played with his feet.

Jason relaxed a little. For Robert, sitting crosslegged on the sidewalk and playing with his feet was low-key.

A few minutes later, Jason pointed at a white Cadillac that was leaving the parking lot. "Is that Solomon whatsisname?"

Martin squinted. "Could be."

The Cadillac drove away.

The next hour went quickly. Jason found Car Talk just starting on an NPR station, so they listened to that. Martin didn't know much about cars, but he liked the show anyway. Jason tried to diagnose the callers' car problems before the hosts could, and invariably failed.

When Car Talk ended, they listened to The Best Of The 'Eighties on another station and agreed only upon the Police and Thomas Dolby.

At ten-twenty, people came out of the church.

Martin looked inquiringly at Jason. Jason nodded and climbed over the seat into the back. Martin started the car, put it in gear, and pulled into traffic. Half a block down, he made a U-turn and entered the long parking lot at the far end, put it into Park, unlatched the passenger door, and sat there with the engine running. Robert didn't acknowledge their presence, though they were close enough to overhear the louder conversations of the people leaving the church. Jason pulled his cap lower to cover his face, and Martin did the same.

The Preacher came out.

"That's him," Jason said.

There was no question. The Preacher was close to seven feet tall, a slender man with dark skin. He wore a gray robe and carried a black-bound Bible. His bearing was that of an important man, and Jason had no doubt that he was very rich.

As the churchgoers paid their respects to the Preacher, Robert lurched to his feet, picked up his *Nigerian Times*, staggered a few steps, fell against the Preacher, and yelled, "I can see! It's a miracle!"

The Preacher's back was toward the CVCC, but after a pause of only a fraction of a second, Jason heard the Preacher say, in a mellifluous, unaccented baritone voice, "Amen, brother. The Lord has truly blessed you."

"Smooth," Martin said in the CVCC. Some of the churchgoers said, "Amen."

"It's a miracle! A miracle!" Robert yelled, whipping off his pink sunglasses and flinging them against the church wall. "I can see!"

The Preacher said, "The power of the Lord has made itself manifest here today, brothers and sisters."

Robert said, "Hallelujah!"

Several more churchgoers said, "Amen!"

A look of shock passed over Robert's face, and he said, "Let me hear you say Amen again!"

The churchgoers said, "Amen!"

Tears appeared in Robert's eyes and he shouted, "I can hear! It's a miracle! I can hear again!"

"We are thankful for the blessing of our God," the Preacher said, with a slight edge to his tone. "Because we know that the Lord punishes those who do not deserve His mercy."

Some of the congregation looked at each other uncertainly. Robert frowned in concentration and made snuffling sounds in his nose. The Preacher turned to his flock. "Brothers and Sisters—"

Robert made a very loud snuffling sound and yelled, "I can smell!"

The Preacher laid his hand on Robert's shoulder and said, "Let us pray for this poor soul."

Robert flinched and canted as though the Preacher were squeezing his shoulder painfully, and whined, "Ow, ow, ow, ow." The flock exchanged uncertain whispers.

Two bulky men in gray suits and white shirts stepped onto the sidewalk from inside the church. One of them was Tony. His face was still puffy and bruised.

Robert swiveled toward the Pastor, did his tough squint, and grated, "Who killed Monica Gleason?"

Tony pointed excitedly and said, "This is Big Bob, Pastor!" He took a step out of the doorway. The Preacher took his hand off Robert's shoulder and stayed Tony with it without looking away from Robert.

Robert whispered dangerously, "I'm sorry. I didn't quite hear your answer." He inhaled deeply, put his face up into the Preacher's, and bellowed, "Who killed Monica Gleason?"

The Preacher angled his hand slightly, and the staying gesture turned to a beckoning one. Robert saw it and held one hand away from his side with two fingers pointing down.

Martin said, "There's the signal," put the CVCC in gear, and pulled forward. Robert said, "That's okay, never mind," twisted out of the Preacher's grip and off the curb, pulled the passenger door open, and jumped in. Martin accelerated smoothly. Jason turned around in the back seat and looked out the window. Tony and the other bulky man were standing with the Preacher, looking at the car. The Preacher's arms were up to encompass his people, as in a benediction, but his gaze was on the CVCC as it reached the end of the parking lot and exited onto Martin Luther King Drive.

"Harass your enemy ceaselessly," Martin said.

"Now that we've done it," Jason said. "I'm not quite sure it was such a good idea."

21

Martin dropped Jason off at his car on the third level of the parking structure, where it was parked between a beautiful black 1967 fastback Mustang and a raised Chevy Suburban with primer and no paint. It was covered with a blue, locking car cover.

"See you at the Square," Jason said, after he unlocked and removed the car cover.

Robert laughed.

"What," Jason said.

Robert said, "That's not the kind of car you usually see under a locking car cover."

Jason looked at the Plymouth. Robert was right. Most cars you found under locking car covers had complete windshields and didn't sport gaping holes where their rear windows were supposed to be. And probably weren't dented, and had only one visible layer of paint. And had matching tires.

"It'll be a classic next year," Jason said.

Martin leaned forward to see past Robert and said, "Uh, no, it won't."

"I love this car," Jason protested. "This is a great car."

"Goodbye, Jason," Martin said, as the CVCC slowly crept forward.

Jason said, "Later."

Robert waved, and the CVCC drove away.

Jason bunched the car cover up and put it in the back seat, and got in the driver's seat. He rolled down the window, and put the key in the ignition, and a fortyish man with tea-colored skin and long brown hair got out of the passenger side of the Suburban and squatted so his face was in the Plymouth's window. He rested his forearms there, pointed a very small handgun at Jason, and said in a friendly voice, "I wouldn't suggest turning the key."

Jason didn't move, except to turn his eyes toward the man. He had brown eyes, and long, deep crow's feet, and was wearing a dark green T-shirt and a wristwatch with a brown strap. His straight hair was parted in the middle and fell loosely past his shoulders. His moustache was slightly darker than his hair, and his expression was amiable, which Jason found difficult to reconcile with the handgun.

The man's expression didn't change, and the gun stayed where it was, not quite pointing at Jason, but rather simply an informal part of the tableau, like an hors d'oeuvre.

Jason said slowly, "The Suburban suits you better than the Marquis did."

The man grinned suddenly, and the crow's feet deepened. He said, "It runs better, too."

Jason said carefully, "Why wouldn't you suggest that I turn the key?"

The man said, "Get out of the car," and stood up and stepped back. He was wearing gray corduroys and tan sneakers. Jason opened the door and got out. The man had about an inch on him, but wasn't as tall as Robert.

"Open the hood," the man said. Jason walked to the front of the car, found the lever that stuck through the grill, and hit the hood with his fist while he pulled it. The hood opened an inch, and Jason reached in with two fingers, released the catch inside, and raised the hood.

On top of the valve cover, toward the firewall, were four sticks of dynamite, bundled with electrical tape. Two wires ran down into the engine compartment. A wave of coldness washed through Jason's body. He put the fingertips of one hand on the fender as an anchor.

"I think that's a good reason," the man said. "Don't you?" He put the handgun in the waistband of the corduroys and pulled the T-shirt over it.

"Oh my," Jason said. It was all he could think to say.

"Do you know someone who drives a white Cadillac?"

"Uh, um, a guy named Solomon."

"He was in the front seat of the Lincoln I totaled the other day. The guy with the missing teeth."

Jason said, "Yes."

The man squatted again, in front of the exposed engine compartment, and looked at the bomb. "Lousy craftsmanship. Sloppy work. Nobody takes any pride in anything any more. Do you know how long it took him to install it?"

"No," Jason said. "How long?"

"It took him ten minutes." The man shook his head. "He didn't even have the sticks bundled together in advance."

Jason said, "Is that a long time?" The conversation seemed inappropriate.

"I could do it in less than one."

"Who are you?"

The man offered his hand. "Norton Platt. Nice to meet you."

Jason shook his hand and said, "Norton Platt?" He felt overloaded.

"Yes." Norton Platt stood up. "Well, I guess I'll be going." He walked to the Suburban. "See you around."

Jason said, "Well, wait!"

Platt stopped and waited.

"What do I do about this?"

Platt said, "Best thing would be to find someone to disarm it."

Jason said, slowly, "Would you disarm it?"

"Well," Platt said, wandering back toward the open hood, "I guess I could. What's it worth to you?"

Jason said, "Um, I ... I don't know. What do you usually charge?"

Platt shrugged and pursed his lips. "It varies according to the situation." Jason tried to think and couldn't. "Often," Platt said after a few seconds of silence, "I'll barter services for goods."

Jason said, "Oh." He looked at the bomb. "Oh! How about if you keep the dynamite?"

Platt said, "And the fuse?"

"Sure, yes, and the fuse. Everything."

Platt grinned. "Okay." He reached into the engine compartment and picked the bomb up off the valve cover. The wires came with it, with clips at their ends. They weren't attached to anything. Jason's brain spun. Platt shrugged and said, "I disconnected it before you got here. It's not safe to have this stuff lying around, waiting to go off."

He reached into the Suburban's open window and put the dynamite on its floor. "The hardest part was getting the hood open."

Jason said, "You have to hit it over the latch."

"Yes, I figured that out."

"You've been following me around."

"Yes. More or less."

"Why?"

Platt said, "Let's go somewhere and talk. Do you drink coffee?"

22

Sitting at a strange, welded table under a long chalkboard, Jason and Norton Platt ate small blue soft tacos and drank coffee in Hollywood. Jason's was a double mocha, and Platt's was a decaffeinated Kenyan blend with sugar and no cream. The chalkboard had faces drawn on it in different colors of chalk. Some of them were very skillfully drawn, and took advantage of the contrast between the light chalk and darker board.

Platt said, "What do you want to know?"

Jason took a sip of his mocha and said, "'What's going on?' seems to be a good starter. I assume this is all because you got my note."

"Yes." Platt finished a soft taco and picked up another one.

Jason said, "I'm not sure what else to ask."

"Well," Platt said. He ate half the taco and drank some coffee. "You could start by asking me if I killed Monica."

"Did you kill Monica?"

"No."

"Okay. What do I ask you next?"

"Why I've been following you around."

"Because you got my note on MUSE and or in your mailbox and decided to find out about me."

"And why I bothered to get involved when you screwed-up, tailing that Lincoln."

"Because ... I don't know why."

"Because I liked that shovel maneuver."

"You mean ... you saw that? How long have you been following me?"

"Since I got your note."

"Where were you?"

"I rented an apartment in the building that faces your back door. Where have your strategies been coming from?"

"Did some research on large and small forces. *The Art of War*. Robert, the tall guy, thought of the shovel idea."

Platt said, "Good choice of research material. Tell me, why did you pick Sun Tzu over Clausewitz?"

Jason said, "Who's that?"

Platt smiled and said, "Oh. Well good job, anyway. What did you use to drive them toward the back?"

"Sound effects. Footsteps and a shotgun being cocked."

"A man after my own heart."

"Do you really do sound design?"

"Yes, I do. Among other things." Platt ate the rest of his taco. "Your ideas aren't bad, but your skills need some work. Like getting stuck in the middle lane at the church." He reached halfway toward the last taco and raised his eyebrows at Jason, who gestured for him to go ahead. "That was a beginner's mistake, and if you plan to continue this thing you're doing, you can't be making beginners' mistakes. Also, remember to always look for people who are doing the same thing you're doing. Like, when you're tailing someone, also look out for someone tailing you."

"I would have seen you?"

"Probably not, but you get the idea. My point is, you have

to get smart pretty fast, if you're going to keep this up. I've got some leeway for you, because you seem potentially useful, but there's only so much I'll do."

"What kind of leeway?"

"Well, for instance, have you seen Detective Johns since she last went out to visit you?"

"Uh, no."

"Don't you think she would have been interested in what you've been up to, if she knew about it?"

"Uh, yes."

"Don't you think she knows about it?"

"Oh. I guess she would."

"That kind of leeway."

"Oh."

"I have to ask you: What were you trying to accomplish at the church?"

"'Harass your enemy ceaselessly.'"

"Oh. Did it work?"

"I don't know."

"Did he look harassed?"

"Well, no."

Jason drank some of his coffee, and Platt finished his.

Jason said, "Where did you get the Marquis?"

"About fifty feet from your house."

"Oh." Jason drank some more of his coffee, unsure how he felt about that.

Platt noticed and said, "No, it belonged to the two goons who broke into your place."

Jason said, "Solomon's car?"

"Yes."

Jason thought about it and chuckled. Then he thought about it again and chuckled again. "So you're involved in this. Why? It can't be just an appreciation for good craftsmanship."

"'Good?' I wouldn't say that yet. It's partly because Monica was a friend, and you've gotten somewhere poking into it. That could be useful. You've gotten somebody mad at you, which is always a good sign."

"That's what I thought."

"Well, you were right." Platt put down the taco. "Now, let me ask you something. Why are you involved?"

Jason said, "I really don't know. It's just something that feels necessary."

Platt narrowed his eyes thoughtfully and said, "Tell me what was happening in your life just before all this."

"Why?"

"Because maybe it will answer my question."

Jason said, "Well, okay." He had to think about it. "Um, I'm working days at a water filtration plant, reading meters and patrolling pipelines. You've seen where I live, and it doesn't look any better on the inside."

"Yes, I've seen the inside."

"Uh, my divorce will be final in a couple of weeks ..." He shrugged. "That's about it."

"Tell me about the divorce."

"It's a divorce."

"First girlfriend? High school sweethearts? First girl you ever slept with?"

Jason stared. "Yes."

"Okay." Platt picked up the taco again.

Jason said, "That's it? You got something out of that?"

"Yep."

"You want to tell me what it is?"

"Nope. That might mess things up. I think you have a delicate balance going, and I don't want to be what tips it over."

"Balance between what?"

"The fact that you don't know is part of the balance. You'll figure it out eventually."

"Okay," Jason said irritably, and then wondered why he was irritable. He said, "Okay," again in a better tone.

Platt said, "You'll get it." He finished his taco and stood up. "I have to go. Check under your hood and undercarriage every morning and every time you leave your car unattended, and have your friend with the little Honda do the same. Better yet, you check them both yourself. And don't use that ugly red wig any more."

Jason said, "Auburn. Auburn wig."

Platt said, "It's an ugly red wig." He offered his hand and Jason shook it. "I'll be around."

Platt left. Jason put two dollars on the table and walked out. He checked under his hood and looked underneath the Plymouth before getting in and driving away.

23

"We don't know we can trust him," said Martin.

The Plymouth and the CVCC were parked next to each other on the top of a parking structure at an indoor mall in Sherman Oaks. Jason knew the spot because he'd lived there in the Plymouth once during one of his breakups with Marisa before they were married. It had been an outdoor mall then, but someone had since decided to cover it. There was a place at the topmost part of the ramp where the lot widened, and it was impossible to see into it from lower down, especially when the lights went out at midnight, which was still an hour away. He wondered if anyone had ever broken up with Monica and then lived in their car. Then we wondered why he was wondering.

He was sitting with Martin and Robert in shirtsleeves in the lawn chairs near the cars, eating off the blue camping plates. Nine hinged, yellow Styrofoam containers from a Korean BBQ take-out place were spread out on the pavement. The CVCC's hatchback was open and somebody was playing a soulful trumpet on the radio. The radio was turned down very low so the sound wouldn't attract anybody. Robert was reading his *Nigerian Times*.

"No, we don't," Jason said. "But I almost do."

Robert read from his newspaper, "'Head-turning Miss Dolly

Sesay is looking for a marriage-minded African man without children.'"He looked up and said, "Anyone?"

"Pass," Martin said.

"Jason?"

"Maybe next time."

Robert folded the paper and kneeled on it among the containers, taking seconds.

"What's that stuff?" Martin asked doubtfully, as Robert served himself something that looked like seaweed. "I was going to try it, but I can't tell what it is."

"I don't know," Robert said. He tried some.

"How is it?" Martin said.

Robert said. "Mm, kind of salty."

Jason held his plate out. "Let me try some."

Martin said, "How can you eat something when you don't know what it is?"

Jason said, "But we do know what it is." He and Robert looked at each other for a beat and then said, together, "It's food."

Martin said, "Hey. A cheeseburger is food. Duck á l'Orange is food. This is ... I don't know ..." He held up a forkful. "Actually, what is this?"

Jason leaned forward and said, "That's squid."

Martin said, "Squid. I see. Yes. Squid." He put the fork down. "Thank you very much. I will now be ill."

Robert said, "I'll take it." Martin handed over his plate without looking at it. Robert took it and sat in his lawn chair.

"If you really want to eat something unidentifiable," Jason said, "we can go get you some McDonalds."

"No, I'm fine," Martin said. "Let me see that newspaper."

Robert picked it up and held it out, but his eye was caught by something on the back page, so he took it back as Martin reached for it.

"Whoa," he said.

"What," Jason and Martin said.

Robert kept looking at whatever it was.

"What," Jason said again.

Robert said, "Look at this," and handed it to Jason.

It was a slightly out-of-focus picture of the Preacher smiling and shaking hands with a man in a business suit. The caption said: The Reverend Billy Cryer receives the African Community Award for his work on behalf of the School for the Blind in Lagos, Nigeria. There was no accompanying article.

"A selfless man," Jason said. "A dedicated and devoted servant of his people. Do you think the money really goes to the school?"

Robert thought and then shrugged. "It could go anywhere."

Jason nodded. "You're right. This doesn't do us much good at all."

"Can I see that?" Martin said. Jason gave him the newspaper. He peered closely at the picture and then said, "Do you mind if I keep this?"

Robert said, "Go ahead."

Jason said, "You have an idea?"

Martin said, "Maybe. Let me think about it a little." He folded the paper. "Actually ..." He glanced at Robert. Robert nodded.

"What," Jason said.

Martin put his plate down and got up from the chair. "Robert and I ran some errands while you were out."He walked to the CVCC, put the newspaper on the front seat, and got a white paper bag out of the back.

"What is it?"

Robert stood up so he was next to Martin.

"Stand up," Martin said.

Jason put his plate on the ground and stood up. Robert intoned gravely, "Jason Keltner: Whereas, you have performed courageously in the face of evil; and, Whereas, you gave us two hundred bucks each and didn't tell us what to do with it; and, Whereas you always buy the food, we hereby induct you into ..."

Martin reached into the bag and pulled out something flat and round, about four inches across, and said, "The Screamin' Pink Tigers."

Jason twisted his head around to try to see it. "What is it?"

Martin handed him one. It was an embroidered patch, round, with a navy blue background bordered by gold braid. Gold letters around the top perimeter said "Screamin' Pink Tigers," and smaller ones around the bottom said "First Unarmed Division." In the middle of the patch was a pink and black Hobbes tiger with an army helmet on, holding a white flag tied to a stick, and looking cranky.

Jason looked at the patch in his hand and felt a grin start and get wider. "This is great!" He examined it further. "Did you do this, Martin?"

Martin said, "Yeah. I know this place where they've got an embroidery system that you run off a Macintosh, and the guy owed me a favor. It just cost materials."

Jason held it up to the side of his arm. "Here?"

Martin said, "Looks good to me." He reached into the bag again and withdrew a smaller bag. "We got needles and thread."

"Let's put them on," Jason said. He got his purple ski jacket and Robert's black one out of the Plymouth, and Martin got his denim jacket out of the CVCC, and then they sat down in the lawn chairs and sewed the patches on.

Martin was done first; his stitches were small and even. Jason ended up with loops of thread that wouldn't pull flat and puckered fabric where the patch had shifted position in mid-application. Robert sewed his sleeve shut.

"Robert," Jason said, "do you do these things for effect, or are they truly accidental?"

"I swear," Robert said, "it was accidental."

Martin fished a small Swiss army knife out of his pocket, flipped out the can opener, and said, "Here, use this as a seam ripper." When Robert's patch was redone, they all stood up and put their jackets on.

"Looks great," Robert said, twisting his arm to look at his own. "Looks like a man's work."

"A man who doesn't know how to sew," Jason said, looking at his own. "Where'd you learn how to sew, Martin?"

Martin said, "I don't know. Just something you learn how to do when your mother's drunk all the time, I guess."

Robert said, "I guess so. That's a nice job of patch-sewing."

Jason said, "Have you seen your mother recently?"

"I went and visited her just before I moved into Marengo Manor," Martin said. "She said to say hi to you."

"Martin," Jason said, "these are really nice. Thank you."

Robert said, "You're a good artist. I still think you should finish Mega Mole."

Jason said, "Yeah, did you just get tired of it, or what?"

Martin made a sound that sounded like *hfff*, and said, "What is this, an AA confrontation?"

There was an uneasy pause. Jason looked at Robert. Robert had a look of utter surprise frozen on his face. Jason looked back at Martin and said, "No, it wasn't supposed to be."

"Good," Martin said. "What do you guys care if I finish my damn comic book, anyway?"

Jason said, "Uh ..." He gestured helplessly. "I'm sorry. I didn't mean to insult you or anything."

Still looking shocked, Robert said, "No! I never did either! I'm sorry if I did! I think you're a very talented artist."

Martin looked quickly between to the two of them, and then relaxed a little and said, "I'm sorry." He looked at his hands for a minute and then said, "I guess I just felt a little ... attacked there for a minute."

Robert gaped at him. "By us?"

"Robert," Martin said after a moment, "you have no idea what kind of gift you have. I can't tell you how many times I've just stopped talking as you did these ... these amazing loops and rolls. It makes me feel insecure."

Robert said, "I always wished I could draw."

Martin snorted and said, "Drawing's nothing. Anybody can draw."

Jason said, "I used to think that anybody could do music."

They didn't say anything for a while. Then Martin said, "Robert, what if MC Shrew doesn't die when he goes off the top of the burning warehouse?"

Robert said, "MC Shrew has to die, because how else could the insect mutants get the power crystal from him?"

Martin said, "He could be almost fatally injured."

Jason got up and said, "I'm going to get some sleep. Wake me up when it's my watch." He opened the front door of the Plymouth, took out his sleeping bag, stepped into it and pulled it up to his neck, and got into the front seat. The lights went out.

He half-listened to Martin and Robert discussing Mega Mole as he fell asleep. At one point, he thought he heard his own name, and talk of music, but he was too sleepy to remember it for long.

Martin and Robert woke him four hours later, and he sat in a lawn chair in the dark until it started to get light. Then he knocked on the roofs of the two cars, and the day started.

24

Martin made Robert look for the Fugitive Pope leaflet from the Rose Parade. Robert found it in the back pocket of the pants he'd worn to the Rose Parade, which were the same ones he was wearing. Then they went to Smokey Joe's coffee shop on Coldwater, and Martin explained his idea while they had pancakes. When they left the restaurant, Jason checked both cars for tampering, and they drove to Hollywood.

They rented four hours of time on a Macintosh with a scanner attached to it, at a print service bureau that Martin knew about on Sunset. The scanner was a flat thing with a glass top like a Xerox machine, only instead of making a paper copy of an original, the scanner made a digital description of the original. The digital description went into the Macintosh, where it could be displayed on the screen and altered, and then the altered version could be printed on paper.

Martin sat in front of the Macintosh and scanned the *Nigerian Times* picture into the Macintosh. Then he said, "Give me the flyer."

Robert gave him the crumpled Fugitive Pope leaflet from the Rose Parade. Martin examined it closely. "Robert," he said, "do you think you could have put any more creases through this?"

"Hey," Robert said, "it's not as though anybody knew we'd need it. Just be grateful that I didn't throw it away."

Jason said, "And, further, that he never does laundry."

Martin flattened the leaflet, put it face-down on the scanner, and scanned it. Then he made both scanned images appear on the screen and said, "This should be pretty easy. The shadows are both coming from the left. I'll just have to soften them in the newspaper photo. The hardest thing will be erasing the creases from Robert's thing."

"Shut up, Robert," Jason said, before Robert could make a joke about how best to erase the creases from his thing.

"What?" Robert protested.

Jason and Robert sat for two hours and watched Martin take elements from one picture and put them into the other, resize things, crop things, blur things, and mutter to himself a lot.

At the end of the two hours, Martin said, "What do you think?"

Jason looked at the picture of the Preacher shaking hands with Castro and said, "Martin, you are a genius."

Robert said, "That's really great."

Martin said, "I altered the Preacher a little so he wouldn't look exactly the same as the original photo." He clicked the mouse, and the picture zoomed in to twice its size. "I just want to do a few more things here. The Castro part still isn't quite the same kind of grainy as the Preacher part. And I think the clipping path needs tweaking, and the whole thing needs despeckling."

"Right," Robert said, seriously. "Despeckle that clipping path."

Martin made a series of alterations. Jason couldn't see any difference. After twenty minutes, Martin said, "Voilà," and rolled back his chair. "Let's print it out."

The best quality printout was thirteen dollars, and came out on shiny white paper. Jason and Robert used another thirty minutes thinking up and typing a caption—"Reverend Billy Cryer Finalizes Cocaine-for-Uzis Deal"—which they printed at a lower quality, for a dollar. Then Jason spent the rest of their four hours at typing into the Macintosh. When the time was up, he had an account of everything that had happened to them. He bought three floppy disks from the counterperson and copied his account onto each, and then gave one to Martin and one to Robert.

They took the picture and the text to a twenty-four hour copy place, pasted the text under the picture with rubber cement from the self-service counter, and made five hundred copies with some of Solomon and Tony's money. At a hardware store across the street, they bought three paint rollers, a paint tray, and a lot of glue.

Then they killed the late morning and early afternoon at a bowling alley on Ventura Boulevard. Martin won four games out of five. His high score was 63. Everyone got bored in the middle of the fifth game, so they awarded it to Martin because he'd had a spare in the second frame.

They returned the shoes and played video games for an hour, and ate lunch at the Jewish delicatessen next door. Robert harangued Martin into trying the potato pancakes, and Martin finally gave in, ordered them, and liked them.

"There," Robert said in a middling Yiddish accent. "Now you're a Jew."

"Some bacon would go good with this," Martin said through a mouthful.

"Oy vay," said Jason.

"It ain't ribs an' black-eyed peas, that's for sure," Martin said, when he had swallowed. "I gotta take you guys for soul food sometime."

Robert said, "Tonight? Sure! Thanks, Martin!"

Martin shrugged. "Fine by me."

They left the delicatessen at three o'clock, drove down Ventura to the Sherman Oaks Galleria, and bought more books. Robert got a P.G. Wodehouse collection and a book by Langston Hughes called *The Ways of White Folks*. Martin bought more comic books. Jason looked for "Clausewitz," but couldn't find anything under that name, and settled for an anthology of science fiction from the 1940s.

"More comic books?" Jason said at the counter.

"They're not comic books," Martin said. "They're graphic novels."

Outside the mall, it was getting darker, and people were turning on their headlights. They drove both cars South on the 405 freeway to the 10 East, and then transferred to the 110 South. When they got off on Martin Luther King Drive, the sun had set.

The Church of the Believers seemed to be empty. The front door was barred, and no light came through its cracks.

Stopping with his engine running across the street, Jason thumbed his walkie-talkie and said, "See anybody?"

The CVCC was stopped behind him. His speaker crackled and Robert's voice said, "This here's the Rubber Duck, and we're about to lay the hammer down. Over? Ten-four?"

Then it crackled again, and Martin's voice said, "I don't see anybody."

Jason said, "Let's wait a while. Something feels weird."

They sat and waited for half an hour. No one entered the church, and no one came out. No lights went on.

"It does look empty," Jason said. "I don't know. What do you think?"

Robert's voice said, "Let's go."

Jason said, "Okay," put the walkie-talkie down, and pulled into traffic. The CVCC followed.

They glued one hundred flyers to the church wall, and another hundred to most of the nearby stationary objects. Robert took another hundred around to the back of the building and ran around the rear parking lot, throwing them up in the air.

"What do we do with the rest?" Martin said, holding up a one-inch stack.

Jason said, "Nothing. We've been here way too long already. Let's get out of here before somebody gets too interested."

"Gotcha." Martin turned and called, "Let's go, Robert!"

He waited for the answer.

There wasn't one.

"Let's *go*, Robert!" he yelled again. After a few more seconds, he rolled his eyes and said, "Jeez, you'd think—"

Jason cut him off with a sharp hand motion. Martin looked puzzled. Jason held up his hand in a gesture that said, *Give me a moment.*

"Martin," he said. He turned all the way around, looking at the lot. Robert wasn't there.

"Yeah," Martin said tensely.

Was he sure? He looked around again. Did he have to be sure? He went to the Plymouth's trunk, opened it, took the Macintosh case out, and held it toward Martin without looking at him. He said, "Get in the CVCC and go to the bumper car place on the Santa Monica pier. If I'm not there by eleven, take the Macintosh and the floppy disk I gave you to a telephone and do that thing I showed you how to do on the Net. Watch for a tail as you go."

He glanced at Martin. Martin looked stunned, holding the stack of flyers. Jason said, "Now."

Martin stared at him for maybe a second and then took

the case to the CVCC, got in, started the engine, and drove out the driveway to the street. The drone of the engine faded.

The wind picked up. Trying to stay aware of everything around him, Jason reached into the trunk and took out a crowbar and a four-foot section of aluminum tubing from his keyboard stand. The dirty metal of the crowbar was cold. He closed the trunk, went to the front of the church, and moved left along the sidewalk to where the church front ended, at the driveway to the rear parking lot.

At the corner, he waited and listened.

There was a very slight howl of wind between the church and the building on the opposite side of the driveway.

There was a soft skitter and swirl of leaves on the driveway and the parking lot, and of the flyers that Robert had strewn there.

There was traffic noise from Martin Luther King Drive.

There was faint birdsong from atop a billboard half a block away.

Jason waited and listened.

There was nothing else.

He swiveled off the curb and into the driveway, tense and bent slightly at the knees and waist, holding the tubing down against his side and the crowbar up at an angle.

What he could see of the rear parking lot was empty. Jason stood, motionless, straining his hearing. There were no new sounds. He took one step toward the parking lot, and then another, and another. With each step, another fraction of the parking lot came into view.

At the end of the driveway, he took a final step into the parking lot. There was nothing but leaves, flyers, and wind. Jason looked carefully both ways, walked forward a few steps, and twisted to see the church behind him. There was a back door, and a window above it. Both were shut, and no light was visible through either.

If he tried to enter the building, he'd be at a huge disadvantage; even more than he already was by allowing Robert to be taken. He hooked the crowbar over his belt, hefted the aluminum tubing in his right hand a few times, and threw it as hard as he could, end-over-end, at the window. The window was made of thin glass, and shattered. The tubing bounced off the exterior windowsill. Taking the crowbar from his belt, Jason moved quickly to the other side of the doorway. The tubing clattered to the ground and rolled away from him. He stood and waited, listening again for any change in sound, and wished the tubing would stop rolling so he could hear better.

As the tubing came to rest in a small ridge of leaves, Jason heard something inside the church: a movement sound, maybe a foot on a floor. He gripped the crowbar with both hands, and then took his left hand off so he was wielding it only with his right. Which was better? He put the left hand back on and waited.

No more noise came from inside.

Real smart coming back, he thought.

He stood in the wind and waited.

There was a click from behind the door, and it popped open half an inch. Adrenaline surged through Jason's body, and he raised the crowbar, trembling and unblinking, awaiting another action.

It didn't come. The metal door wobbled very slightly in the wind. No gun barrel pushed through the opening. An invitation.

Jason's vision swam a little, and he realized that he had been holding his breath. He let it out slowly and controlled his breathing, despite the urge to gasp.

He could enter the door, or he could leave. Or he could wait and see if someone else came out. He liked none of the choices, but that seemed to be the game.

Or, he thought, still trembling, *I could do what Robert would do, and make up a new game.*

It was hard to think with the adrenaline exciting his reflexes and blurring his mind.

What are my available resources? What's in the trunk?

He shook his head. It seemed to help. *Keyboards, keyboard stand, road cases, camping stuff.*

What else? Earthquake stuff, oil, water, duct tape, Squeegee, dirty plates, spare tire, bumper jack, backpack, propane tank.

He thought about the propane tank. After a few seconds, he backed away from the door and edged around the corner and into the driveway, shuddering from the cold wind, oxygen debt, and dissipating adrenaline.

There was no window on the front wall of the church, and the metal door looked solid. As far as Jason could tell, the people inside couldn't see him.

He worked as quickly as he could under the open trunk lid. It was difficult to detach the hoses that dangled from the lantern and the stove, because they had been attached for so long that the fitting surfaces had oxidized a little, but he did it eventually, connected them to each other with a brass fitting, and screwed the resulting length into the nozzle of the propane tank.

A seam along the side of the backpack tore when he forced the propane tank into it. He took a butane cigarette lighter from the lantern box and held it between his teeth, slung the backpack over his chest, looped the hose around his left hand, and went back to the open door.

He flicked the tab on the cigarette lighter and put the

small flame in front of the hose, offered a short plea to who-ever might be listening—*Please, please, let this not be the wrong way to do it*—and cracked open the nozzle on the propane tank. The propane hissed and the flame caught, and Jason flinched, waiting to be blown to pieces.

He wasn't blown to pieces. He pocketed the lighter, waited to see if he would continue to not be blown to pieces, and then opened the door slowly and stepped in.

A concrete staircase led up from the doorway. Jason trans-ferred the hose to his right hand and rested his left on the nozzle valve, stepped up onto the first step, and then the second, and listened. There was no noise. He continued up the stairs.

Three-quarters of the way up, something moved at the top, and a male voice that sounded like Tony said, "Stay where you are or we will shoot you."

Jason stopped and called, "This guy's skydiving for the first time." His voice was shaky. He paused and tried to con-trol it. "And he jumps out of the plane, and gets to the place where he's supposed to pull the ripcord. He pulls it, and noth-ing happens. So he pulls his backup and nothing happens. He's getting really worried, and he sees another guy, coming up at him from the ground. This is a little surprising, but he doesn't have time to worry about it. As the other guy passes him, the first guy yells, 'Hey, do you know how to work a parachute?' and the other guy goes, 'No, do you know how to light a propane stove?'"

There was no response.

Jason stepped onto the next step and called, "This is a ten-gallon propane tank I've got on." He opened the valve slowly with his left hand, and the hiss deepened in pitch, the flame growing to two feet. The heat against his right hand increased, and the hose wobbled a little. "If you shoot me, and you hit it, this whole building goes up in a big fireball and we all die."

Still nothing. Jason called, "What say we find out how big this flame can get?"He opened the valve farther, and the flame grew to four feet, the low hiss becoming a soft roar. The hose wanted to wobble more, and Jason held it more firmly, beginning to feel pain in his right hand from the heat. He couldn't move the hand back too far from the flame because he'd lose control of the hose. He took another step up.

The voice said, "If we all die, your Jew Boy friend dies too, American Boy."

Jason clamped his jaw together and opened the valve farther. The flame increased to about eight feet, reaching the top of the staircase, and the roar increased as the hose wriggled in his grip. He had an impression of someone moving suddenly away at the top of the stairs. He took another step and carefully transferred the hose from his right hand to his left, and the heat hit his left hand. He brought his right hand to his mouth and licked the hurt part. Evaporation cooled it slightly and brought a small amount of relief, but it was clearly damaged. He couldn't tell how badly. He rested it on the propane valve and tried to accept that it hurt worse than anything he could remember.

"Ask my Jew Boy friend about Entebbe," Jason called. Anger rose in him. He forced it down. "I'll wait."

He reduced the flame to three feet and grunted as the sudden reduction of pain made his left hand throb. He was halfway to the top. Past the upper landing, someone whispered something, and then someone moved away, back into the church, and there was the sound of a door opening and closing.

The door hinge behind him creaked, and he lost his balance and jumped, startled. The flame roared up over his head, but he kept his grip and clutched the handrail with his hurt right hand. With the flame again under control, and again aimed ahead of him, he turned his head, panicked.

Standing in the doorway, with his back to Jason, and the open door resting against his right shoulder, Norton Platt said, "If you flambé either one of us, I've wasted an evening." Cradled in the crook of his right arm was a compact, long gun that looked like the one Jason remembered from the videotape of Ronald Reagan being shot.

Jason couldn't think of anything to say, so he turned back and took the rest of the stairway slowly. The top landing was empty: ten feet of concrete that ended at a closed door with a small window in it, with criss-crossed wire embedded in the glass. No light shone through it. Avoiding the window, Jason turned the flame down until it was the length of a finger, and opened the door an inch. Then he opened it wider and stepped through.

He was in a dark corridor. A flat, dark carpet covered the floor, but it still felt like concrete under the carpet. The corridor led to the right. To the left was a door, ajar. On the other side of the door, a telephone began to ring. Jason went to the door, listened at it, and nudged it open with his foot.

It was a small, empty sound booth situated above and behind where the congregation sat. Jason stepped in. A broad window faced forward; there was a mixing console on a desk under it and a rack full of audio equipment to its right. None of it was turned on. The window was dark, and Jason could only barely see the church interior below.

The ringing telephone was on the desk, next to the mixing console. Jason ducked so he wouldn't be framed in the window and moved awkwardly across the room, with the backpack banging into his knees. He picked up the receiver. It was an intercom, with a talk button on the handpiece.

Nobody said anything for several seconds. Then there was a click, and a fluid baritone voice said, "Hello?"in the handpiece speaker.

Jason depressed the button and said, "Mm hmm."

The voice said, "One moment."

Lights came on in the church below. Rows of wooden benches began under the sound booth and ended in front of a carpeted stage. On the stage were the Preacher's pulpit, a drum kit, an amplifier, three microphone stands with microphones on them, four big thugs, the Preacher, and Robert. The Preacher held a white telephone receiver. Two of the thugs flanked him, and two more stood behind Robert. One of them was Tony.

Jason's chest tightened. Robert was bound in a chair with something tied around his mouth. Jason exhaled sharply through his nose and said, "Hell," very softly.

The Preacher spoke into the telephone, and his voice said, "I believe we can come to an understanding."

Jason pressed the button and said, "We already have one. We understand that this situation is not acceptable and will not continue."

The Preacher said, "Yes. I did understand the Entebbe reference." Robert looked at the Preacher when he said "Entebbe," and then looked up at Jason. The Preacher said, "And so, it seems, does your friend."

"Say what you have to say," Jason said.

"May I remind you," said the Preacher, "that you are not in control of this situation. I am. You are caught in a small glass box, suspended in the air, eighty feet away, and even if you break the window, I sincerely doubt that your little toy flamethrower has that kind of range."

"Say what you have to say," Jason repeated.

The Preacher inclined his head graciously. "I have something you want. You have something I want. Let us attempt to reach an equitable solution."

Norton Platt appeared in the doorway to the sound booth, crouching, and said, "Those four are the only muscle here. If things get weird, do something to distract everyone, and I'll shoot some of them."

Platt disappeared. Jason said into the telephone, "What do you want?"

The Preacher said, "I want to talk to you, face to face, like men."

Jason said, "Men don't plant car bombs and shoot at people on their porches."

The Preacher said, "I know of no one who shot at anyone on their porch. As for the car bomb, Solomon did get somewhat overzealous. He has been disciplined. If you leave that room, there is a hallway that leads to several classrooms. I will meet you in one of those, Jason."

Norton Platt reappeared in the doorway and said, "I heard that. I can't cover those classrooms."

Before Platt could disappear again, Jason said, without depressing the talk button, "What time is it?"

"Nine-thirty," Platt said.

Jason said into the handpiece, "Thanks for the offer, Billy, but you say what you have to say now or not at all."

The Preacher said, "Some things must be discussed between leaders."

Jason said, "Let him go, and we'll talk."

The Preacher said, "And remove your motivation for meeting? No. We will meet first. This is not subject to discussion. These are the terms. If you do not accept them ... then we shall see."

Jason lowered the receiver and thought about it. With access to the mixing console, it wouldn't be difficult to blast the whole area with feedback, assuming at least one of the onstage microphones were turned on. Chances were good that one was; leaving a mike turned on was a common oversight. That would certainly catch everyone off-guard, and give Norton Platt his distraction.

But then Platt would kill people.

He raised the receiver and said, "No thugs."

"No flamethrower," the Preacher countered.

"Agreed."

"Agreed."

Jason hung up the telephone and left the sound booth. In the dark corridor, he closed the valve on the propane tank, extinguishing the flame.

He removed the hose from the tank, coiled it, and held it in his left hand as he walked down the corridor toward the classrooms.

25

At the end of the corridor, another stairway angled down toward the church interior. There was a door facing Jason at the end, and two on the wall to his right. He didn't see Norton Platt anywhere, and guessed that he was keeping an eye on the four armed men on the stage.

He stopped at the end of the corridor. A door at the bottom opened, admitting light, and the Preacher looked up at Jason and ascended the stairway. The Preacher's eyes were at the same level as Jason's when he was still three stairs from the top. Jason held up the coiled hose and said, "It's disconnected."

On the landing, the Preacher swept one arm toward the open door facing Jason and said, "After you."

Jason walked forward and entered the room, suppressing the impulse to look behind him after he passed the Preacher. The classroom contained twenty small chairs with attached writing desks, two whiteboards with colored markers in their trays, a bookshelf full of Little Golden Books and educational materials, an American flag, a wall clock, and a teacher's desk and chair.

The Preacher entered and closed the door, and said, "Please, have a seat." Jason half-sat and half-leaned on the edge of the teacher's desk, the propane tank preventing him from really sitting. The Preacher remained standing. Jason shrugged, got off the desk, and stood up.

The Preacher chuckled, pulled the teacher's chair out from under the desk, and sat in it. Jason leaned on the desk again.

The Preacher sat and watched Jason. Jason watched him back. The wall clock ticked very softly.

The adrenaline surge had gone, leaving a slack, irritable exhaustion that made the silent tactic annoying. Jason gave it another full minute and then got off the desk and walked toward the door.

"Let us talk," the Preacher said.

Jason turned around. "Yes. Let us. Let us neither waffle nor mince."

"I want your help," the Preacher said, spreading his hands. "Only your help."

"What help?"

"There's something that we both want."

"Peace in our time? A new windshield?"

"The person who killed Monica Gleason."

Jason said, "Pardon?"

"The person who killed Monica Gleason. You and I both have business with him. It would be worth my while to assist you in delivering him." The Preacher leaned back in the chair and did his silent trick again.

Jason said, "Who is he?"

The Preacher said, "I will not give you any information until you agree to cooperate, Jason."

Jason thought about it. Then he said, "No deal, Billy. Get one of your trained boulders to do it." He turned toward the door again.

The Preacher held one hand up. "Wait. Perhaps I was too hasty."

Jason said, "Perhaps your trained boulders can't, you mean."

The Preacher said, "What I am offering is assistance in your quest. Surely you cannot be offended by that."

"No, you're not. You're trying to get cheap labor for your own quest. Come to the point or shut the hell up."

"You have me at a disadvantage."

"Wriggling in the vise-like grip of reason," Jason said. "Get to it. This whole thing will be on the computer screens of a couple million people in about forty-five minutes unless I'm out of here in half an hour."

The Preacher tipped his head back and looked down at Jason. "Very well." He made calming motions with his hands. "I have business with the person you're looking for, and my associates"—he inclined his head toward the stage—"may not be up to the task. They follow orders well, but I need someone more resourceful."

Jason said, "Then hire someone."

"That is, unfortunately, not an option at the moment."

"Why not?"

The Preacher didn't answer. Jason said, "Unless you want The Adventures of Pastor Billy to be worldwide public reading material."

"I cannot afford to." The voice was steady, but Jason thought he saw something—pain?—in the Preacher's eyes.

"Why not?"

"Because the man we both seek has stolen all my money." It was probably pain.

"You mean all the money you stole from your congregation?"

"Not only that," the Preacher said, apparently missing the irony, "but additional funds as well."

"And you want me to find him so you can get your money back."

"Yes."

"And I want to find him anyway, and I don't cost anything, so you'll give me what you have, and set me after him."

"Yes."

"Call me Mr. Bloodhound."

"There is one further detail."

"That figures."

"You must deliver him before Friday."

"What's today?"

"Monday."

Jason said, "Why Friday?"

"I have arrangements that conclude Friday."

Jason thought about Robert and said, "Okay. Let Robert go and give me everything you know, and I'll bring your quarry here when I find him."

"Perhaps you would have a further incentive to find my quarry if your friend were to remain my guest."

Jason walked a few feet farther into the room, carefully, and said, "Pardon?"

"You will get your friend back when I get what I want."

"No Robert, no deal. No discussion."

The Preacher began, "Now understand my position, Jason—"

"Your position?" Jason said. "Your position is irrelevant. No Robert, no deal."

"You are foolish," the Preacher said. "I can hurt him a lot."

Rage bubbled up in Jason's chest. He said nothing while he controlled it. When it had reduced to a simmer, he said, "If you do, I will give up music and you will be my new hobby. You're jerking me around. I'm getting crabby."

"I don't think you understand," the Preacher said.

"You want your damn money back or not?" The rage had almost burst through. He compressed it again. "Twenty more minutes and it's a great big moot point."

The Preacher glared at him. Controlled violence surged in Jason's chest, and he wondered vaguely and disconnectedly about the etymology of *moot*.

The Preacher nodded in acquiescence, stood up and smoothed his robes. The regained advantage of altitude must have reinforced his ego, because he looked down at Jason and said, "You will learn the advantages of compromise as you grow older."

Jason said, "Yeah." Unexpected sadness broke the surface of the rage. He pushed it down and tagged it for later analysis.

26

The Preacher was sitting behind the teacher's desk, and Jason had pulled up one of the students' seats, and was sitting on the attached writing desk. The propane tank was on the floor, still in its backpack.

"I do not know the name of the man you are looking for," the Preacher said. "I do not have a photograph of him, and I have never met him face-to-face, so I cannot describe him to you." He withdrew a white slip of paper from a deep pocket somewhere within his robe. "This is his telephone number and address. I was able to find the address from the telephone number. He will not be at that address any more."

Jason took the slip and put it in his pocket, and said, "How did he steal all your money?"

"He transferred it by computer to another account, the account of a gold broker."

"So get the gold broker to transfer it back."

"The gold broker transferred it to another broker last week. That broker transferred it to a personal bank account."

"How much?"

"One point eight million dollars. One point five million was withdrawn from the personal account in the form of several cashier's checks. The remaining three hundred thousand was apparently abandoned."

Jason said, "Cleaning out the account would have aroused someone's suspicion. How do I know you're not just telling me all this so I'll find him for you?" He paused. "How do I know he really killed Monica?"

"I'll tell you how he did it."

"That's been in the newspapers. Tell me something I can surprise the cops with."

"No cops."

"Cops if I say cops."

The Preacher looked displeased, and said, "He had a thing for this Gleason chick."

Jason said, "What we in the clergy refer to as 'impure thoughts.'"

The Preacher looked patronizing and said, "Do you want to hear this or not?"

"Ten minutes and counting," Jason said. "You're the one who wants me on the Secret Four-Day Bounty-Hunting Plan."

The Preacher said, as though Jason hadn't spoken, "He determined that she would be at a conference—"

"The TechnoArts show?"

"I do not know the name of the event. He discovered with his computer that she had shipped one of her lasers—I understand that she used lasers in her act—across the country for repair. I am not precisely familiar with the exact process, but he was able to use his computer to reroute the laser's return shipment to his own address, where he installed a second laser."

Jason said, "A second laser."

"Yes."

"Alongside the first one, in the same casing."

"Yes."

"With a beefed-up power supply, probably."

"I really have no idea. Then he used his computer again to erase the record of the delivery to his address, repackaged the laser in its shipping box, put it in the lobby of another building, called the shipping company, and reported a mistaken delivery to that address."

Jason said, "The shipping company picks up the 'mistaken delivery' and delivers it to the TechnoArts show, and there's no record of the diverted shipment."

"Yes. I doubt that the police have unraveled it yet."

"They may have. That's a nice little plan."

"He is not stupid."

"Then what is he?"

"He is ... creative in the sense that he is able to find unusual opportunities for himself and take advantage of them."

"That's what he did with you?"

The Preacher looked wryly philosophical. "Those who become too arrogant, who believe themselves untouchable by lesser men, are subject to the Lord's lessons of humility."

Jason said, "Uh huh."

The Preacher said, "He handled some of the church accounts. I unwisely allowed him to gain more control than was prudent."

"Why don't you know his name or what he looks like?"

"All our business was done through e-mail."

"Who contacted whom?"

"He contacted me. I never had a telephone number for him until a few days ago. He sent me a message over the Net, requesting assistance with a problem he was having."

He leaned back in his chair, as though waiting for a prompt. Jason said, "What problem?"

"You."

"And you sent Solomon and the other guy."

"Tony. Yes."

"What we in the warfare business refer to as a 'tactical error.'"

The Preacher said, "That is all I know of him. His messages to me were always over the Net. I never even heard his voice until he sent me the telephone number."

"Describe the voice."

"Careless elocution, almost as though he had a speech defect." The Preacher looked thoughtful. Then he shrugged and said, "That's all."

"Baritone?"

"Tenor."

"Fast talker or slow?"

"Slow."

"Background noises?"

"Not that I can recall."

"Did he say anything that was not related to his 'me' problem?"

"No. It was a very short conversation. He said 'I need your help in the matter we have discussed' and I said 'What do you need' and he said 'I need you to persuade someone to leave me alone' and gave me your address. That was the extent of it."

"Were his Net messages always business-related?"

"Most of the time. The only exceptions were that he was always trying to convince me to learn more about computers and the Net. He knows quite a bit about both."

"What did he write about the most, regarding the Net?"

"Well ..." The Preacher narrowed his eyes and pursed his lips. "Ah. I don't quite understand how this would work, but he claimed to have an extensive collection of pornographic pictures from the Net."

"What about his thing for this Gleason chick?"

"It was his belief that she was leading him on. He claimed to have had sex with her, but I understood that it was in some form of correspondence. I did not entirely comprehend what he was really saying."

"Hot chats. What else did he mention, besides dirty pictures and hot chats?"

"Just computers."

Jason stood up. "Okay. Time for Robert and me to go."

The Preacher stood. Jason picked up the backpack, and began to put it on.

The Preacher said, "Jason, I assure you. That will not be necessary."

Jason attached the hose, opened the valve, and started the flame with the cigarette lighter.

"After you, Pastor," he said, gesturing at the door. The Preacher's expression was one of injured hospitality.

Robert was still in the chair onstage, the four thugs were still looking tough, and Platt was still nowhere. The Preacher said to Jason, "I'll go ahead and release your friend."

Jason said, "Heck, yeah," and kept walking with him. He looked at Robert. Robert was staring straight ahead, expressionless.

At the front of the church, the Preacher mounted the stage, called Tony aside, and whispered to him. Halfway through the whispering, Tony looked at Jason for a few seconds, and then turned his attention back to the Preacher. Then he nodded and said something back, straightened up, and dismissed the three other thugs with an uncourteous hand flick. As they left, Tony untied Robert's hands and unknotted and unwrapped the gag. It was a bandanna. Tony dropped it in Robert's lap, gave Jason a dirty look, and followed the three thugs out through a side door.

Jason looked at the Preacher. The Preacher bowed slightly and exited behind Tony.

Robert was still staring straight ahead. Jason said, tentatively, "Robert?"

Robert's eyes moved a little bit and he slowly looked toward Jason, but didn't seem to see him.

Jason said, again, "Robert?"

Robert's gaze drifted. Uncertainty stirred in Jason. He stepped onto the first step to the stage, and snapped, "Robert!"

Robert looked at him.

Jason said, "Are you ..." He gestured emptily.

"That," Robert said very slowly, and paused.

The low hiss of the propane flame was very loud in Robert's silence.

"Was," Robert said. Jason watched him closely.

Finally, as though pondering each word weightily, Robert said, "A very ... weird ... space."

He nodded slightly to himself, and his gaze drifted away.

Jason coaxed him outside and into the Plymouth. They left the Church and headed North on the 110 Freeway.

27

Jason turned onto the 10 West. Robert didn't say much in the car. After fifteen minutes, Jason said, "Are you okay?"

Robert didn't respond. He was looking out the passenger window, with his forehead leaning against it. Wind blew through the car. Jason caught sight of himself in the rear-view mirror. He looked tired.

He took the 10 to the Pacific Coast Highway and then went north to the Santa Monica Pier, with the ocean on Jason's side of the car. He tried to look at the ocean, but it was too dark, and hard to see beyond the other lanes until he turned left across the highway and parked for three dollars near the pier.

The pier was not crowded on a Monday night. A few couples with arms linked wandered past the tacky shops and carnival games, and a stiff wind gusted across the pier and parking lots. Jason and Robert went to the bumper cars at the pier's end and collected Martin. Then they drove both cars five minutes to a Denny's and ordered coffee, and Jason told Martin uncomfortably and as briefly as possible about what had happened at the church.

There was an awkward pause when he was done.

"So," Martin said coldly. "McGyver here makes a flamethrower out of Coleman supplies and storms the Bastille like the Human Torch. Is that about the size of it?"

Jason said, "Yes."

Martin said, "Am I missing something, or was that probably the most moronic and irresponsible thing he has ever done?"

"Hey—"

Martin said, "Shut up, Jason. I'm talking to Robert. Robert?"

Robert said, "Huh? Oh. Well, it did work. Of course, that doesn't necessarily discount stupidity."

Jason started to say, "Hey—" again, but before he could get it out, Martin said, "Jason, why don't you go fight a duel or kill a hydra or something? I'm too mad to even talk to you right now."

Jason got up, put his jacket on, and walked toward the door. Behind him, Martin said, "You okay, buddy?" to Robert.

He went outside and looked back, and thought of the Denny's restaurant on Burbank, after leaving Marisa at the fern bar. It seemed that he was always standing outside places where people were.

The street he was on was called Colorado, and Jason wondered if it was the same Colorado as the one in Pasadena. It ended at the pier. He walked halfway up the pier and then off its side down a set of very wide wooden steps to the beach. It was too cold to go barefoot. He sat down on the last step and took his shoes and socks off, put the socks in the shoes, and carried them across the beach. The sand was cold, and the wind wrapped around his ankles.

There was enough light from the pier for Jason to discern the darker, smooth part of the sand that marked the sloping reach of the tide. He walked along the perimeter of the dark part, moving out of the way whenever the flat remains of a small wave approached.

He walked that way for twenty minutes, looking at the

beach and the ocean and, to his right, the condominiums and parking lots that filled the space between the beach and the Pacific Coast Highway. Then, feeling a little foolish, he walked into the dark area and let the frigid water roll over the tops of his feet. He hadn't been to the beach in years. Only people from out of town or those who lived within walking distance ever went there. Native Angelenos, five or ten or thirty minutes away, went every few years.

The water was freezing, and the wind chilled Jason's feet between waves. He hugged his arms around his chest and withdrew his hands into his sleeves as far as he could while holding his shoes. The warmth inside the sleeves felt like a furnace against his burned hands, so he stretched his arms forward to move his sleeves up to his wrists. He sat down a few feet past the dark region, put his shoes down on the sand, and lay back on the beach with his legs out toward the water.

He noticed the trace of the sadness that he had felt earlier, and tried to tease it into the open, but the more he wanted it to come, the more it wouldn't. He lay and looked up at faint stars, and forgot to think about the sadness. The wind numbed his scratched face, and the sand soothed his hurt hands. He wiggled them into the sand, down a few inches to where it was damp, and felt the coolness absorb their heat.

Distractedly, he thought about divorce papers. It cost one hundred and thirty dollars to get a divorce if you didn't have children or property. An easy divorce. What would he do with the papers when they came?

The cold tide reached the soles of his feet. A while later, it reached the middle of his calf. He wondered how high it would go. The wet denim would chafe later.

The first time she had cooked for him, she had made spherical hamburgers, raw on the inside and black on the outside. On white bread. It always reminded him of a Droodle: Tomato Sandwich Made By Amateur Tomato Sandwich Maker.

The sadness came and racked him. He heard himself sob, noted it, tried to hold it, and the sadness receded. The icy tide reached the crook of his knees.

Martin and Robert came looking for him some time later, and found him shivering on a bench on the pier with his jeans sandy and soaked to mid-thigh. They sat on the bench with him. Jason said, with his teeth chattering, "I'm sorry. I'm sorry."

Martin said, "Let's get you dried off and warm," and Jason said, "Okay."

Robert drove the Plymouth. Jason turned the heater on, but its effect was negligible against the wind that roared through the broken windows and chilled the wet denim further. At the Manor, Jason took a pair of pliers from the soap dish in the shower and turned the stripped shower handle stems. He took a shower without a lot of heat or water pressure and shut the water off with the pliers, dried, and put on a pair of gray sweat pants and an oversized T-shirt.

Coffee was brewing in the pseudo-kitchen. In the front room, the piano had been placed back upright. Its keys were at odd angles. A small space heater battled the cold.

Martin came through the front door with a paper bag and made Jason sit on the couch, took a tube of topical antibiotic and a roll of bandages out of the bag, and bandaged Jason's right hand. Then he pushed a blanket against the bottom of the door against drafts, took a bottle of Irish whiskey out of the same bag, and went into the pseudo-kitchen. Jason sat and looked at the glass and cardboard in the door.

Someone clumped down the inside stairs on the other side of the wall, and then Robert's silhouette appeared against the door. Robert knocked, came in, sat down on the piano bench, and said, "Weird day."

Jason nodded.

Robert said, "Martin and I had a long talk at Denny's. He postulated that you might think that this whole thing was your fault, and that you'd let us down."

Jason nodded.

Robert said, "We're not your sidekicks. We're your friends. We have our own volitions and our own motivations. We're not marionettes, and although the case might be presented that you failed tactically or strategically, you didn't fail Martin, and you certainly didn't fail me."

Jason nodded.

Robert said, "I got myself caught."

Jason nodded again.

Robert said, "That nod means you disagree."

Jason said, "I railroaded you into helping me."

Robert said, "You didn't railroad either of us into anything. We talked about it and decided to help."

Jason said, "I let you go off by yourself."

Robert said, "You didn't *let* me do anything. You're the one who's always saying that people choose what they do."

Martin came into the room with three coffee mugs on a black lacquer tray that Jason had forgotten he owned. It had been a wedding gift from Robert. The mugs were wedding gifts, too. So were all his dishes. So was everything but the coffeemaker, and he'd bought Marisa the coffeemaker for her birthday.

Martin put the tray down and distributed coffee. One of the mugs was separate from the other two on the tray, and Martin took that one for himself. Jason took his and raised it to drink, and hot alcohol vapor came into his nose. He said, "Is this Irish coffee?"

Martin said, "Yes."

Jason said, "I never had Irish coffee." He took a sip. It didn't taste as he expected.

Martin said, "So?"

Jason nodded and took another sip.

Robert said, "Do you understand that what happened today was not your fault?"

Jason said, "No." He felt annoyed and tense. "I also don't understand why you're trying to make me feel better, when it should be the other way around."

Robert said, in a falsetto Pollyanna voice, "Because we're your friends, you chowderhead!"

Jason said, "Chowderhead?"

Martin said, "I'm sorry, Jase. I was just worried."

Jason nodded again and looked down at his coffee, which became more blurred as he watched it. His chest shook and he felt his jaw muscles clench and unclench. He kept looking at the coffee. Martin said, "You know we both love you, man. I'm sorry I got mad."

Jason looked at Robert. Robert said, "I'm sorry he got mad, too."

Jason wanted to say, "I love you guys, too," but he couldn't get it out, and felt bad about it.

Martin said, "Maybe this isn't the time to talk about it."

Robert said to Jason, "Maybe so?"

Jason nodded and sipped his blurry coffee, and then, after a long time, his chest stopped shaking and he put the coffee mug on the floor, and the room faded as he fell asleep.

He slept fitfully for a few hours, but his hands and face hurt too much, and then he started thinking about his left arm where he'd bashed it against the rental car window frame, and it started hurting, too. He got up and went into the pseudo-kitchen and looked through the little basket where he'd kept his Percoset. There was only off-the-shelf Ibuprofen. He took five in a Tom and Jerry jelly glass of lukewarm water from the bathroom tap. The clock in the pseudo-kitchen said 4:30 A.M., so it was actually 4:15. He'd gotten so used to Marisa's weird clock habits that to actually set the right time would throw him off. He wondered if Monica had set her clock ahead. Maybe it was a girl thing. He should have looked when he was in her apartment.

He went through the bathroom and looked into the bedroom. Martin was asleep on the futon. Jason went into the front room, called the filtration plant, and left a message for his foreman that he'd be off on personal leave for the rest of the week.

A little green light blinked on the answering machine on the bookcase. Jason pressed the playback button and carried the machine as far into the room as it would go, while it rewound. He put it on the floor and sat next to it.

The tape reached its beginning and clunked into playback.

There were a few seconds of blank-tape hiss, and then a low click, and then Jason's chest clutched as Marisa's voice said, "Jason, pick up the phone." But the clutch wasn't overpowering.

"Jason, we should talk about this. Please pick up. I hope you don't do anything stupid. Are you there? Hello? Well, I'll call you later. Please don't do anything stupid, like go to Paul's house. Okay? Please call me."

The next three messages were also Marisa, saying essentially the same things over again.

The next one was also Marisa, but the tone was different. "Jason, I don't see what you're so upset about. If I want to go to a music festival, or whatever, I don't see how it concerns you."

Jason decided not to listen to the rest of that message. He pressed the fast-forward button, and the machine skipped to the next message.

The rest of the incoming message tape was filled with Marisa, alternately contrite and obdurate, but consistently impatient. Jason listened to the first few seconds of each message, and then skipped ahead to the next.

When the tape ended, he sat on the floor in the dark, and experienced a curious lack of anguish.

He sat and thought, and after thinking hard about it for the better part of an hour, it gradually came to him that although he'd have to consider the point more extensively, it could conceivably be possible that Marisa might not be such a prize.

And then, as he was mulling that over, something else came to him.

He got up and went to the computer.

28

Morning sunlight began to shine around the edges of the blue towel that hung on the front door, and Jason realized that he had been sitting in front of the computer for hours. He got up and looked around for a big piece of paper, and ended up tearing Martin's brown paper bag along its folds and flattening it. He found a thick black marking pen in the front room, sat on the floor, and drew a big silhouette of a bat on the bag. It was strange drawing with his left hand, and the marker moved oddly.

He looked for a roll of tape, didn't find one, and used three Band-Aids from the bathroom cabinet to tape the bag on the back door, facing the parking lot. Then he sat down again at the computer, brought his account of events up to date, and copied it onto two floppy disks from a box on the table.

Somebody tapped on the door. Jason got up and moved the blue towel, and then let Robert in. Robert had a pink cardboard box, its top open to display two rows of glistening donuts. He stepped into the room and said, "Have a donut. Not the chocolate one."

Jason said, "I'll fight you for the chocolate one," and went into the pseudo-kitchen to make coffee. Robert held the box with one hand and ate the chocolate donut with the other.

"I hope espresso beans work for regular coffee," Jason said. "There's no more regular ones. They look darker. Maybe I should have used less."

"Maybe you should have used more."

Jason wondered which was right, and then said, "Caffeine is your friend," and dumped the contents of the grinder into the coffeemaker.

Robert took out a crumb donut and ate it while he said, "How are you feeling?"

Jason said, "Like I just took a short intermission from banging my head against a big post office. I guess I don't recognize when I get stressed and intense."

"Well, that's why you have friends," Robert said. "So we can have the pleasure of recognizing it instead."

"Sorry," Jason said. "I guess I've been less than fun recently."

"You've been really tightly wound. You seem a little better today."

"Maybe I am. How many donuts are you going to eat?"

Robert said, "Eight," and extracted a maple bar from the box. Before eating it, he held it poised before his lips and said in his thin Alistair Cooke accent, "Donut go gently into that good night," waited a beat, and then stuffed the whole thing into his mouth.

"Wow," Jason said, "You're literate and classy both. Marry me."

Robert said, "Mmf mmm drm nnn."

Jason said, "Thanks," and took an old-fashioned butter-milk donut from the box with his left hand.

The telephone rang, and Jason dropped the donut back in the box and went into the front room to answer it.

"Acme Carrot Ranch," he said in a receptionist voice. "Carrot speaking."

Norton Platt's voice said, "Is that chicken for me?"

"It's a bat," Jason said. "Gotham needs you. The donut population is mysteriously diminishing."

Platt said, "Robin, to the chicken cave!" and then hung up.

Jason hung up and said to Robert, "Norton Platt's coming over for donuts. He has a big gun. Leave that disgusting custard-filled thing for him."

Robert said, "Okay," and looked at the pink cruller. "You don't usually see much pink food."

Martin shuffled blearily out of the bedroom and said, "Thanks for keeping it down so I could sleep, you jerks."

Beaming happily, Robert extended the box and said, "Good morning, Mr. Sunshine!"

Martin looked in the box, said, "Gross," and rummaged in the dish cabinet for a coffee mug. There wasn't a sufficiently clean one, so he took out a Flintstones jelly glass and poured coffee into it. Then he took a plain cake donut out of the box and got a carton of milk out of the cube refrigerator.

The back door shuddered open until its lower edge scraped against the floor and wedged tight. Norton Platt, wearing a faded orange T-shirt tucked into light blue jeans with a belt, stepped in and said, "Nice door."

Martin sniffed the milk and poured a little into his jelly glass. It disappeared. He looked hatefully at Jason.

Jason said, "Robert Goldstein, Martin Altamirano; Norton Platt."

Platt said, "Hello. What kind of coffee is that?"

Robert held the tip of his forefinger to his thumb and enunciated, "A very special coffee, lovingly blended from a plentiful extravaganza of aromatic espresso beans."

Platt looked at the espresso part of the coffeemaker and said, "Why didn't you just make espresso?"

Jason said, "It's a poor mind that can only think of one way to make coffee."

Martin said, "He doesn't know how." He poured more milk into his coffee until the glass was full. The coffee became very slightly less dark.

Jason said, "So dense, not even light can escape."

Martin said, "You or the coffee?"

Platt rooted through the donut box and said, "No maple bars?" He took a bear claw.

Jason looked in the box. His buttermilk donut was gone. He took the custard-filled one. "Let's go into the other room so we can sit down."

The answering machine was on the piano bench. Robert sat on the floor, Martin sat on Jason's amplifier, Platt sat on the couch, and Jason sat next to the answering machine and said, "Thank you all for coming today." Something vaguely familiar buzzed in him, and it took a few moments to blow the layered dust off and identify it as enthusiasm.

"I put something together when I was listening to my answering machine messages from last week. Listen." He pressed the Play button.

Marisa's voice said, "—don't see what you're so upset about. If I want to go to a music festival, or whatever, I don't see how it concerns you."

He stopped playback.

Martin said, "So?"

Jason said, "That festival was in Santa Barbara. Robert, look on the Macintosh screen. What do you see?"

Robert put down his coconut donut and rose from the floor to look. "There's a folder out called 'SB Show.'"

"Open it."

Martin got off the amplifier to watch, and Platt leaned

around to see the screen. Robert clicked the mouse and the folder opened onscreen to reveal a list of file names.

Jason said, "Open the one called 'SB Show Details.'"

Clicking the mouse again caused text to appear on the screen.

Jason said, "Read that first paragraph."

Robert read, "'Artist and co-performers shall be present at least two hours before scheduled curtain time. Festival will make every attempt to provide one assistant per act to assist in setup, sound check, and breakdown. Artist is urged to contact the assistant in advance to discuss details. Artist agrees to forfeit one sixteenth of his or her payment for every fifteen minutes of tardiness. Artist agrees—"

"That's fine. Remember the part about the one assistant per act. How was Monica killed?"

Platt said, "Somebody installed a powerful ruby laser into the same case as her show laser, and when it came time for the show laser to write on her, the ruby laser kicked in instead and killed her."

"Did the show laser work properly until that point?"

"Yes."

Jason shifted on the bench. "So something switched the lasers."

Platt said, "Yes. Probably a unique MIDI event."

Jason said, "Very good guess. That is the case."

Martin said, "What's a unique MIDI event?"

Jason gestured for Platt to explain if he wanted. Platt made the same gesture back, and Jason said, "You know how I use my Macintosh for making music?"

Martin said, "Yes."

Jason said, "It probably seems like I'm recording and playing back sounds from the computer, because there are Record and Playback buttons depicted on the screen. But what I'm really doing is recording *actions*. When I play a keyboard, messages are sent to the computer. The messages represent actions like what note is played, how hard it's struck, when it's released, things like that. As each of those messages is sent to the computer, the computer notes it, and adds it to a list of actions. Get it?"

"Got it so far," Martin said. "Keep going."

"That's what happens when I'm 'recording.' Then when I stop recording, I can 'play back,' which consists of the computer sending all those messages back to the keyboard, so the keyboard thinks it's being played, and makes noise. It's called sequencing. It's kind of an evolutionary step up from a player piano."

Martin squinted and then said, "Yeah, I got it. That's why you call it sequencing, right? Because you're making lists of sequences of actions?"

"Right. Each of those action-messages is called a MIDI event, and each of the message-lists is called a sequence. There are lots of kinds of MIDI events, not just representations of actions. Some represent things like volume, or placement in a stereo field, or *vibrato*, all expressed numerically."

Platt interjected, "For instance, if your volume is set at, say, a value of sixty-four, and you send a volume MIDI event with a value of one-twenty to the keyboard, the keyboard will suddenly get louder."

Robert said, "So if you send a *vibrato* MIDI event of one-twenty, the sound being produced by the keyboard will get more *vibrato-y*."

Jason said, "Right. So what Mr. Fluffy did—"

Robert said to Platt, "We call the killer Mr. Fluffy."

Platt said, "Right."

Jason said, "What Mr. Fluffy did was to use a MIDI event to cause the laser controller to switch from the show laser to the ruby laser when it recognized that event."

Platt said, "How do you know that?"

Jason said, "Same as Mr. Fluffy. I looked in the event list. Robert, close that one and open the one called 'SB Sequence.'"

Robert clicked the mouse and the text went away. Then he clicked again and the contents of *SB Sequence* came up on the screen. Platt got up off the couch and came around for a better look.

He looked back at Jason and said, "How did you get this?"

"I downloaded the contents of Monica's hard disk way back when this all started. I just never made the connection before that 'SB' stood for 'Santa Barbara,' so I never thought to look through it."

Platt said, "May I?" to Robert.

Robert said, "Sure," and got up. Platt put his bear claw on top of his coffee mug and sat down and clicked the mouse a few times. "Where's the unique event?"

Jason said, "In the track called 'Lights.' Bar number two-forty, beat one."

Platt brought the contents of the track up on the screen. At bar 240, beat one, in the MIDI event list, it said: *#9 127*.

"There it is," Platt said. "Controller nine to a value of one-twenty-seven. Controller nine has no standard meaning. What do you think she was using it for?"

"I don't think she was using it for anything," Jason said.

Robert said, "Then what's it doing there?"

Jason said, "Someone else put it there."

"How?"

"Steal the sequence data, insert the MIDI event, and then put the sequence back into Monica's Macintosh, replacing the original one, and she'd never know the controller nine event was there, unless she went hunting for it."

Robert looked fascinated. "Steal it how?"

Jason said, "My sequencer—and Monica's—run on a Macintosh, but some sequencers are little boxes that you can carry around easily. They call them 'lunchboxes.' Two things, though: the first is that she didn't know that there was anything to hunt for, and the second is that she didn't have time to."

"Because ..." Platt said.

"Because the tampered-with data was dumped into her computer from the lunchbox just before curtain time."

Robert nodded, thoughtfully. "By whom?"

"By the same person who stole it and gave it to Mr. Fluffy in the first place. Someone who had access to her equipment while it was being set up, and had time to dump data back and forth, and edit it."

Martin said, "The assistant you told us to remember."

Robert said, "Who is ..."

Jason said, "Who is Paul Reno."

29

Robert's eyes widened and he said, "Paul?"

At the same time, Platt said, "Paul Reno?"

Robert said, "You know him?"

Platt said, "Why do you think it was Paul Reno?"

Jason said, "When Marisa—the voice on the answering machine—mentioned the music festival, she was referring to the Santa Barbara festival. She went with Paul. He worked the show."

"She told you this?"

"Yes."

Martin said, "Even if he's a sleazoid, just because he was there it doesn't mean he did it."

"He did it," Jason said. "I know it. Paul doesn't volunteer for anything, and a little skullduggery like that would be just his thing."

Platt said, "Then how do you know that he didn't kill Monica? He had access to the lasers at the same time as he had access to the sequencer data."

"I thought of that. Three reasons. The first is, the Preacher told me about an elaborate scheme that Mr. Fluffy used to alter the laser, and it's not Paul's style. Paul would just walk off with it and then bring it back. He could pull off an explanation so well that no one would even remember that he'd been gone with it. Second, he's too smart to show his face around a murder scene, if he's the murderer. Third, I've known him a long time. He probably likes to think that he could kill somebody cold-bloodedly, but he couldn't."

Platt said, "Then ..."

"I don't think he knew what he was involved in. I think he thought it was something else. Data theft, maybe, or a bad practical joke. Music piracy. I don't know."

Platt nodded. "That fits what I know of him. I tend to agree."

Jason said, "How do you know of him?"

"I know people who like to keep an eye on the minor leagues."

Martin said, "To watch for trouble, or to get the good draft picks?"

Platt said, "Same thing. Reno wants to be in the majors, but ..." He smiled and shrugged.

Martin said, "Why not?"

"He's not honest with himself," Platt said, "and that can lead to problems working with other people."

Robert said, "A self-centered spook is such a drag to share space with."

Platt said, "We prefer 'G-Man.' It makes us feel like Robert Vaughn."

Robert said, "Us who?"

Platt smiled apologetically. Robert returned it with a tacky talk-show smile that he tried unsuccessfully to wrestle into apology, twisting through a variety of rubber-faced attempts. Everyone watched him fail, and then Martin said, "Ladies and gentlemen, this moment of surrealism brought to you by Mutual of Omaha."

Jason saw Robert latching onto the Wild Kingdom theme

and said, "Before Jim wrestles the rhino, let's get back to the subject."

Platt said, "Then Paul Reno is a possible link with the ... with Mr. Fluffy."

Jason said, "What do you know about Paul?"

It was a moment before Platt answered. "Reno does odd jobs for an unusual clientele. He has several Net accesses that he thinks are secret, and uses the Net the way you might use a middleman; as a way of removing himself from the transaction. He's not believed dangerous, but his potential has not quite been dismissed, either. Someone will probably snap him up within a few years and let him think he's playing first-string."

"When in reality ..." Robert said.

"He'll be, oh, fifth-string."

Jason said, "Which means, what, clandestine back-alley meetings with short, limping informants in rumpled white linen suits?"

Platt said, "Yes, that is exactly, precisely, what it means."

"So he was probably contacted over the Net for some innocent—well, not exactly innocent—data theft."

Platt shrugged and said, "Could be. I'll ask around if anybody's heard anything."

Jason nodded. "Ask whom?"

Platt smiled again.

Jason repeated, "Ask whom?"

"Jason," Platt said, "the enigmatic smile means 'I'm not going to tell you.' It is considered poor form in tonier G-Man circles to press the issue when presented with the enigmatic smile."

Robert said, "G-Manners."

Platt snorted and said, "You guys are too much."

Jason said, "Mr. Platt, with due respect, I don't particularly care where all the better feds are wintering this year. My two friends, God knows why, have decided to follow me around and poke into things. I have a responsibility to them to poke into said things first and see what's there, whenever I can. I apologize if I'm out of line, but the question stands. Ask whom?"

Platt picked up his bear claw and said, "I understand that, Jason. Now you need to understand something, too. As valid as your question is, I'm not going to answer it, and don't ask me again." He took a bite.

Another "Ask whom" threatened to emerge. Jason stifled it and said instead, "I want to go to this address and look at what's there."

Platt said, "What address?"

Jason smiled enigmatically.

Platt said, "Okay, see you there."

30

They drove past the address twice before Martin spotted it. Jason parked the Plymouth alongside a nearly wrecked Chevette in a dirt lot between two badly painted blue apartment buildings, and they got out. Platt was not in evidence, but Jason had no doubt that he was lurking somewhere.

Robert said, "Hey, this is almost as nice as our house!"

Martin looked at the blistered paint and said, "Nicer."

Each apartment had its own fractional address, and the one they were looking for was 1/4. They found it up a swaying flight of stairs. Its door was the color of dirty cream, and the remains of a doorbell had been painted over, thickly, more than once. Jason tried the knob. It was locked. The doorframe was rotted and flimsy. Martin said, "Try breathing on it."

Jason said, "Here goes," backed up a step, concentrated, and kicked the knob straight on. The doorframe came apart without making much noise, and the door opened.

Martin said, "Nice work, Danno."

Jason beat his left fist against his chest and said, "Jase strong. Jase open door."

It was a ratty single-room apartment with an ugly rust-colored carpet and a kitchenette. A plastic window, with closed red curtains, looked east. Under the window was a table made from two sawhorses and an interior door with no knob; on the table was an IBM personal computer with its case cracked open and wires ripped out.

The kitchenette had a refrigerator, a stove, a countertop and sink, a wooden chair, a single cupboard, and a small table on hinges that folded against the wall. The table was unfolded down over the chair. There was nothing on the walls, and nothing in the refrigerator or its freezer compartment but soft, built-up frost. A toaster-oven sat on the counter next to the refrigerator. Jason opened a drawer under the toaster-oven and found a few forks and table knives. He went into the bathroom: ugly linoleum with sparkles in it; a torn plastic shower curtain; and some cracked, fish-shaped blue-green non-skid stickers in the bathtub.

A sliding door next to the bathroom revealed an empty closet with a high shelf. There was nothing else in the apartment.

Jason felt uneasy, and said lightly, "Well, this was useful."

Robert was looking thoughtful. He said, "Not so fast. We just started. Let's start in the kitchen."

Martin looked at Jason. Jason shrugged and said, "Okay."

The kitchenette was too confined for all three, so Jason and Martin waited in the doorway.

Robert opened the refrigerator door and poked around inside. After thirty seconds, he said, "Refrigerator's empty but not clean, so you'd expect to find some trace of veggies in the veggie trays, but nothing's there. Mr. Fluffy didn't eat a balanced diet. Or if he did, he didn't cook, though he could have done TV dinners in the toaster-oven. No open box of baking soda that most people leave in when they clean out their refrigerators when they move, which supports the no-ingredients theory."

He opened the freezer compartment. "No real ice trays. Just these little baby ones. If he'd ever had guests, the baby ones would be in the cupboard, and there would be real ones in here. The freezer hasn't been defrosted in a long time." He looked thoughtful and then said, "I don't know if that means anything."

Closing the refrigerator, he opened the cupboard and said, "One plate. No shelf paper. He didn't have a girlfriend."

Martin said, "No friends over, no girlfriend, no real food."

Jason said, "Sounds like me, except for the friends part."

Robert continued, "Dust on the shelves."

Jason said, "Thank you both for ignoring the obvious straight line."

"It wasn't easy," Robert said.

Martin looked at both of them and said, "What obvious straight line?"

"So," Jason said, "Mr. Fluffy is a solitary person." He moved aside so Robert could exit the kitchenette and enter the bathroom.

"Nothing here," Robert said, after a minute.

"Nothing here either," he said, after looking through the closet.

Martin said, "What's with the ripped-up computer?"

Jason looked more closely at the IBM. "I don't know for sure," he said, "but it looks as though a hard disk might have been removed from it. To keep whatever data was on it from falling into the wrong hands. Like ours, maybe."

Norton Platt appeared in the doorway and said, "This is very interesting. We're not the only ace private eyes here."

Jason said, "Who else?"

Platt tipped his head toward the street. "Two men in a gray Chrysler. Well-dressed. Not government."

Jason said, "Who, then?"

"They look like organized crime to me." He shrugged. "I could be wrong, though."

Robert said, "If I were a well-dressed organized criminal, the only relationship I'd have with a slovenly, dishonest programmer would be an employer-employee dynamic."

Martin said, "And if I was a slovenly, dishonest programmer who suddenly disappeared, and then two organized criminals camped outside my door, I bet I'd be gone with some of their money."

Jason said, "Point them out to me."

Platt stepped back from the doorway so Jason could see out, saying, "Past the end of the dirt lot, half a block down, on the left. They don't look like the Preacher's people, so I'll take a stab and say they work for whoever he owes money to."

Jason looked for the gray Chrysler and found it, parked in front of a tan house under an avocado tree. He left the apartment, went down the stairs, and walked toward it.

Above and behind him, Platt's voice said, "Somehow, I knew you would."

When Jason was fifty feet from the Chrysler, its doors opened, and two men got out. They were in their late thirties or early forties, and interchangeable, with short, dark, conservative hair, muted slacks with black shoes, and white shirts. They didn't look like anything from a Bogart movie. They looked like district sales reps between customer calls. Software, or paper goods. The one on the driver's side had high cheekbones.

"Good morning," Jason called, still walking.

"Good morning," Driver's Side said. His tone was friendly and impersonal.

Jason stopped a few feet away and said, "We're both looking for the same person."

Driver's Side glanced at the other man and said, "I beg your pardon?"

Jason said, "My name is Jason Keltner. It's possible that we can help each other. I'm in the Pasadena phone book."

Driver's Side said, "I don't exactly know what you mean."

"You're looking for the man who lives in that apartment. So am I. I've made some progress. Feel free to call."

"Thank you for the offer," Passenger's Side said. His voice was higher than Driver's Side's. "But I think you've made a mistake. We were just trying to figure out how to get to the Interstate."

Jason said, "Down this street, hang a left to the Ventura Freeway, five minutes to the Interstate."

"Thank you," Driver's Side said.

Jason said, "You're welcome." He smiled, turned around, and went back to the apartment building.

Martin and Robert were waiting by the cars. Platt was gone again.

Martin said, "So?"

"I offered our valuable assistance," Jason said. "Any further useful clues inside?"

Robert raised one eyebrow and said, "I believe the man we are looking for is a four-foot-tall Alsatian, albino, with one eye, a pronounced limp, and a curious predilection for mango chutney."

"Yuck," Jason said.

"What the heck is chutney?" Martin said.

"A fruit relish," Jason said. "Let's look around the outside here."

"For what?"

The Chrysler pulled into the street and drove away. Jason walked toward the side of the building. "Smoking pistols. Secret one-way spyholes. Mysterious and elusive women with husky contralto voices."

They found no spyholes. They did find a corroded car battery, several piles of hardened dog excrement, a broken syringe, a trash dumpster, and a lot of rusted wire nails in the weeds along the side of the building. The trash dumpster was empty.

"Darn," Martin said. "No women."

"Look in the dumpster again," Jason said. He knocked on both downstairs doors, but no one seemed to be there. All three went up the stairs again. When Jason knocked on the upstairs door, a small white rat-dog poked its pointed face past the thin lace curtains in the window, but no one opened the door. The rat-dog stood on the windowsill and yapped at them. It had a pink collar with fake diamonds on it, and brown gums, and its eyes were milky and bulging.

"Hello, pooch," Jason said.

"Jesus Christ," Martin said. "What the hell is that?"

Robert said, "Eek. The mutants have come."

The rat-dog yipped at them and fell off the windowsill.

Robert said, "Never mind. They're not dangerous."

They left in their cars, stopped at a hot dog stand, and got chocolate egg creams and chili onion cheese dogs in yellow paper bags. They ate them on the way back to the Manor. No one spilled anything. Everyone was impressed.

At the manor, Jason took five more Ibuprofen tablets, hoped they'd work better than the last five, and went into the front room. The green light on the answering machine was blinking. Jason hit the playback button while Robert and Martin sat on the floor and sucked noisily at the spare remains of their egg creams.

The tape rewound, the machine clunked, and then a man's voice said, "This message is for Mr. Jason Keltner regarding an apartment in North Hollywood. My name is Mr. Matthew Davies, and I would be interested in speaking further with you. I can be reached at—"

Jason said, "Wow, that was quick," hit the pause button, got a pencil from the computer table, restarted playback, and wrote the telephone number on his chili onion cheese dog bag. The number had a Los Angeles area code. He called it.

A female voice said, "Mr. Davies' office."

Jason said, "Mr. Davies, please."

"May I ask who is calling, please?"

"Jason Keltner, returning his call."

"One moment."

Light jazz played tastefully. Jason's brain glazed over.

The light jazz stopped. "This is Matthew Davies. Thank you for returning my call, Mr. Keltner."

"My pleasure."

"I understand you have shown an interest in an apartment in North Hollywood."

"Yes," Jason said. "That is my understanding of the situation as well."

"If I may ask, what is your interest?"

"I'm trying to find the person who used to live there. As are you, I think."

"What makes you think that?"

"Because you're there and he's not, and he has a history of taking things that belong to other people. I would like to meet with whoever in your organization is in charge of dealing with this kind of, uh ..."

He was stuck for the word.

After a few seconds, Davies said, "Contingency?"

"That's it," Jason said. "Contingency. It seems to me that it would make more sense to combine efforts."

"Although the offer is generous," Davies said, "what makes you think that you have anything that this organization does not have?"

"Nothing at all," Jason said. "What makes you think I don't?"

Davies said, "How is this afternoon?"

"Satisfactory. I'll take the kids to a movie some other time."

"You don't have kids. How is this afternoon?"

"Where and when?"

"Do you know Rosa's on Wilshire?"

"Vaguely. What's the address?"

Davies gave it to him. "Five o'clock."

They hung up. Jason turned around and said, "Watson, the game is afoot!"

"Sounds like Twister," Robert said.

31

Rosa's was the kind of faux-Mexican restaurant that Jason liked. It was not too dark, served large portions, used shredded beef instead of ground beef, and had no roving mariachis. The salsa verde was medium-hot. The margaritas were large and slushy, and were not available in peach or strawberry flavors.

Matthew Davies looked like a black-and-white photograph of a Fortune 500 executive. He had dark hair with gray at the temples, slate-gray eyes, and a confident handshake, all contained in a well-made dark gray suit. His tie was pinstriped and understated, and a charcoal-gray overcoat lay on the seat beside him. In their contrast to his otherwise monochromatic appearance, the normal fleshtones of his hands and face were mildly surprising in the amber light of the table candle.

Jason was not wearing a gray suit. He was wearing a long-sleeved white shirt and dark blue jeans with black boots. His hair was tied back with a thin, soft black band and he had foregone his Screamin' Pink Tigers ski jacket for a brown leather jacket that he never wore because he never went anywhere nice enough. New white bandages on his right hand afforded a subtle and stylish counterpoint to his shirt. *The word*, Jason thought, *is "flair."*

Davies had decaf. He took a sip and said, "What is it you would like from this organization?"

Jason ate one of the free tortilla chips that came before the dinner. *Bond. James Bond.* "Information," he said.

"What information?"

"If I knew that, I'd be out acting on it. We're both nosing after the same rabbit. I contacted you because it seemed inefficient not to, but I don't have a specific agenda."

Davies nodded and sipped his coffee. Jason ate more free chips and salsa and noticed that the surface of Davies' coffee trembled slightly when he raised and lowered the cup. Either Davies was nervous or he just had shaky hands.

Davies put his coffee down without rattling the saucer and said, "What's your interest in the rabbit?"

"It's personal."

"I understand that you believe he killed Monica Gleason."

Jason waited. Davies said, "I also understand that you have an arrangement with Billy Cryer. How did he get you on his team?"

"He didn't. I don't work for him."

Davies said, "We would like to bring you on board with us."

Jason said, "Who's us?"

"The organization I represent."

"Yeah, I got that part. What organization?"

"The people for whom I work prefer to remain anonymous."

"Now there's something I've never heard before."

Davies shrugged. "It's a secretive business."

A needle of impatience stabbed Jason. *What's a secretive business?* He said, "You work for SMERSH, don't you?"

A red-haired waiter brought their dinner. Davies' was *arroz con pollo*, and Jason's was a chicken enchilada with beans and rice on the side.

Jason ate some of his enchilada and then said, "So, do you guys offer a competitive retirement plan?"

"The people for whom I work have followed your progress with approval, and would be very pleased to recruit into the organization an individual with a sense of discretion and a respect for the affairs of others."

"But since one wasn't around ..." Jason said. When Davies didn't smile, Jason squelched the impulse to make a rimshot sound with his mouth. "Thanks for the offer, but this is just a hobby for me. My true passion is the exciting and lucrative water filtration industry."

Uncertainty flickered across Davies' face and was gone in an instant, but Jason saw and enjoyed it.

Davies leaned forward again. "The people for whom I work understand that to acquire such an individual would require sufficient and appropriate compensation."

Jason thoughtfully scooped up some beans with a free tortilla chip. *Bond. Savings Bond.*

"This isn't about work," he said. "This is about paying me to get me out of the way."

"Not at all," Davies protested. "Simply put, you have impressed some people who are not easy to impress. This offer is not extended to many people." He removed a thick off-white business envelope from his inside coat pocket and dropped it on a clean part of the table. It went *thunk*, and the amber candle flickered.

"Let me guess," Jason said. "There's more where that came from."

"Indeed there is," Davies said.

Jason picked up the envelope. It was not light. "How much is in here?"

"Ten thousand dollars."

"Ten thousand."

"Yes."

"In small, unmarked bills?"

"Yes."

"Pretty soon you're talking real money."

"Pardon?" The uncertain look was back, briefly.

"Never mind." Jason dropped the envelope back on the table. "I'm flattered and everything, but I'm just not interested in being acquired."

"Perhaps you have an idea of a more suitable sum."

"I have many ideas," Jason said. "None of them involve taking on yet another day job. Illegal or otherwise."

"Then what exactly do you have in mind?"

"If the people you work for really want this guy, there are better ways to spend ten thousand dollars than bribing me with it."

"It's not—"

"Yeah, yeah, it's not a bribe."

Davies didn't seem to have anything to say.

Jason said, "I'm not looking for employment. However, I might be intrigued by the prospect of a joint venture. Tell your people that."

Davies didn't look well. He picked up his decaf and sipped some more. Then he said, "Please excuse me for a moment," and left the booth.

Jason finished his food and looked covetously at Davies' plate.

Davies came back and said, "It looks as though you may tell them yourself. Shall we?"

Jason said, "Now? Uh, sure."

Davies gathered his overcoat, Jason stood and ate the last tortilla chip, and they left the restaurant.

Bond, Jason thought. *Erasable Bond.*

Davies' car was a creamy white Lexus with a leather interior. The radio station that came on when Davies turned the key was one that advertised "continuous soft hits." Davies turned it off. Usually when someone said "continuous soft hits" around Jason, he'd hit them gently and steadily in the arm until they got the joke and told him to cut it out. Davies didn't seem to be someone to appreciate that species of razor wit, so Jason opted instead to look out the window.

The Lexus hummed subtly through the Miracle Mile district of Wilshire Boulevard, swept with a subdued hush into Beverly Hills, arced gracefully onto a broad, flat avenue with correct trees, and shimmered unbumpingly into a driveway, settling to an easy stop at a large iron gate. The Plymouth rarely shimmered. It had hummed once, though, just before a wheel came off and Jason had to climb down a freeway embankment to retrieve it.

The large iron gate was separated from a tall concealing hedge by two large metal lions with calcified streaks on their faces. Davies waved somewhere and the heavy gate halves opened silently inward. The Lexus engine purred, and the car whispered forward onto a circular cobblestone driveway and parked in front of a mansion from the movies, a tall and sprawling building that somehow managed despite its expense to appear squat and ungainly.

A cobblestone path led through a mannered jungle of broad-leafed plants with leathery stems to a big ungainly front door flanked by two big ungainly men, one short and dark, and the other tall and light. The tall one wore aviator sunglasses. Both had been standing with their arms folded, but unfolded them and looked dimly aware as the Lexus drew up.

There was a heliport with a bubble-bodied orange helicopter perched on it atop a small rise to the east. Jason had the feeling that anywhere within two hundred feet of the house, the weather stayed at 72 degrees and balmy, by special arrangement.

An attached carport provided shelter for a red Lamborghini, a black Bentley, and a very old, but flawlessly restored, green Karmann Ghia. Next to the Karmann Ghia was a silver car of angles and slopes, which Jason didn't recognize.

Jason looked at the heliport and said, "You don't work for SMERSH. You work for Madonna."

Davies got out, so Jason did too, and noticed a video camera mounted on one of the uprights of the carport. He looked at everything again and found more cameras on the house and the heliport.

Davies said, "After you," and gestured toward the front door. As they walked toward it, Davies nodded to the two men, who nodded back. The tall one opened the door and Jason and Davies went in.

Jason had once gone to the Norton Simon Museum in Pasadena just after he and Marisa had separated, during one of the times when he'd found it necessary to keep very busy. The front room of the mansion reminded him of it. The room was large and white, with paintings and small sculptures arranged around its perimeter, discreetly lighted. There were no Lucite cases around the sculptures, and Jason curled his fingers into his palms, conscious of the possibility of knocking something over. Two red doorways faced each other across the room. In the center of the white tiled floor, on a square mahogany stand, was a massive black iron sculpture of what appeared to Jason to be a cancerous turkey giblet.

Next to the huge giblet was a slender man of medium height and bad skin, in another gray suit. As Davies and Jason stepped into the room, the slender man came forward.

Davies said, "Mr. Pascal."

The slender man inclined his head and said, "Matthew." Then he looked at Jason and said, "Mr. Keltner." He had an accent that Jason couldn't place.

Jason said, "Call me Warren."

Pascal said, "That's very funny," in a friendly voice, without laughing. His eyes were casual and unwelcoming. Jason thought of an amiable cobra. Pascal nodded at Davies again, and Davies bowed a little and went outside. Jason wondered if he would sit in the car and sing continuous soft hits.

Pascal looked at Jason appraisingly. Jason smiled pleasantly. Then, although Pascal's face didn't change tangibly, his expression suddenly shifted from appraisal to something else that was unblinking and unfriendly. Jason recognized the trick, but it worked anyway, and he got the cobra feeling again.

After an uncomfortable time, Jason said, "Can you do this?" He crossed his eyes and then moved the left one back and forth.

"I was told that you are not serious," Pascal said.

Jason uncrossed his eyes and said, "You have no idea how many staring contests I've been in this week."

Pascal said, "We shall talk in the study." He gestured toward one of the red doorways and then followed Jason through a richly carpeted and paneled hallway. There were several closed doors with solid-looking polished hardware, and then an open archway on the right that overlooked a broad stairway and a big room with bookshelves, couches, and a long grand piano with a silver candelabra, and then more closed doors. At the end of the hallway, Pascal opened a door on the left and went in, after Jason.

The study was all leather and wood. Two black leather chairs framed a small round table in the middle of the room.The walls were full of books from floor to ceiling, with the exception of a space left for a red brick fireplace that had no fire in it. Many of the books were leather-bound, and bore gilt lettering on their spines. Jason tipped one toward him and looked at the title: *Lehrbuch der Geshichte der Philosophie.* He pulled it off the shelf and said, "Did you read this? I love the part where Skipper saves Muffin from the burning barn."

Pascal said, "I hope you amuse yourself, Mr. Keltner, because I find the effort pointless."

"Always," Jason said. "What kind of car is that silver thing in your carport?"

"It is called a Vector." Pascal sat. Jason put the book back and sat in the other chair.

Pascal said, "Do you know who I am?"

"No."

"Why is that, do you think?"

"Why don't I know who you are?"

"Yes."

"Uh ..." Jason groped for an answer. "Because you never introduce yourself when we bump into each other down at the malt shop?"

"You do not know who I am," Pascal said, "because you are an amateur."

"An amateur what?"

"There are plenty of things that you do not know because you are an amateur."

"Name two."

"Number one: you do not know who I am. Number two: you do not know why Mr. Platt is involved in your affairs."

"Because he's a friend of Monica's."

"That is not the case, and you would know it, if you were not an amateur."

"Ah."

"Why 'ah?'"

"Um, because it seemed to be my turn to talk, but I had nothing substantial to say."

"Here is what I want. I want you to accept Mr. Davies' offer."

"No."

"Why not?"

"Because I don't want to."

"Because?"

"Because I don't want to."

"You put yourself at a considerable disadvantage by your insistence upon maintaining your amateur status."

"Don't say amateur. Say enthusiast."

"Semantics. You are at a disadvantage."

"Or hobbyist."

"Obfuscation. What is your answer?"

"My answer is 'How would you like to drop the subject and talk about something else?'"

"Specifically?"

"Specifically cooperation. We have similar goals."

"You have nothing to offer me."

"Imagine my embarrassment," Jason said, standing. "I better leave before I start to cry."

"Sit."

Jason sat. "Woof," he said.

"What is your plan?"

"I'm not going to tell you."

"Because?"

"Because I don't know who you are."

"Then it is impossible for us to discuss anything."

Jason considered that. "Okay," he said. "Here's what I want. I want resources."

"What kind of resources?"

"I don't know yet. But when I know, I'll want them."

"What else?"

"I want information. Again, I don't yet know what information."

"And in return for these undefined resources and information, you offer what?"

"Same answer. I'm not about to barter away something concrete for something this vague."

"Then what you wish is merely the opening of a potential avenue."

"Yeah, that."

Pascal opened a drawer in the small round table, extracted a white card with a telephone number on it, and gave it to Jason. "Call this number when you know what resources or information you wish, and what you are willing to offer in exchange, or when you are prepared to stop being foolish and become a professional. Is there anything left to discuss?"

"Duh, nope."

Pascal stood. Jason put the card in his pocket and got up. Pascal opened the door, and they went back through the paneled hallway and into the art room. Davies was in the art room, next to the cancerous giblet. Jason went with him to the Lexus and they drove back to Rosa's. Davies dropped him there and glided away in the Lexus.

Jason got into the Plymouth, reflected on how little it resembled the Lexus, and remembered a Peanuts cartoon in which Charlie Brown said to Snoopy, "How come you couldn't be a pony?"

He said, "How come you couldn't be a pony?" to the Plymouth and went back to the Manor.

32

The blue towel on the front door was drawn to one side, casting mid-day light onto the floor and walls. Water dripped occasionally from a wet hole in the increasingly yellowed ceiling plaster under the second-story bathroom. The drops made metal sounds of varying pitches and timbres when they landed in Jason's mixing bowls.

Robert, Martin, Jason, and Platt were hunched around a lot of notepad papers strewn over the back of Jason's carefully overturned amplifier. The papers had handwritten notes on them.

Platt straightened and said, "Jason, you have a truly twisted mind."

Jason smiled warpedly and said, "Why, thank you." He looked back down at the papers, and then up again at Platt and said, "So could it work?"

Platt studied the papers again. "It needs refinement."

"Right."

"And some serious resources."

"Yes."

"And some favors called in."

"But."

"But ... it could work. If some deranged maniac really went to the trouble of setting it all up, it could work. Maybe."

"You're too kind."

Martin said, "Wanna know what I think?"

Jason said, "Oh, probably not."

Martin said, "I think this is one of the best comic book plots I've ever seen. Really. It's clever, original, and unexpected. Perfect for a comic book."

He paused. Everyone waited for him to finish.

"However," he said, "as for real life, it's the most idiotic, lamebrained, ridiculous idea I've ever heard in my life. And believe me, I've heard lots of them."

"No, don't sugar-coat it," Jason said. "Tell us how you really feel."

"Okay, I will, you moron," Martin said. "Remember when you were a little kid, and there were bigger kids called playleaders on the playground who were supposed to keep the littler kids from walking into traffic and eating dirt? But they never could? That's how I feel."

"Well put," Platt said.

Robert said, "Yeah, Martin. You can really be eloquent when you're pissed off."

"Shut the hell up," Martin said, furiously. "It's risky and dangerous."

Platt said, "Yes, it is. But it could work."

Jason said, "Does anybody have a better idea?"

Robert said, "I think the risky and dangerous one makes sense."

Martin folded his arms. "It would be hard to find a worse plan. Just think about how many things could go wrong."

"It still needs refinement," Jason said.

Nobody said anything for a while, and everyone looked at the papers without actually reading them.

"It still needs refinement," Jason said again.

Martin looked at him balefully. Jason said, "*Nececita más refinamente.*"

Martin's expression didn't change. Jason said, "Let's mull it over and talk about it again soon. How's that sound?"

Robert said, "Okay," and Platt nodded.

"Martin?" Jason said.

"What."

"Talk again soon?"

"Fine."

"Okay, then why don't you and Robert go get us some lunch?"

Robert got up and said, "Lunch!"

Jason said, "Do you need money?"

Robert said, "No," and he and Martin left.

"This is really twisted," Platt said, picking up a piece of paper.

Jason said, "Why are you involved in this?"

Platt put down the paper. "Didn't we already cover that?"

"Yes."

"Then ..."

"I had a meeting last night with a Mr. Pascal, who said that I only believed that you were Monica's friend because I'm an amateur."

"I see. And what did this Mr. Pascal have to say about himself?"

"He didn't."

"I see."

"So it seems reasonable to raise the question again. Why are you involved?"

"Because Monica was my friend, and you seem to have made progress."

"Okay."

"You don't believe that."

"At this point, with the data I have to work with—or the lack thereof—my only option seems to be to accept the assistance and keep my eyes open for more information. I don't know enough to decide whether I believe it."

Platt spread his hands. "That's life."

"That's what people say. Who is Mr. Pascal?"

"He's about what he seems to be."

"Very intelligent? Shrewd? Dangerous? Powerful? Sparkling sense of humor?"

Platt smiled. "I do sometimes like how you put things. That's the guy."

"Well-connected?"

"No. People who know him are well-connected."

"Oh," Jason said. "Wow, I'm so glad I annoyed him."

"You annoyed Mr. Pascal?"

"Yes."

Platt looked at him for a long time. Then he said, "Is this a pathology with you, or what?"

"Seems to be. I should join Irritants Anonymous. First step: accept that you are obnoxious. So what does Mr. Pascal do?"

"International finance, buying and selling public servants, construction, things like that. Things that are large. Jason, unless you're really that tired of life, try not to annoy Mr. Pascal. Try very hard. I know it'll be difficult for you, but try anyway."

"I'll bring him some Almond Roca next time I go."

Platt looked down and shook his head very slightly.

Jason said, "Anyway, what refinement do you see as necessary with this plan?"

Platt gathered the papers. "I'll take this with me and go over them some more, if that's okay with you."

"Fine with me. I have it all on disk."

"I may find it necessary to contact outside people about some details. I have some people in mind."

"I'd rather you didn't."

"I don't know everything, Jason. Almost everything, but not quite. There will be fine points that I'm not up to speed on, and I need to be able to call out when I see fit."

Jason thought about it and said, "How many people?"

"Three. Four. Something."

"All right. Please let me know who and what."

"Two are called Bookman and Delahugh. We do each other favors sometimes." Platt stood. "What are you going to do in the meantime?"

"I thought I'd take a better look through the stuff I got from Monica's hard drive."

"Okay. I'll be in touch."

Platt left, and Jason started his Macintosh and sat down in front of it.

Phone Courier had a "phone book" feature that allowed a user to store frequently-dialed numbers for later recall, instead of having to type the number each time. Monica had seen fit to include all her usernames and passwords, along with her phone numbers. Jason thought about that. With all the passwords, he could ostensibly connect to her favorite online services disguised as her.

He got up and got a little radio from the pseudo-kitchen and tuned it to a local blues show, and then selected an entry at random and had Phone Courier call it.

CONNECT 2400

*** Welcome to The party Board ***
Please enter your user number: 4311

If you are user 4311, you are Ms. Mo from NoDopes, OK
Please enter your password: Aileen

Welcome back, Ms. Mo!

<u>Who's online now:</u>

Line#	Username	City	St.	Age	M/F	Chat Status
Line 1:						
Line 2:						
Line 3:	Dr.Strangeluv 416		FU	42	MS	Chatting
Line 4:	Big Joey 81	Happy	HA	26	MS	Chatable
Line 5:	Ms. Mo 4311	NoDopes	OK	27	FS	Page Me
Line 6:						
Line 7:	Bo'Peep 880	Baaaaa	CA	38		Chatting
Line 8:						

Ms. Mo has no new mail.
> Big Joey 81>> /p4311 hi would you like to chat?
>

Jason looked at Big Joey 81's message. The "/p" meant
that Big Joey 81 had sent "Monica" a private message that
could not be seen by anyone else. "Why not?" Jason said to
the screen. He typed, "/p81 Sure. How do we do that?" and then
hit ENTER on the Mac keyboard.

> /p81 Sure. How do we do that?
> Big Joey 81>> just type c and then choose A
> /p81 Okay. hold on.
> c
Welcome to the chat area.
(a,p,m,n)> a
You are now available for chats.
>

Now entering chat mode.
Chatter: Big Joey 81 from Happy, HA   26   MS
<u>Chattee: Ms. Mo 4311 from NoDopes, OK</u> 27   <u>FS</u>
Big Joey 81> so how are you today

   Jason typed, "I'm fine. How are you?" and hit ENTER.
Ms. Mo. 4311> I'm fine. How are you?
Big Joey 81> been worse. so are you new here?

   Beats me, Jason thought. He typed his reply and hit ENTER.

Ms. Mo 4311> Not really. I just usually don't log on very
often. What about you?
Big Joey 81> oh ive been on here for about six months.
what do you like most about this BBS?
Ms.Mo 4311> I haven't decided yet. What about you?
Big Joey 81> i like to chat with people one on one like this.
its easier this way
Ms. Mo 4311> Why is that?
Big Joey 81> well i get shy around most people. so do you
want to hot chat?

   "Hell no!" Jason said to the screen. *Monica did this?*

Ms.Mo 4311> Why would you ask that?
Big Joey 81> you should try it, its fun
Ms. Mo 4311> No, I don't think so. Thanks for the offer,
though.
Big Joey 81> dont be scared, its fun, can't i make you feel
good? let me lick and suck your crotch real good, i like to
be controlled

Jason screwed up his face in disgust and said, "Yuck!" He hit control-C, the key combination on the Macintosh keyboard that severed communication with Big Joey. Then he typed, "bye," and the BBS disconnected. The words, "No Carrier," appeared on the Macintosh screen to signify that Phone Courier could no longer sense contact with the BBS.

The front door opened and Robert and Martin came in with full white paper bags. Jason said, "Bleah!"

"What," Martin said.

"Bleah!" Jason said again.

"What," Martin said.

"I just logged onto a BBS as Monica and got hit on by some slug. Bleah!"

A wide grin cracked Robert's face. "Really?"

"Gross!" Martin said.

Jason said, "And he was pretty damn crude about it, too."

Still grinning, Robert said, "Do you need to go take a shower now?"

"A shower wouldn't do it," Jason said. "Somebody get me a belt sander."

Martin put his paper bag on the back of the amplifier, and Robert followed suit. Jason said, "Sorry. What did you get?"

Robert took two wax-paper-wrapped things out of one of the bags, held them aloft, and declared in a 1940s continental accent, "Grilled cheese for everyone!" Then he made cheering crowd noises. The wax paper was transparent in some places.

"And chocolate shakes," Martin said.

"Stop with all the nutrients," Jason said. "I'll have mine with grease, please."

"Ah," Robert said grandly, handing over the one in his left hand. "That would be this one."

After they ate, Jason said, "Okay, well, let's get Phase One over with," and he and Martin walked to an adult book store on Colorado Boulevard. Robert declined to accompany them.

Inside, Jason tried not to look at any of the tackily colorful cellophane packages hanging on the wall, but couldn't help glancing sideways. Not that it really made much difference—he couldn't deduce the functions of most of the flesh-colored objects anyway. Most of them had straps, but Jason couldn't figure out where the straps would go.

There were only two other customers, both of them men in business suits. The counterman was a blonde man of about forty, with sparse hair and a tiger tattooed on his forearm.

From the magazine rack that ran the length of the shop, Martin picked up a previously thumbed magazine called "Blonds 'n Blacks" and opened it. Although the cover was garishly colored, the pictures inside were black and white, and depicted nothing of surprise to anyone sufficiently literate to sound out the title. Martin didn't seem uncomfortable.

"How about this?" he said to Jason.

Jason looked at it, self-consciously casual. "Too busty and hippy."

Martin said, "Okay," and flipped through the magazine. "This one?"

Jason looked. "No, nothing with, uh, props."

Martin nodded. "Right. Good point." He flipped quickly through the rest, and then put the magazine back on the rack and took down one called, "Sucking Sluts."

"It's got that alliteration thing going for it," Jason said.

Martin opened it and said, "This?"

"No."

"This?"

One of the businessmen passed in front of them and murmured, "Excuse me," as he picked up a magazine called "Double-D-Lite."

Jason said, "Uh, no, not that one either."

"This?"

It was a brown-haired woman and a carrot. "The body is pretty close."

The businessman glanced at the picture to see what they were talking about. Martin brought the magazine up very close to his eyes and tilted it so it was more in the light. "This isn't bad, though we should really lose the carrot. Let's see what else we've got in here." He turned the pages slowly, saying, "Nope. Nope. Nope. Nope." He peered closely at another picture. "How's this?"

Jason looked at it. It was a picture of the same brown-haired woman, *sans* carrot. "Okay. That'll work. Does it work for you?"

Martin looked closely again, and said, "It's almost in focus." He turned it upside-down and looked at it that way. "Yeah, I think this will work."

They paid the counterman twenty dollars for the magazine, then Martin went to the same print service bureau in Hollywood, where they had done the Preacher/Castro picture.

Jason went back to the Manor and called Paul.

33

It was afternoon and Jason was sitting inside the E-Bar, drinking coffee and waiting for Paul. The counterperson was somewhere in back; the only other customers were a quartet of what Jason guessed to be students from the Art Center. They were seated at a table to Jason's left, and appeared to be in their mid-twenties. One young woman sported close-cropped artificially black hair, and a worn pea coat hung on the back of her chair. The other wore her red hair long, and rolled up the sleeves of her denim jacket. Jason couldn't figure out what it was that was so similar about them despite their divergent fashion choices.

The red door opened and Paul entered the room, raised his eyebrows once at Jason, and sat at the table.

"So," he said. "I thought we weren't friends anymore."

"I don't know if we are," Jason said, "but we've known each other a long time. Maybe history is worth something."

"Is that supposed to make me feel better?"

"It's not supposed to do anything. It's just how I feel."

"It was pretty lousy what you did."

Jason said, "Maybe."

"So now what?"

"I don't know."

Paul nodded noncommittally. Jason drank some coffee.

They both looked around the room and avoided each other's eyes. The art students laughed and one of the young men hit the other one playfully on the shoulder.

"Going back to work on Monday," Jason said.

Paul looked at him and said, "Really? Now, that's a surprise."

"Why a surprise?"

"I didn't think you'd take my advice."

"Well," Jason said, "The dudes turned out not to be that heavy-duty. The computer guy is just not very good." He shrugged. "So."

Paul looked a little stunned. He started to say something, stopped, and then said, "I'm here to tell you, Jason, that you're making a mistake. I don't think you have any idea who you're dealing with."

Jason frowned in dismissal. "Sure I do. He's a hack. No balls, no style, no power. Now he's off hiding someplace with his little computer, probably bragging to all the virtual babes on the Net, when the truth is that he's just a sick little toad who got a little too lucky."

"Jason, this person can make you dead."

Jason laughed. "Right."

"Jason—"

"Paul," Jason said, "You wouldn't know."

"I have my ways of knowing. Believe me."

"Sure," Jason said.

"Listen—"

"He's a loser. And even if I'm wrong, why should I listen to some sorry little tapeworm who gets off on playing Super Spy?"

Paul's expression slackened. "You really are an arrogant prick, aren't you?"

"I'm arrogant because I finally have your number, and we both know it. But tell you what." Jason made his face show mock pity. "I won't tell anybody if you don't sic your scary powerful friends on me, okay?"

"What's happened to you, Jason?"

"What's happened to me? Nothing, buddy. I just realized that the reason you're such a worm all the time is your lack of a life. Really—government contact for witness relocation? Please. What are we now, Secret Agent X? Is it lots of fun, Paul?"

Paul's face showed no expression. He got up.

"Oh, don't go away mad, Paul. You haven't told me the password to the top-secret underground missile complex yet."

Paul said conversationally, "You know, Jason, Marisa's a lot of fun."

Jason nodded.

"I especially like those little gasps. You know the ones?"

Jason pursed his lips and didn't respond.

"So did a lot of your friends," Paul said.

Paul held the look for another moment and then turned and walked away. When he had almost reached the door, Jason said, "Paul."

Paul stopped and looked.

"You were right. We're not friends."

Paul let out a laugh that went *humph*, and said, "Big loss." He turned away and left.

The counterperson came back from wherever she had been and started combining half-empty bottles of fruit juice. Jason stared at the door for a long time after it closed. The art students laughed some more.

34

*A*n *unexpected message comes from Pollux. He reads it several times, and sweeps the computer monitor off the table. It crashes on the floor and goes dark.*

He stands and moves across the room to a television set and VCR, turns both on, and presses Play.

The woman dances to the front of the stage, turns one ... two ... three ... four times ... and stops.

Freeze.

The satisfaction is gone.

"Fuck you!" he screams at the frozen image. "I did not get lucky!"

The woman is motionless. He feels no thrill at her stillness, and kicks the VCR. Its cable becomes detached from the television, and video snow fills the screen. The snow pleases him.

"Fuck you," he says again, panting. "You just watch."

35

Martin came in the back door only a few minutes after Jason had returned from the E-Bar. He was carrying a flat brown bag sealed shut with a small round sticker. He looked at Jason's face and said, "Tough time with Paul?"

Jason said, "Yeah."

"Sorry."

"Had to be done. No way to reach Mr. Fluffy without using Paul." He shook his head. "Oh well. Let's see the printout."

Martin picked the sticker off with a fingernail, took an oversized piece of shiny white paper out of the bag, and said, "Ta da."

Jason took it. It was the picture of the naked brown-haired woman with Monica's face transplanted seamlessly onto it.

Jason studied it closely.

"Turn it upside down," Martin said. "That way you can look at it without being distracted by what it is."

Jason turned it upside-down and looked for seams again, but didn't find any.

Martin said, "I was a little worried because the show program from the TechnoArts show was printed on a textured paper, but the texture wasn't a problem."

"It's perfect," Jason said. "How do you do it, Martin?"

"Black magic."

"You can't fool me," Jason said. "You're only half black."

"Maybe so," Martin said in a John Wayne voice, putting his fists on his hips. "But it's the lower half, Pilgrum."

"You've been hanging out with Robert too much," Jason said.

"Robert's John Wayne probably sucks," Martin said.

Robert opened the front door and walked in.

"Robert," Jason said, "Martin says your John Wayne probably sucks."

Robert squinted and said, "Howdy, Pilgrim," in the Clint Eastwood whisper.

"See?" Martin said. "He can only do Jack Palance."

Robert assumed a more sauntering posture, and the squint changed somehow. Then he said in a flawless John Wayne, "I think you'd better take that back, partner."

Martin looked stunned. "Wow! I didn't know you could do that!"

"Guess you never asked, Pilgrim." Then he said in a fast, fruity accent out of a 1930s screwball comedy, "There are many things you don't know about me, Madeline; many, many things; but this is neither the time nor the place. A man's duty calls and he answers. They call it patriotism, Madeline; patriotism!"

He strode purposefully to the sofa and stepped up onto it. "Because when a man's country calls, Madeline, it is for him to neither waver nor hesitate."

Jason started to hum the Star-Spangled Banner, and Martin caught on after a few notes. Robert's voice gained depth and purpose. "No," he boomed over the humming, "rather it is for him to stride forward with bearing regal to take up the banner of freedom; to march with pride along with his fellows; to show the world and the enemy what he is made of! That, Madeline; *that* is a man!"

Jason and Martin reached the part about the rockets' red glare. Robert clasped his hand to his chest, looked with feeling at unseen horizons, and projected passionately, "Because when the enemy comes from the north with his black boots and his rifles; his tanks and his bombers; his drooling, dribbling fangs and his red, rabid eyes; when he smashes in the doors and windows of honest fisherfolk and yogurt makers"— Martin lost it and stopped humming for a moment. Without breaking his pace, Robert shouted—"of simple shoe repair specialists and good, trustworthy satellite television installers; that, Madeline, that is when the true muster of a man calls him—nay, beseeches him—to take up guns and sharp, pointy objects and fight for his country. For truth, Madeline ... for truth and justice! For checks and cash!"

Jason and Martin applauded as they hummed the last few bars of the Star-Spangled Banner. Robert continued to gaze nobly at Destiny. Something went *thump thump thump* on the ceiling and Patrice's voice upstairs yelled, "Shut up!" The telephone rang.

"Bravo, bravo," Jason said, walking backward toward the telephone.

"*Bravissimo!*" Martin cried. Robert inclined his head graciously.

Jason said, "The critics agree! The feel-good movie of the year! A modern masterpiece!"

"I couldn't put it down," Martin said.

"I laughed, I cried." Jason said, picking up the receiver. "Now get your muddy shoes off Martin's bed. Hello?"

Platt's voice said, "Will you be home for awhile?"

"Planning on it."

"I'll be over. Clear out the front room and make some coffee."

Platt hung up. Jason replaced the receiver.

Robert was twisting his shoes up one at a time to look at them. "They're not muddy," he said.

"Then please," Martin said graciously, "don't miss my pillow." Robert stepped heavily down from the sofa.

Jason said, "Martin, do you have the floppy disk with the naked Monica picture on it?"

"It's in the bag."

"Is it ready to upload?"

"Not yet."

"Okay. Um, could you disconnect the Mac and set it up in the bedroom? You can use it in there."

"Sure," Martin said. "Now?"

"Yeah," Jason said. Martin shut the computer down and began to detach its cables.

"Robert, would you help me put the furniture in the pseudo-kitchen?"

"Okay. What's up?"

"I don't know. Platt says he needs the room cleared."

There was no good place for the piano and sofa in the pseudo-kitchen, so Jason and Robert just wedged them into the space between the dish cabinet and the wall, blocking passage through the apartment. Jason covered the middle of the sofa with a beach towel, so it wouldn't be soiled by people climbing over it, and started a pot of coffee brewing.

The beeping alarm of a truck backing up in the parking lot was followed by a knock at the back door. Jason climbed over the sofa, looked through the orange towel at Platt, and opened the door. Behind Platt, a long white cargo van with a black hydraulic lift was parked tail-in to the Manor. The lift motor whined as it lowered.

Platt looked pointedly at the sofa and piano, then at the truck, then back at the furniture, and then at Jason.

"Where did you think I was going to put them," Jason said. "On the roof? You didn't mention cargo. We'll move them into the parking lot so you can get through, and then put them back when we're done loading in."

Platt said, "Okay."

There were footsteps on the outside staircase and then Patrice's voice said, "What's this?" Jason stepped outside. Patrice was standing on the lowest step.

Platt smiled a pleased smile, walked toward her, and said, "You must be Patrice! Hi, I'm Norton Platt. I'm a friend of Jason's." He extended his hand. Patrice took it and they shook hands.

"You're moving in," she said suspiciously.

"Only for a few days. We're just getting Jason's show together, and then we'll be out of here."

"What show?" Patrice said, looking at Jason.

Platt said, "You haven't told her about the show, Jason?"

Jason said, "You know me."

Platt said, "You know Jason. He doesn't like to talk about his big projects until they're done."

"What's in the truck?" Patrice said.

"Just stuff for the show."

"Are you going to be making a lot of noise?"

"No, not at all," Platt said. "We'll practice at low volume levels, and if you do happen to hear anything, we'd love to know what you think of it." He smiled brightly.

Her concerns apparently addressed, Patrice smiled slightly back, turned to mount the stairs again, and said, "Just as long as you're not too loud."

"Thank you very much," Platt said. "We'll do our best to be thoughtful and considerate." Patrice climbed the stairs and went up to the second story.

As soon as the door shut behind her, the doors to the

truck's cab opened and two people stepped down. The driver was a slightly-built man in his forties with dark blond hair, small hands, and a scar across his left cheek. The passenger was a tall, good-looking dark-haired woman with some gray who favored her left leg a little as she walked toward the Manor. Both were dressed casually in blue jeans, the man with a green La Coste shirt with the collar turned up, and the woman with a plain tan T-shirt with a pocket.

The man looked at the back of the Manor and said, "Here?" He didn't look pleased.

"Jason," Platt said, "This is Vince Delahugh. Vince, Jason, Jason, Vince."

"Hi," Jason said. Delahugh nodded sourly.

"And Leslie Bookman. Leslie, Jason, Jason, Leslie."

"Hi," Jason said. They shook hands. She smiled. She had good crow's feet.

"Nice to meet you," she said. "Ready for us?"

"Not quite," Jason said. "Give me a couple of minutes." He turned toward the open door and yelled, "Robert!"

In a few seconds, Robert leaned out the back door and said, "Your honeyed voice wafted gently?"

"Dulcet tones and dulcet mind," Jason said. "We gotta move the piano and the sofa out here so Platt can get his stuff through the pseudo-kitchen."

They bumped things against the stairway a couple of times. Platt opened the back of the truck. It was three-quarters full with equipment racks that ranged from carry-on luggage-size, to four that were as big as apartment refrigerators.

It took forty-five minutes to empty the truck into the pseudo-kitchen. Then Leslie Bookman drove the van away somewhere and Platt began to arrange the racks the way he wanted them in the front room, with the four big ones side-by-side against the wall, where the sofa had been. The racks were padded and covered in blue canvas, with zippers around their fronts.

Jason went into his bedroom, where Martin was sitting on the floor, intent on the Macintosh, which sat on the futon. Martin looked absorbed, so Jason left him alone and went back into the front room. Leslie Bookman was back, and she and Platt and Delahugh were unzipping the racks. Robert was standing around, poised to do something as soon as someone told him what.

"Coffee?" Jason said.

Platt said, "Is it coffee, or is it espresso impersonating coffee?"

"Espresso."

"Could somebody go get some real coffee?"

Robert looked alert and said, "I'll go. Be back soon." He reached for the front door knob and said, "Do I have to be sneaky and go out the back or anything?"

Delahugh said, "Never let your guard down."

"Yes," Robert said, overpatiently. He smiled falsely. "Indeed. Even so. Does that mean go out the back?"

Delahugh looked pained and said, "Just watch it. This ain't the Girl Scouts."

Robert did his plastic smile at Jason, said, "Okay then," and went out the front door. Jason shot a glance at the back of Platt's head, which seemed to be ignoring everyone.

Next to Platt, Leslie Bookman turned from the rack she was unzipping, looked over Delahugh at Jason, and made an apologetic face. Delahugh was busy unzipping a rack and didn't notice. Jason shook his head a little and angled one hand in polite dismissal, and she smiled warmly at him. The warm smile caught him off balance. His heart thumped a little, and he felt decidedly unsophisticated.

"I'd like some espresso coffee," she said. "One sugar, no cream."

"Coming right up." Jason went into the pseudo-kitchen without tangling his feet together, edged around the few blue racks which hadn't yet made it into the front room, and got her coffee. She smiled warmly again when he gave it to her. He didn't think he blushed.

"Where's Platt?" he said.

She pointed with her chin. "Outside, getting electricity."

Delahugh snorted. "This wiring is so old, I'm surprised this place hasn't burned down."

"It can't," Jason said. "The wood stays soggy year 'round. All it can do is steam a little."

"Great," Delahugh said. "What a dump."

Jason looked at him and didn't say anything.

"Yeah, sorry, whatever," Delahugh said.

Jason looked at him some more and then turned and went over the sofa into the bedroom.

Martin was still sitting on the floor, his gaze fixed on the Macintosh screen, which showed the falsified picture of Monica. Below the top inch-and-a-half, the picture turned into a chaotic mess of lines and dots.

Jason said, "Is it done?"

Martin said, "Uh ..." and didn't look away from the screen. Jason waited. After fifteen seconds, Martin looked glazedly at him and said, "Huh?"

Jason said, "Is it done?"

"This is a goddamn slow computer."

"Want some coffee?"

Martin said, "Yeah," and turned back to the screen.

Jason got Martin's coffee and gave it to him, complete with saucer. Martin grunted and didn't look at the coffee.

Jason went back into the front room. Platt was running a beige cable into the front room through a hole in the wall that had once had a TV cable in it.

Jason stood and watched for a few seconds. "Where's the other end?"

Platt said, "One foot out from the curb and eighteen inches down."

"Can I do anything, or am I just in the way?"

"You're in the way," Platt said. "Did you talk to Mr. Pascal yet?"

"No. Is it a good time?"

"As good as any."

"Okay."

The white card with the phone number was still in the back pocket of his dark blue jeans. He found the jeans under the futon. Martin was still doing something with the Macintosh, but seemed somewhat better connected with reality. Jason sat on the futon next to him and dialed the number.

Someone with a brusque voice said, "Yes."

"Mr. Pascal, please," Jason said.

"Who is calling, please?"

"This is the National Brain Trust. We're calling a representative sampling of Americans to let them know that we trust their brains."

There was a pause on the other end, and then the brusque person hung up.

Jason held the receiver and said, "He hung up," to Martin in a surprised voice.

"No!" Martin said. "And you didn't even get to do Prince Albert in the can."

"Martin," Jason said as he pressed the redial button, "why do I do these things?"

Martin said, "Just guessing. Because you're a moron?"

"Oh yeah. It's reassuring that I can always count on— Hello? Mr. Pascal, please. This is Jason Keltner."

After a very short time, Pascal's voice said, "Yes."

Jason said, "I understand you have construction interests."

36

By early evening, Platt had all the racks set up where he wanted them, and he and Vince Delahugh began to switch things on and run tests. Leslie Bookman said to Platt, "I'll take a break and be back in half an hour." Platt nodded at her, and she said to Jason, "Care to take an evening stroll?"

"Sure," Jason said.

The old-fashioned streetlights on Marengo Avenue came on as they left the Manor, and a gusting breeze pushed dead leaves around in front of the porch. On the sidewalk, Jason tried to be subtle about getting around her and walking on the outside.

"I like this area," she said, as they passed a narrow lot with half a dozen bungalows on it that had been converted to offices.

"Me too," Jason said. "I like the turn-of-the-century architecture. I grew up in the Valley, and nothing there is older than the 'fifties or so. That square, tacky look."

She smiled at him. He couldn't think of an appropriate facial expression, so he looked away.

After a while, she said, "Norton tells me you're almost divorced. When is it final?"

"Um," Jason said, trying to remember the date. "It'll be final—" he stopped walking, shocked. "Oh my gosh. Two days ago. Oh my."

She said, "I guess you've been pretty busy."

"I guess so!"

"How does it feel?"

"Weird. No, not weird. Strange. Um, I don't know how it feels." He stood still and tried to determine how he felt. "Actually, it feels pretty much the same, only I'm divorced. Wow."

He thought about it some more, and then they started walking again. "I wonder if the papers came. I haven't checked my mail in awhile. It's kind of like having a birthday, isn't it? You don't feel different, but there's a new number associated with your life."

They walked a few blocks to California Street and turned left.

"What's in your future?" she asked.

"Music."

"Nothing else?"

"No."

"That's a hard life."

"Not as hard as some."

"Harder than most."

"Could be. I'll let you know when I get there."

"What kind of music do you do?"

"Honestly ... right now, I don't do any."

"Why not?"

"I just can't. It doesn't come. I sit there and stare at the little blinking lights and the computer screen, and nothing good happens. I haven't really put it into words before. I know Martin and Robert are worried about me, but I can't talk to them about it."

"Why can't you?"

"I ... don't know why not."

"They seem nice to me."

"They are. Very nice."

They turned left again at Los Robles, and looked at the old, wide California bungalows that shared the street with newer condominiums.

"Why can't you talk to them, then? I bet it's some male thing."

"You might be right."

"Do you have a hard time talking about your feelings?"

"Not at all. I have a hard time seeing why I should. What does it get me? That kind of thing."

"That sounds like the same thing to me."

"It's not. I just have a hard time seeing the relevance of my feelings. Talking about them doesn't change them or their causes."

"But it might make you feel better."

"Maybe."

"You don't think so."

"No."

"Why wouldn't it?"

"Because it never has."

She shook her head and sighed. "On a few things," she said, "I think men got the short end of the stick."

"Yeah, I suppose. But we also get things you women don't."

"Like what?"

"I don't know if I can reveal the secret male knowledge to you."

"Oh, do."

"Okay. This is the secret male knowledge: Every man is born knowing two important things: How to make spaghetti sauce, and that he could kill an alligator barehanded."

"I see."

"I never said the secret male knowledge made sense."

"Men are weird."

"*Men* are weird? Explain to me about home shopping."

"It's convenient." She narrowed her eyes and said, "Now you explain to me about monster trucks."

"Makes us feel like we're hunting mammoths. What about going to the bathroom in platoons?"

"Safety. How about *Hustler* magazine?"

"Yuck. What about romance novels?"

"Um, you got me there. What about Jean Claude Van Damme movies?"

"We enjoy a well-wrought drama. See? All you had to do was ask, and now you know the secret male knowledge."

"I'm so glad I did."

"Next week we'll discuss how to find just the wrong person and maintain a long-term relationship with them."

"How'd you get so cynical so young?"

Surprised, he said, "I'm not cynical."

"Yes, you are."

"No I'm not. I'm not at all cynical."

She stopped, put her hands on his shoulders, and said, "Jason, believe me; you are cynical." It was too dark to tell, but he thought her eyes were blue.

"I'm too much of a romantic to be cynical," he said. "Can somebody be romantic and cynical both?"

"Oh, heavens, yes," she said. "Oh, yes."

As they turned onto Del Mar and cut through the parking lot to the Manor, a slight rain began to fall. At the back door, she said, "Well, congratulations on your divorce. Or should it be condolences? What does one say about a divorce?"

He got his keys out of his pocket. "Good question. I guess *gesundheit* is already taken."

She laughed, and so did he. Then she looked down at the ground, and looked up and said, "Isn't it funny how timing is everything sometimes?"

He unlocked the door. "What do you mean?"

"Oh," she said, smiling a little, "Nothing." She looked at him for another second and then opened the door and went in.

What timing?

Waldo the cat came halfway down the stairs from the second story, looked quizzically at Jason, and meowed rustily. Jason leaned over and scratched Waldo on the top of the head, and then followed Leslie Bookman into the Manor, as Waldo trotted down the stairs and lay down in the newly-wet grass.

37

Robert and Martin were sitting on top of empty cases in the front room. All the equipment in the racks had been turned on, and little colored indicator lights flickered on the faceplates. Four beige telephones sat in a row atop a medium-sized rack that contained three small computer monitors. The room light was off, and the little lights and screens reminded Jason of a time when he and Marisa had gone to Disneyland and waited in line at the Star Tours ride.

"Ground control to Major Tom," Jason said.

Platt craned his head around from where he was squatting with Delahugh in front of a rack and said, "Commencing countdown, engines on."

Leslie Bookman stepped around a rack and joined Platt and Delahugh. "Isn't that some song?"

Delahugh said, "It's David Bowie. Where you been?" He gave Jason a just-us-guys headshake. Jason pretended not to see it.

"Oh," she said. She made a face at Delahugh that he couldn't see. "I guess I just don't know the really good music."

"Yeah," Jason said. "You should be hip and current like Delahugh. What do you listen to?"

"I like older stuff, mostly."

Robert said, "Me too. I think my favorite song right now is 'One Bourbon, One Scotch, and One Beer' from a tape Jason lent me."

"Thorogood!" Delahugh said.

"No," Robert said condescendingly. "Howlin' Wolf."

"Who?" Delahugh said. Robert smiled pityingly.

Platt straightened. "Okay, Jason," he said. "We're ready for you. Let's have the picture."

Jason said, "Martin?"

Martin held up a blue floppy disk and said, "Right here." He tossed it to Platt, who gave it to Delahugh. Delahugh inserted it into a slot in one of the racks and typed on a keyboard.

"Okay," said Delahugh after a minute. "It's online."

"Speaking of music," Leslie Bookman said, "Where's my boombox?"

"In the truck, I think," Platt said.

"Oh, darn."

Robert slid off the case he was sitting on, said, "I'll get mine from upstairs," and went out the front door. A few seconds later, heavy clomping sounds reverberated through the Manor.

Martin said, "We really need to carpet those stairs or something."

An upstairs door opened, the ceiling creaked, and the door closed, followed immediately by a reprise of the clomping sounds. Then the front door opened and Robert came in with a portable AM/FM/cassette/CD player and a handful of tapes. He put the player on top of one of the rack cases and pushed Play. Etta James began singing "Baby, What You Want Me To Do" in midphrase.

"So now what?" Martin said.

Platt shrugged. "Dinner? What's good and delivers around here?"

"How's wonton and guacamole sound," Jason said.

"Wonton and guacamole?" Delahugh said, looking pained. He made it a hard *g*.

"Wonton," Robert enunciated slowly at Delahugh. He smiled. "Guacamole," he concluded, nodding lovingly. Delahugh looked at him as though he were roadkill.

"Fine with me," Leslie Bookman said.

"Sure," Platt said.

Robert said, "Get some crúco for Vince."

Delahugh said, "What's that, what's crúco?"

"Oh, yeah, get me one too," Martin said. "It's ... how would you explain it, Robert?"

"It's really good," Robert said. "Do you like tuffte? It's a lot like tuffte."

"Uh," Delahugh said.

"You've never had tuffte?" Robert's expression was incredulous.

"Really?" Martin said.

Jason said, "Do they serve their crúco with the poo sauce?"

Martin said, "No, you're thinking of crassits. Crassits is different from crúco."

Delahugh looked back and forth as he followed the conversation.

Jason said, "What's the difference?"

"No sauce."

"Oh. Then what do they dip the slugs in?"

"Don't worry," Martin said to Delahugh. "They're not the same as the slugs we have here." To Jason, he said, "We could get that brown pasty stuff instead, if he doesn't want the slugs."

Robert said, "I really liked those little bloated purple things in it."

"No fucking slugs," Delahugh said.

Jason looked past him at Leslie Bookman, and said, "Want some slugs in poo sauce or some little bloated purple things?"

"Gracious, no."

Delahugh must have caught the amusement in her voice because he turned around to see her expression and then looked disgusted and said, "Ha ha, very funny."

Robert leaned in toward Delahugh, squinted at him, and grated, "Always. Always watch your back." He pointed meaningfully. "This ain't the Girl Scouts." Then he said in a Groucho voice, "Which is a shame, because I could really use a box of Savannahs."

"You just take care of your own back," Delahugh said, "and let me worry about mine, bozo."

Robert looked happy and said, "'Bozo!'"

Delahugh said, "Listen, dickweed—"

Robert's joy doubled and he said, "'Dickweed!'"

Platt was looking pointedly at Jason. Jason raised his eyebrows to acknowledge the pointed look and said, "Robert, you have a delivery menu upstairs, don't you?"

Robert looked as though he were about to say something else, but then said in an overhelpful tone, "Why don't I go get it."

"Thanks."

Robert left and clomped up the stairs.

"What a loser," Delahugh said.

Jason looked pointedly at Platt. Platt's lips twitched in the barest smile, and he raised his eyebrows in acknowledgment and said, "Vince, if you're done, I'm not sure the telecom connectors are seated completely. I don't have dial tone on line three."

Delahugh looked annoyed and said, "There was dial tone before." He got up and reached toward one of the four telephones. Platt picked it up first and listened to it.

"Nope," he said. "Why don't you go outside and wiggle the connector and I'll listen to the phone. Grab your jacket— I think it's still raining out."

They ate Chinese food in the front room, spooning servings from the black rectangular plastic containers onto the transparent rectangular lids. Everyone used chopsticks to eat. When they were done, and Jason had thrown away the containers, Robert said, "How long do you think it'll be before Mr. Fluffy will call?"

"There's no way to tell," said Platt. "He has to log on to the Net, see the anonymous announcement that there's a new nude picture of Monica to be had, download it, discover that he can't see the good parts of the picture, try to fix it with a graphics program or whatever, log on to download it again, because he figures his first one got messed up while downloading, and then notice the modem phone number at the top of the photo, call it, and try to get the 'uncorrupted' .GIF file. It might be a while before it happens."

"If it happens at all," Jason said.

"Exactly. I think it's got a good shot, though."

Robert said, "So what do we do in the meantime?"

"Whatever you usually do."

Martin looked at Jason quizzically. "What exactly is that?"

Jason said, "I don't think we have a usual, do we?"

Robert said. "Sure we do. About this time, Martin and I walk into Old Town and talk to girls who give us fake phone numbers, and you go to bed."

"At eight-thirty?" Leslie Bookman said.

Jason said, "When you have to get up at four-thirty in the morning to be at a filtration plant at six o'clock, eight-thirty's about right."

Platt said, "If you go to bed at eight-thirty, when do you play out?"

"I don't."

Leslie Bookman said, "Play out?"

"Play music someplace," Platt said.

"Ah."

"It's musician talk," Jason said. "Maybe soon."

Robert went upstairs and came down with his game of Risk, and played two games with Platt and Leslie Bookman. Platt won the first game and Leslie Bookman won the second. Robert seemed intensely focused, and Jason guessed that he was having a great time being trounced by people from whom he could learn.

Delahugh sat in front of the rack with the computer in it, and listened to something on a Walkman, and Jason and Martin read. At 11:00 PM, Platt unrolled two olive-colored sleeping bags with ducks printed on the inside onto the floor of the front room, and everyone but Delahugh went to bed. Jason looked back as he left; Delahugh's headphones made soft cymbal sounds in the room as he watched for something to happen on the three little monitors that glowed milk-blue in the padded rack.

38

In the morning, Delahugh slipped into one of the sleeping bags and Platt and Leslie Bookman alternated eight-hour shifts watching the monitor. Jason, Robert, and Martin watched daytime television and listened to music in Jason's bedroom and Robert's apartment. Robert's apartment looked like Jason's room had looked when he was fifteen: sprawled clothes choked the walking areas, and things sat where Robert had dropped them. Jason and Martin tried to spend most of their time downstairs.

Lunch was bagels from a bagel place on Colorado Boulevard. Robert walked there to get them. No one shot at him or forced him into a black limousine with mirrored windows.

Robert and Martin played Risk with Leslie Bookman after lunch. Jason picked up *The Art of War*, tried to read it, and put it back down. He went out the back door and whisked a thin stick back and forth in front of Waldo the cat for half an hour, and then let Waldo kill the stick and went back inside. Then he went back outside and tried to play with Waldo again, but Waldo didn't want to kill any more sticks.

Delahugh came out of the front room at about two o'clock, drank a Pepsi from the little refrigerator, and sat on the sofa with a vinyl cassette case, listening to his Walkman and reading a bodybuilding magazine with a huge oiled veiny male person grimacing on the cover next to an oiled veiny female person.

Robert won a game of Risk and went out with Leslie Bookman to rent a video. Jason and Martin sat on the back steps and talked about Mega Mole until they came back, and then they all went upstairs, opened the windows in Robert's apartment, and watched *Wizards* and *All of Me*. Then Leslie Bookman went downstairs and relieved Platt, and Robert and Martin went to return the videos and get new ones. They came back with *Silverado* and *A Fish Called Wanda* and a paper bag of burrito ingredients, made burritos in the real kitchen next door to Jason's section of the house, and ate the burritos and watched the movies. At 11:00 PM, everybody but Delahugh went to bed; Delahugh sat up and watched the monitor and listened to his Walkman. When Jason got up in the morning, Delahugh was sleeping in one of the olive-colored sleeping bags; Platt was up, watching the monitor and listening to Delahugh's Walkman.

Leslie Bookman and Martin got coffee beans and more bagels. Jason made coffee. Nobody said much during breakfast. Then Martin returned the videos and got *Modern Times* and *The General*. At lunchtime, Robert and Martin went out and came back with barbecued ribs, cole slaw, corn on the cob, onion rings, *Monty Python and the Holy Grail*, and *Road Warrior*. Leslie Bookman said, "Oh, Mel Gibson," and went upstairs to watch with them.

While they were all eating in Robert's apartment and watching the movie, Robert's phone rang. Jason answered it.

"Come downstairs if you want," Platt's voice said. "No telling if it's him, but it looks like we got contact."

39

SORRY, OUR 28.8 KBAUD LINES ARE DOWN RIGHT NOW.
WE APOLOGIZE FOR THE INCONVENIENCE, AND ARE TRYING
TO FIX THEM AS QUICKLY AS POSSIBLE

Time is billed at $0.25 per minute, $2.00 for the first minute. Charges are billed discreetly on your credit card, and appear as "SPT Entertainment."
Welcome to The Foto Shop. We are pleased to offer a wide selection of adult picture files. Most of our photos are in .GIF format. If you don't have a means of viewing .GIF files, you may download our .GIF viewer from the main library.
Enter "LIST" for a list of library categories or enter the number of the library you wish to browse.
> list
1. Beautiful Women   4. Men On Men
2. M/F Action   5. Whips and Chains
3. Gay/Bi Babes   6. Kinky Korner

Enter "LIST" for a list of library categories or enter the number of the library you wish to browse.

```
> 1
BEAUTIFUL WOMEN: (s)earch by keyword (d)ownload
(b)rowse (e)xit
> s
SEARCH BY KEYWORD: enter the keyword you wish to
search for
> monica
SEARCHING....
FILE              SIZE          DESCRIPTION
MONICA.GIF        42,064        Monica having solo
                                fun on bed
Keyword: "monica": 1 selection found
BEAUTIFUL WOMEN: (s)earch by keyword (d)ownload
(b)rowse (e)xit
> d
Name of file to download:
> MONICA.GIF
What transfer protocol? (x)modem (y)modem (z)modem
> z
Beginning transfer of file MONICA.GIF...

File transfer complete. Elapsed time 9 minutes
BEAUTIFUL WOMEN: (s)earch by keyword (d)ownload
(b)rowse (e)xit
> e
Thank you for using The Foto Shop. Come back soon!
NO CARRIER
```

"That's it," Platt said. "Our first call. That one came from ..." He consulted an LCD display in the rack. "Minneapolis. He gave us his name and MasterCard number before you got here."

"Nice how they stay connected for so long, so we can trace them," Jason said. "It's very considerate."

"That's the idea behind the faster lines being down," Platt said. "It's an excuse to keep them online longer."

"So now you check the MasterCard?" Robert said.

"Yes, I'm about to do that."

"I never asked you," Jason said. "Are you actually going to bill people for their online time?"

Platt grinned. "Charges are billed discreetly to your credit card, and appear as 'SPT Entertainment.'"

Martin said, "SPT?"

Jason and Martin looked at each other. Robert looked thoughtfully up in the air.

"What's SPT?" Jason said.

Robert hooted and said, "Screamin' Pink Tigers!"

"Yup," Platt said. "By the way, I want one of those shoulder patches."

"I gotta make some more," Martin said. "I only made three."

Jason said, "Who gets the money?"

"Defrayment of expenses," Platt said. "We just made six dollars off that one call. Another, uh, two thousand calls and we break even on this."

Martin said, "Do you really have all those pictures in there?"

"Yes." He pointed to a unit in the rack. "They're all on this hard drive. It would look awfully strange if Martin's fake Monica picture were the only dirty picture available on the whole system."

Jason said, "Where does one acquire a hard drive of dirty pictures?"

Platt said, "I don't know. The dirty picture hard drive store?"

Robert said, "Smut-R-Us."

"I mean, is this a standard-issue thing, or did you have to assemble it?"

Platt said, "Let's just put it this way: all kinds of things are available to those who know where to look."

"You are indeed a font of information."

"An oblique font," Platt said. "Watch it or I'll break out the enigmatic smile again."

"Watch it, *Buster*," Robert corrected.

"Oh, right," Platt said. "Sorry."

Jason said, "Or *Jack. Buster* or *Jack*."

Robert said, "*Jack* is archaic."

"That's true," Jason said.

Platt said, "Everybody go away."

Two days later, in the early evening, he said, "Got him."

40

"Here," Platt said, pointing at a telephone number that showed on the middle monitor. Everyone was crowded around the rack. Pointing to another telephone number on the right-hand monitor, he said, "And here."

"The numbers are different," Martin said.

"But the area codes are the same. Both nine-oh-nine. It's unlikely that one person from one area code would call the X-rated foto number and also call Municipal Water's computer access number, and that the same person wouldn't know the Municipal password. See? Connection to the Municipal Water computer—or, more accurately, our fake Municipal Water computer—at oh-nine-thirty-two this morning." He tapped the third monitor. "See? This is him. He's still trying to find the password so he can get in."

Jason looked at the third monitor. Every few seconds, an unseen hand entered a string of numbers and letters, and the computer responded with "Incorrect password. Please try again."

Unable to look away, Jason said very softly, "We see you."

Another string of numbers and letters appeared.

Incorrect password. Please try again.

"He bit," Jason said.

"It was a good bet," said Platt. "How better to find out about your daily schedule than to rifle through your personnel record?"

"I know," Jason said. "But I'm still a little surprised that it worked. Where's he calling from?"

"Well, nine-oh-nine is San Bernardino. Colton, Redlands, around there. But I checked the number, and he's using a stolen cellular phone. We can't trace his location. Same thing with the call to our little Foto Shop scam, but from a different stolen cellular phone. That's another reason it's probably the same guy."

Incorrect password. Please try again.

"Just keep trying," Jason said to the screen. "What if he doesn't get the password?"

Platt said, "He will. He's just playing around, so far. He hasn't gotten serious, yet. I give him two days at the outside before he has your route, the fake pipeline shutdown schedule, the phony patrol truck radio frequency, and everything. You'll be going back to work soon."

"Okay," Jason said.

The unseen hand entered another string.

Incorrect password. You have exceeded the allowable number of attempts. Please contact MIS.

Disconnecting...

NO CARRIER

"Don't worry," Platt said. "That won't stop him."

41

It was cold outside the covers. Jason hit the snooze button on his clock-radio at 4:10, 4:19, 4:28, and 4:37. At 4:46, he turned the alarm off and sat on the edge of the futon for ten minutes with the covers around him, staring blankly and waiting for the disconnected, swimmy feeling of interrupted sleep to go away. It didn't. He got up anyway, with the covers still on, and went into the bathroom.

The only advantage of being the first person awake in the Manor was the reduced likelihood of sudden scalding or chilling in the shower. It wasn't a sure thing; Chuck, who lived upstairs, kept irregular hours and ignored the shower schedule, but he was out of town. Jason fumbled the pliers from the shower soap dish and turned the stripped and handleless brass stems until a small stream of water trickled from the cracked plastic showerhead. When the water pressure had built sufficiently for the stream to arc slightly, he tossed the covers into his bedroom and stepped in.

The water wasn't hot or plentiful enough to really warm the cold shower stall, so he shivered through his shower and then dried off as briskly as he could. He called the filtration plant and left a message for his foreman, Don, that he'd be there. Then he dressed in blue jeans, sneakers, a black T-shirt, and his Tigers ski jacket. He took the flat, circular retracting keychain from his jacket pocket and hooked it to the top of his jeans, and then went into the front room where Platt and Leslie Bookman were drinking coffee from the mugs he'd owned with Marisa.

Platt handed him a blue knapsack. "The channel's already set," he said. He opened the knapsack to show Jason the two-way radio inside. "This is the power switch. The battery should be good for at least a week, but there's a fully-charged extra in there, just in case. It works just like the one in your truck."

"Break a leg," Leslie Bookman said.

Jason took the knapsack, waved goodbye, and went outside at 5:20 AM.

He breathed out in a huff through his mouth and watched the silver cloud of his breath in the moonlight. Sorting through his keys, he walked to the Plymouth and looked at the low, dark apartments next to the Manor. A single window was lighted, its glass fogged with condensation. It was half-open and framed nicely the pleasant morning movements of a naked female upper torso.

"Good morning," Jason said softly enough so the owner of the torso wouldn't hear. The male tenants at the Manor called her the Topless Blow-Dryer. As far as Jason knew, the female tenants had no word for her. Sometimes an inconsiderate calico cat sat in the window and obstructed the view, but this morning there was no cat.

Jason got into the Plymouth, started the engine, and wiggled the accelerator pedal to keep it from dying. He pulled a cheap blue-and-white Mexican blanket from under the back seat and wrapped it around him as he watched the Topless Blow-Dryer and listened to his teeth clatter. When the automatic choke shifted and the engine rhythm smoothed out, he backed away from the Manor and pulled onto Del Mar, turned on his headlights, and headed north on the 210 Freeway, a torrent of wind pouring in through the broken windshield. He drove with one hand so he could use the other to hold the blanket closed, switching hands every few minutes to allow the non-driving hand to thaw.

In Sylmar twenty-five minutes later, he entered a small lot through a wheeled gate and parked next to a chain-link fence. Past the fence, dozens of silent pickup trucks with black plastic storage boxes installed across their beds, a few compact pickups with smaller boxes, and two big ten-wheeled utility trucks with specialized machinery welded onto metal brackets, were parked on gravel. Every truck was white, with red diagonal stripes on the tailgate or back panel, and every truck had a whip antenna mounted somewhere, a small orange rotary light on the roof of the cab, and an *E* in a diamond on the license plate.

Jason shut off the lights and engine, walked across the parking lot to a long, flat, beige building, and went through a brown door into the auto mechanics' bays. It was no warmer inside. Two trucks and a sedan were on the hydraulic lifts. The sedan didn't have red stripes.

Three mechanics with half-shut eyes sat on a bench near the door, sipping industrial coffee from Styrofoam cups and looking blearily across the room. Jason walked around one of the lifts and down a short corridor, and entered the pipeline crew's breakroom, which was slightly warmer than the mechanics' bays. Seven men sat with cups of coffee around a Formica table, in the middle of the L-shaped space that was left after the supervisor's office took a small rectangular chunk out of the room. The morning newspaper was scattered on the table. A broad window would have revealed the rest of the filtration plant, but it was still too dark to see more than the lights of the main building several hundred feet away, and a row of white trucks parked head-in near the breakroom. A small, tan metal desk stood against the window.

A tall sunburned man with blonde hair looked up and grinned. "Jase, we missed ya!" he drawled.

Jason said, "Morning, Rick."

A small, wiry man was sitting with his back to Jason. He turned around and said, "You have fun fishing?"

Don was his supervisor. "Skiing, Don," Jason said. "Not fishing."

"Oh, skiing," Don said.

"Then I went nude co-ed white water hot-air ballooning."

"Well, today you're patrolling. Think you can handle that?"

"I think so."

Don turned back to the men at the table. "Bob and Willy, keep greasing and flushing up north. You can take off if you finish up early."

Bob said, "Okay." He shook Willy's shoulder and said, "Wake up, Willy." Willy grunted. They both got up and went out. Jason unhooked a set of truck keys from a pegboard near the door and took a new pad of Xeroxed patrol logs from a stack on the desk.

Don said, "Rico and Ernie, head out to San Fernando and help the District guys with the new meters." Ernie rolled his eyes and looked at Rico. Rico said, "Don't worry. We go slow for them." Ernie sighed and pushed away from the table and they left.

"Logan, take Eduardo with you and fix the stair railing at the North Portal."

Jason walked with Logan and Eduardo back through the auto shop, where the mechanics were opening the bay doors.

Logan was a lanky man with sandy hair and an amiable face. Eduardo was new to the pipeline crew. He was a compact man who wore his black sweatshirt with the bottom rolled up to reveal the flat belly of a blue T-shirt.

A gray-haired mechanic yelled, "Hey Jase, what the hell happened to your car?"

Jason said, "Uh ... this guy in a flatbed was transporting long pieces of one-inch conduit and didn't have a red flag tied to the back of the load."

"And you ran into it like a dumbshit?"

"Very much like a dumbshit, yes," Jason said. The mechanic grinned and shook his head.

Logan said, "Hey, safety's nothing to laugh at. You're lucky you didn't get speared through the forehead. You should sue him."

"Maybe I will," Jason said. As the door to the bay closed behind him, he heard the mechanic say, "Hey Sammy, you gotta hear this ..."

In the parking lot, Jason said to Logan, "I miss anything?"

"Nope. Same old same old."

Logan unlocked one of the big utility trucks and he and Eduardo climbed up and swung into the cab and closed the doors, and the noisy diesel engine started. Jason got Platt's blue knapsack out of the Plymouth and carried it to a little pickup truck in the compound.

Logan pulled up next to him in the utility truck, rolled down his window and called down, "What time are you at the North Portal?"

"Twelve thirty-six," Jason yelled over the engine noise. "Plus or minus a couple."

"Want to have lunch?"

"Nah, not today. I got to run some errands during lunch."

Logan said, "Okay, next time."

Jason waved and Logan rolled his window up and shifted into reverse. The utility truck's backup beeper sounded until he shifted again and pulled out of the compound. Jason put the blue knapsack on the passenger's seat, tossed the new patrol logs next to them and then drove the pickup out of the compound and got on I-5, heading north.

During the half-hour drive to Castaic Lake, the morning darkness lightened, and Jason turned off his headlights. At the end of the off ramp, he waited behind a big truck with half a house on it and considered whether to get an apple fritter and coffee before or after he took meter readings at the Foothill pumping plant where he had camped with Robert and Martin. The half a house turned off the off ramp and Jason followed it. He didn't turn toward the donut shop.

At the Foothill Plant, he filled two little plastic bottles with water from a tall, thin spigot that stuck up out of the ground, capped both bottles tightly, put them on the pickup's open utility box, and withdrew a long thermometer from the box. Holding the thermometer under the stream of water, he looked up to where orange light, beginning to fade, brought the hills into relief. Sunrise over Castaic Lake was the second of five things he looked forward to every day. The first was that the donut shop ladies always poured a medium coffee when he walked in.

The third thing he looked forward to was a morning radio show that played music from around the world. The show lasted from about Chatsworth to Hollywood. The fourth thing was deciding where to eat lunch in Hollywood and what to read while he ate it. After that, through Burbank and Pacoima, he just looked forward to going home.

It occurred to him that he might consider quitting this job.

He withdrew the thermometer, wrote "Castaic, Jan. 20, 0640 hrs, 15°C" in black indelible marker on two small Tyvek slips that he bound to the plastic bottles with rubber bands, put the bottles in an ice-filled cooler in the pickup bed, shut off the water, closed the utility box, and drove fifty yards to the same low building that he and Robert and Martin had camped next to. Carrying a clipboard from the front seat, he unlocked two glass doors and took readings from a bank of meters in a small room.

A window on one wall overlooked the cavernous subterranean vault through which ran the huge pipelines that carried lake water to the filtration plant. A switch near the window operated a bank of sulphur lights on the ceiling of the vault. Jason switched the lights on, waited for them to get bright, and looked at the pipes. They were massive. A low vibration ran through the meter room: machinery and moving water.

He locked the glass doors behind him as he left and drove away from the lake and back onto the interstate. Three miles later, out of the hills, he unhitched a two-way radio handpiece from its mounting under the dashboard, pulled on it to untangle the spiral cord that connected it to the radio, pressed the button, and said, "Unit Eight to Municipal Plant."

A thin voice said, "Municipal Plant. Go ahead, Jason."

Jason pulled the clipboard onto his lap and recited the meter readings over the radio.

"Ten-four. Municipal Plant out."

"Unit Eight out."

The two-way radio was kind of fun. He'd always wanted to say, "One-Adam-twelve, handling Code Three." The pipeline crew occasionally transmitted rock music or phone sex recordings because it was frowned upon by management types and the FCC.

He reached into Platt's knapsack, switched Platt's radio on, and laid its handpiece across his thigh with the spiral cable stretched across the seat. A few minutes later, the radio in the backpack crackled and Norton Platt's voice said, "Municipal Plant to Jason Keltner, Unit Eight."

Jason picked up the handset, pressed the button, and said, "This is Unit Eight."

"Jason, what is your twenty, over?"

"I'm Southbound on the interstate, just South of Castaic, over?"

"Ten-four. You expect to be on schedule today, over?"

"Yes, as far as I know. Everything on schedule, over?"

"Ten-four, Unit Eight. Shutdown is on schedule, so you'll be due back at Castaic for pipeline walkthrough by fourteen-forty-five hours. Municipal Plant out."

"Ten-four. Unit Eight Out."

42

The day got warmer. Jason followed the patrol route west into Las Virgenes and Calabasas and south through the Sepulveda Pass. He took samples, ran tests, and logged the results. At the top of the Sepulveda Pass, he unlocked a metal gate and drove up a hill to where two huge water tanks dwarfed an adjoining building. He took water samples outside the building and hydroelectric power readings inside, drove back down the hill, and followed the patrol route through Hollywood and Beverly Hills, and then over the Hollywood Hills into the foothills that defined the southern edge of the San Fernando Valley.

In Burbank, he abandoned his patrol route and got on the 134 freeway, took it to the Interstate, and was back at Castaic at 2:40.

Sitting in the truck next to the low building, he picked up the handpiece from the knapsack and said, "Unit Eight to Municipal Plant."

He waited a few seconds and said, "This is Unit Eight to Municipal Plant, over."

Norton Platt's voice said, "This is Municipal Plant. Go ahead, Unit Eight."

Jason pressed the key. "I'm at Castaic now, over?"

"Ten-four, Jason," Platt's voice said. "This is Frank. Proceed with scheduled walkthrough, over?"

"Oh, hi, Frank," Jason said. "Ten-four. I'm entering Foothill Plant at fifteen-hundred hours, and will enter the pipeline on schedule at fifteen-ten hours. I'll be out of radio contact for approximately thirty minutes."

"Ten four. Valves fifty-six and fifty-seven are full open for visual inspection. Make sure you're out of there by sixteen-hundred hours when they close. Municipal Plant out."

"Unit Eight out."

In the front room of the Manor, Norton Platt released the microphone button and said to Martin, "This is the part that makes me nervous."

"I really wish you wouldn't say that," Martin said.

43

"**H**mm," Platt said suddenly. He leaned more closely toward the second small screen.

Martin said, "What?"

"Bookman!" Platt yelled.

"What!" Martin said.

Leslie Bookman entered the front room from the pseudo-kitchen.

"What is it?"

"Our killer isn't where we thought he'd be." He wrote something on a small notepad, tore off the sheet, and handed it to her. "Delahugh's nearby at the site. Get him there."

Leslie Bookman snapped one of the telephones off the top of a rack and paced as she dialed. Martin said, "What happens if somebody else finds him?"

"Mr. Fluffy is at Castaic," Platt said softly to himself. "Why is he there? Why didn't he tap into the controls from the junction box outside the filtration plant, where it makes more sense? Why is he putting himself at risk by being at the pumping plant?"

Martin said, "What happens if somebody else finds him?"

Leslie Bookman was talking calmly on the telephone. Platt frowned hard at the second screen. Then raised his head and nodded. "Yes. Video. That might be it. If he wanted to watch, he'd have to be at the pumping plant to tap into the local closed-circuit security video."

Martin said, "Answer my frigging question. What happens if somebody else finds him?"

Platt keyed something in on the computer keyboard and watched the monitors. He glanced momentarily at Martin.

"Things could go wrong," he said.

He watches video signal in the empty control room.

Jason Keltner is on time, to the minute. It hadn't been easy to break into Municipal Water's Operations Department's main computer, but it hadn't been that difficult, either. Utility companies were never as secure as they liked to think. It had taken only a few days of poking around to find Jason's personnel file, his truck's radio call sign, and the radio frequency used by Municipal's field units.

And then to find the pipeline shutdown schedule and discover Jason's walkthrough and inspection—that was almost a gift!

He arrived at the empty Foothill Pumping Plant earlier in the day and entered through an open back door, found the control room, and acquainted himself with the interior security cameras and the computerized valve controls, and then tuned the desktop two-way radio to the frequency he'd stolen. For the last few hours, he has listened to the radio and sporadically giggled to himself.

The entryway security camera shows Jason, clipboard in hand, unlocking and entering the building. He leaves the view of the entryway camera and appears in the output of the control room camera. Reading from the bank of meters, he makes entries with a pencil on the raised clipboard. He raises one hand and brushes hair away from his eyes, and leaves the control room. Picked up again by the entryway camera, Jason approaches the door that leads down into the huge vault, unlocks it

*with a key from a belt chain, and goes through the door. The entryway
video monitor shows the door swinging slowly closed.*

    *When the clock in the upper right corner of the valve control
computer reads* 15:12, *he types a chain of commands on the keyboard. In a few seconds, two lines of text appear on the screen:*
  V 56 OPEN 2°
  V 57 CLOSED
    *He watches the picture from the security camera. Jason does not
return.*
    He giggles.
    Something moves behind him, and he turns.
    *"Nighty night," says Delahugh, and hits him hard on the back
of the head with something, and his vision goes white–*

44

Light shot through the crack of the opening hatch. Jason turned to face it. His feet were wet in his shoes from the few inches of water on the floor of the pipe.

Norton Platt's face appeared in the half-open hatch. His hand came up and shaded his eyes.

"You in there, Jason?" he said.

"Right here," Jason said. "And glad to see you. What time is it?"

"Three-forty."

"Still a few minutes before the pipeline fills up. You got a rope or something so I can get out of here? The valves closed early for some reason." Jason made a hurry-up gesture with one hand. "Why don't I tell you all about it later, after you get me out of here."

Platt looked displeased. "There's this little problem."

"Uh, can we discuss this later?"

"I'm afraid not," Platt said. There was a scuffling sound behind him. Platt turned to look over his shoulder, and then swung the hatch door completely open. Behind him was Delahugh, and next to Delahugh was a messy-looking man with his hands behind his back. It took Jason a few seconds to realize that the man was BIGVIRG from the Rust Garden show, and that his hands were behind his back because they were tied there. BIGVIRG seemed stunned, and was drooling a little. He was blindfolded, and a second rope was bound around his chest, under his arms.

"As you can see," Platt said, "we do have rope. Unfortunately, it's in use."

"Uh," Jason said.

"You should have been less accommodating when I wouldn't tell you why I was involved. Bad move." He looked at Delahugh and motioned toward the hatch. Delahugh pushed BIGVIRG toward the opening, but BIGVIRG whipped his bound hands awkwardly out of Delahugh's grip and stumbled away from Jason's line of sight.

Delahugh said, "Shit," and moved after him. Scuffling sounds came through the open hatch, and BIGVIRG reappeared, Delahugh behind him. Delahugh seemed to have the ropes that tied BIGVIRG's hands. He pulled sharply on them as BIGVIRG tried to whip away again, and BIGVIRG fell and struck his head against the rim of the hatchway and lay still, panting. The blow rang dully in the pipe. Delahugh put his foot against the back of BIGVIRG's neck.

Jason said, "Why are you doing this?"

Platt said, "With you and Mr. Fluffy here both gone, things tie themselves up in a nice little package." He shrugged. "As I said, you should have been less accommodating." He said to Delahugh, "Put him in."

BIGVIRG thrashed under Delahugh's foot and wailed.

"Christ," Delahugh said, in an annoyed voice. He reached above him and pulled a cargo hook down from some piece of machinery Jason couldn't see. His foot still against BIGVIRG's neck, he slipped the hook through the rope around BIGVIRG's chest.

He looked up and jerked his thumb into the air. The sound of an electric winch came through the hatchway, and the hook line drew taught and began to hoist BIGVIRG to a standing position. Delahugh pulled a forefinger across his own neck and the winch halted. Platt crouched, grabbed the rope that bound BIGVIRG's chest, and pulled; BIGVIRG fell through the hatch, flailing. The hook and rope held, and the winch started again and lowered BIGVIRG to the pipe floor. Platt reached into his back pocket and withdrew a knife. He cut the rope and stood as Delahugh left the hatchway and disappeared outside.

"Too bad," he said. "You only really made one fatal mistake." He put the knife back into his pocket. "Unfortunately for you, that's all it takes." He squinted at something outside the pipe that Jason couldn't see and said, "His turn."

BIGVIRG moaned on the pipe floor.

Platt looked down at the moan. "You can loosen his bonds if you'd like, Jason," he said. "I don't need him tied up down there."

Jason stepped to where BIGVIRG was and untied the knot that bound BIGVIRG's wrists. When his hands were free, BIGVIRG pulled his blindfold off and stared up at the open hatch. Delahugh reappeared with a second person, a tall man with a black hood over his head and a rope tied around it as a gag. Blonde hair stuck out under the hood.

Platt stood and loosened the gag. "You have my sincere apologies," he said to the hooded man. "I never like to lose civilians."

"Who the hell are you people?" came a deep voice from the behind the gag, frightened, with a pronounced drawl.

"Rick?" Jason said. "Is that you?"

"Jason? What're they gonna do? I'm just here to do stress tests. What the hell's going on? Please, don't do this."

"Platt," Jason said, "What do you want with Rick?"

"Wrong place at the wrong time," Platt said. "You didn't tell me he'd be here."

"I don't know every goddamn thing that every goddamn supervisor decides to do during a line shutdown," Jason yelled. Delahugh snagged a second hook onto the tall man's bonds. He motioned to someone unseen and the winch started up again, raising the tall man a little off the ground.

"What the hell are you doing?" the deep voice cried through the gag, panicked. The sound of the winch changed and the man moved forward, over the open hatchway, and began to lower.

"Platt," Jason yelled. "He doesn't have anything to do with this!"

The winch rope jiggled as its payload struggled."Hey!" the deep voice yelled through the hood. "You assholes, what the hell's going on?" He found the edge of the hatchway with one foot and blocked his descent momentarily, but Delahugh knocked the foot away.

The tall man bucked and struggled. "Oh, god ..." When he reached bottom, Platt cut the rope. He began to close the hatch, and then opened it again and said, "Oh, I might as well introduce you to somebody." He motioned, and the Preacher appeared in the open hatchway and said, "Hello, Jason." He shifted his gaze to BIGVIRG and said, "And hello to you, my good friend. How nice to see you down there."

BIGVIRG wailed.

"Platt," Jason said, "you suck."

Platt closed the hatch.

45

There was a slight breeze and a faint whistling sound. Jason said, "What time do you think it is?"

"Oh, god, I don't know."

"It must be at least three forty-five."

"Oh Jesus!" the deep voice wailed. "Help, please somebody!"

"Keep yelling, Rick," Jason said. "Just in case."

"Why? Why bother? The only people here are the ones who want us here, and the other crews are all doing walkthroughs at other sites! That longhaired bastard made me radio the plant that we were safely out of the pipeline!"

"Christ, Rick."

"He had a gun, Jason! What the hell was I gonna do?"

"Help!" Jason yelled. "Help! Hello? Anybody?"

In a tone of hysterical disbelief, the deep voice yelled, "Jason, we're going to drown down here!" The yell reverberated farther away, subsequent echoes gaining resonance and ringing crazily.

"Shut up, Rick," Jason said shakily. "Sorry, but just shut up. I don't want to hear it. I'm sorry you got involved, but I don't want to hear it right now. There's no way to tell how far sound will carry in this pipeline. It might reach a few miles to the next crew."

"I'm sorry." There was still a hysterical edge to the voice.

"Hello!" Jason yelled. "Is anybody there?" His voice echoed down the dark pipeline.

"Jason, if there was another crew to hear, they'd be yelling back." The scrape of a shoe was followed by a solid thwack, as though Rick had kicked the pipe's interior wall with a heavy shoe. The reverberation was deep and short. "God *damn*! I don't want to drown!"

Jason felt around near where BIGVIRG had landed on the pipe floor. His hands found a shirt collar and lifted. There was only deadweight; no resistance. "You did this, you coward. Guess I was right about you." He let go. "Loser."

A moan came from where the deadweight had dropped. It rose in pitch and repeated eerily as the echoes intersected each other. Jason groped again in the total darkness and found the rope and hook still caught in BIGVIRG's bonds. He detached the hook and hung it over his right front jeans pocket.

Another solid thump reverberated in the pipe, followed by a soft scrabbling from Jason's right. "Open, damn you! Open! Help me, Jason. Try to get hold of the edge of the valve."

Jason felt in front of him and found another pair of hands there at the square edge of a flapper valve, a large, slightly convex disk the same diameter as the pipe that pivoted on large pins to control the flow of water. He ran his hands over it until he found purchase along the edge where it gapped an inch away from the rim of the valve seat, and pulled with all his strength. The valve didn't move.

"Goddamn!"he said in frustration.

He remembered the grappling hook.

"Rick, do you still have that hook they lowered you with?"

"Fuck! Yeah!"

Jason unhooked his and tried to force it into the groove

with his hands, grunting. Just above him, he heard the same sounds of metal levering against metal. Every scrape and clink rang down the length of the pipeline, each echo modulating the last, twisting into a high-pitched scatter of sound. After what seemed like a few minutes, Jason stopped prying and stood panting near the valve. The man next to him followed his lead.

"Jase, forget it," the deep voice said, "we can't open it with our fingers or with these things. We can't open it from here at all."

The moaning from BIGVIRG continued, echoing weirdly.

Jason shouted, "Well, what do you want me to do? Sit here until they reopen the pipeline?" He flung the hook blindly away from the voices. It clanked against prestressed concrete somewhere. The echoes bounced and intersected and clashed and died. "Where is that asshole?" Jason walked unsteadily toward the moaning until his shoe bumped into something soft. "You bastard," he shouted, "you did this!"

The moaning stopped and a broken voice whined, "It's not my fault!"

Jason's reached down and his right hand touched shirt fabric. He grabbed it. "I'm gonna kill this SOB! Gimme that damn grappling hook!"

A sob broke from the pipe floor.

The shirt shifted. Across the pipe, the deep voice drawled, "Why do I have to die? Why?"

Jason said, "Because you were here. You saw Platt and Delahugh here, and they can't let you talk."

"But I wouldn't tell. I wouldn't!"

"Rick, it's too late."

"I wouldn't tell!"

"They can't hear you. Or if they can, they don't care." Jason found the shirtfront of the body on the pipe floor and tapped it. "Nice trap, idiot. I'm glad you got caught in it." He found the side of the pipe with his left hand and squatted carefully, putting his right hand down for balance in the inch-deep water. He felt a small, gentle ridge under the water where there was a seam in the pipe. "You couldn't have trapped us in the Santa Monica line?" he said. "We could maybe kick our way through a seam in that cast iron, it's so old. But not this prestressed. This stuff's got concrete and steel cords and God knows what else. They drive the tour buses through a section of this same stuff, up top. The first bus driver that did it didn't think his bus would fit through, but it did." He grimaced in the darkness and shook his head. "What the hell am I talking about?"

"Goddamn tour buses."

"Sorry."

"We're really dead, aren't we?"

"Yes," Jason said. "I think we really are. But at least we're taking this piece of garbage with us."

The moan from the body on the pipe floor built into words and said, "Fuck you." It didn't sound convincing; the voice shuddered.

"Fuck yourself," Jason said. "If you could do anything right, you wouldn't be in here."

"I do things right," the voice said after a few seconds. "You're the one, not me. It's your fault, not mine."

"Yeah, I forgot; you're a real man. You get real girls," Jason said. "And you never hot chat on the Net, either. What a man."

After a pause, the voice wheedled, "I got your girlfriend Monica, what you got to say about that?"

"What do you mean, 'got her?' Monica killed herself on stage. You had nothing to do with it."

"Did so."

There was a rustle on the other side of the pipe. "You killed Jason's girlfriend?"

"I got her with her tits hanging out and cut her up good!"

The sound of hard breathing came across the pipe. "Jesus Christ!" the deep voice said shakily. "Jesus Christ!"

Wheezing, BIGVIRG said, "I killed the bitch! She had it coming!"

Jason felt his blood rise, but said nothing.

Another shifting sound from the pipe floor, and he said, cagily, "Got the whore with her tits hanging out."

A little hot burst of red, up through his sternum. Jason said, "Listen, shitbag. I don't care how much time we have left. If you don't want yours shortened, you refer to her with respect."

"Got her with her tits hanging out. She was a fucking whore and everybody knew it and I killed the bitch like she deserved."

Jason found the shirtfront again. It squirmed, but he found purchase on the fabric, felt around a little, and aimed a punch at the vicinity of a fat stomach. The punch sank in, and drew a pneumatic grunt and then a sob.

After a few moments, Jason said, "Is that whistling sound louder?" He let go of the shirtfront. Ragged, labored wheezing came from the pipe floor.

A few seconds later, the deep voice drawled, "Yeah. Oh, shit. That's got to be the air vents." Thuds reverberated in the pipe, as though Rick were again trying to kick through the concrete. "They must be reopening the line, and the water's forcing the air out through the vents. Help! Somebody help, damn you! Help!" Metal scrapes and clinks came from the direction of the valve.

"Jason, help me with this valve! We gotta try again."

Jason got up awkwardly in the dark and walked with tiny steps, hands outstretched, toward the sounds until he touched the cool metal of the valve. He found the square edge again and pulled as hard and as long as he could. Nothing moved. He bumped into something soft and said, "Sorry."

"Jase, it ain't opening. Hey you! Get over here and help."

There were soft splashes and grunts from BIGVIRG, and then a hand touched Jason's cheek. Jason jerked his head away and said, "Get a grip on the edge and pull."

The whistling was definitely louder, and the pipe surface vibrated gently. Jason strained to open the valve and heard the other two doing the same. It didn't move at all.

"Goddamn remote control valves." The drawl seemed stronger. "We coulda maybe opened the old-fashioned ones."

"How much time do you think we have?" Jason said.

The response was shaky, "Uh, let me think. Uh ... let's see, at that rate, and, uh, it can't be any nearer than, uh, let's see ..." Jason could hear fast, shallow breathing. "Uh, about ten minutes before the water gets here."

Jason found the hand that had touched his cheek and held it firmly around the wrist. He jerked it. "Hope you're happy," he said.

The wrist struggled to break free. Then the voice insisted, "It's not my fault! You forced me! I had no choice!"

"You had plenty of choice." He jerked the wrist. "You're just wacko. You think you've got power over women, power over money, power over dangerous people. But really, when you really get down to it, all you've really done is play with yourself while you look at a computer screen, and get yourself caught in your own trap and drown in a pipeline. I mean, what the hell are you doing here? *You got away!* What kind of idiot goes and gets himself caught after he's gotten away?"

The wrist yanked free, and something splashed loudly a few feet away. "You don't know anything."

"I know what a big man you think you are. I also know what a fuckup you really are."

"That's what you think! I have more money than you'll ever have! I can do anything I want! I can go anywhere and kill anyone I want to, just like I killed that bitch!"

"Sure you did."

"I did! I switched her lasers and rigged her computer to kill her. I did it!"

Jason didn't say anything.

"She had it coming!" the voice screamed. "She had it coming!" The scream bounced and careened down the pipeline in shrill dissonance.

"That still doesn't explain this money you supposedly have. Where would you possibly get that kind of money?"

"I have ways," the voice said smugly. "It just shows how much you know. I have more than you'll ever see in my hotel room right now."

"Not likely," Jason said, "Last I heard, salaries for chronic masturbators were on the decline."

There was another shifting, scuffling sound, and a whir of air. It took Jason a moment to realize that he had almost been hit in the face by a fist, but before he could step back, another blow came and connected. It wasn't a good punch, but it startled him, and he fell blindly back into the blackness and landed hard on his back in the water with his wind knocked out. The fat body fell atop him, yowling wordlessly. Gasping for breath, Jason hit straight up with the heel of his hand and smashed into something hard, maybe a jaw. The yowling broke momentarily, and then got closer, and got wilder, and Jason felt teeth through his shirt, biting his shoulder. He pulled his knee up sharply and connected with something, and slammed his forearm against the head. There was a yelp of pain, and Jason shoved the body off him and found his way to his feet.

"You got no money," he gasped. "You got nothing. You *are* nothing. Garbage."

"I told you not to call me that!"

"I heard you, Garbage. Even if they haven't found your money yet, Garbage, they will. You can bet on it, Garbage. They're not going to just let it go that easily with you out of the way, Garbage."

"They won't find it!"

"They will."

The whistling seemed higher in pitch, and a soft spray drifted past, dampening Jason's skin. Across the pipeline the deep voice pleaded, "Please. Please stop."

"Rick," Jason said, breathing hard. "I gotta ask you something. When the water gets here, will it be a big wall, or will the pipe just fill up gradually?"

"I don't know, man. Goddamn, I hate waiting for it!" His voice rose and he yelled, "Just get it over with!"

The deep drawl echoed and died. "Where's that accent from, Rick?" Jason said.

"Huh?" Distracted.

"The drawl. Where's it from?"

"Uh ..." Jason could almost see him shaking his head to clear it. "Georgia. Why?"

"I just thought I ought to know, I guess. I didn't know."

"It's from Georgia. My kids grew up here, so they don't have it. Oh, Christ. My kids."

"I'm sorry, Rick. I'm sorry you got dragged into this."

"What the hell, Jase, right?"

"If you hadn't been here when they came for me and Garbage—"

"I said don't call me that!"

"—you'd be back at the breakroom now, probably."

A weak laugh. "Or hiding from Don, probably."

Something clanged dully a long way past the valve, and the vibration of the pipe increased. A deep, steady roar began, thrumming through the pipe all around them.

46

The slight breeze gained strength, ruffling Jason's hair, and the whistling sound rose in pitch and volume and became more strident.

The human sounds in the immediate section of the pipe became more difficult to discern. The sound of a body shifting across from Jason came faintly. "Anybody got anything they want to confess? This looks like the time for it."

Jason said, "Like what, Rick?"

"Well ..." There was another shifting noise. "Well, okay, like I shouldn't have been unfaithful to old Lois. It only happened twice and it didn't mean nothing neither time, but it was wrong and I still shouldn't of done it. Both times was with two different girls, so it wasn't like a real affair, you know?"

Jason didn't know what to say.

"But I was a pretty good father, I think. *I* think I was, anyway."

Jason said, "I bet you were."

The roar didn't increase in volume, but the wind grew in strength. Jason said, "Feel the wind picking up?"

"The water must be passing the last of the upstream air vents, so there's nowhere for the air to go but here."

Jason said, "Maybe the air pressure here will rise enough that we pass out before we drown."

"If we could only get that other valve open, the totally closed one, it might wash us into the forebay, but they're not opening that one until tomorrow."

"Maybe they'll change the schedule."

The deep voice said, "No way."

Jason said, "Let's try to reach the overhead hatch."

The deep voice said, "Hell, let's try it. Get on my shoulders."

Jason reached forward and found the coarse cloth of a work shirt."Kneel down a little." The cloth moved down. Jason found shoulders and a head, got behind them, and settled himself onto the shoulders. "Okay," he said. "You can stand up."

The giddy sensation of motion in the blackness threw his balance off and he almost fell off.

The deep voice below him said, "You okay?"

Disoriented, he said, "Yeah, just hurry up. Here goes nothing."

Jason felt the body below him struggling for balance. It seemed to sway, but he wasn't sure whether that was just his lack of orientation.

"Can you reach it?"

From the pipe floor came, "Oh God, the water's deeper!"

Jason reached up, tense and wobbling. His thighs tightened as he tried to stay balanced in the increasing wind. He stretched his hands up as far as he could, but felt nothing. He detached the hook from his pocket and arced it blindly overhead at arm's length, hitting nothing.

"I can't reach it."

Another sickening motion, and a splashing sound.

"Okay, Jase, get off me."

Holding the shoulder he was on, Jason felt with one foot for the floor, found it, and got off the shoulder. His socks soaked through at the ankle with cold water that quickly filled his shoes. "It's deeper."

"It'll be deeper yet."

There were sniffles and a sob from the pipe floor. "I don't want to die!"

"You're the only one here who deserves to," Jason said.

"Please! Somebody help me!"

"Like somebody helped Monica?"

"She was a teasing slut!"

"There's a crime," Jason said. "What did you do with your new money? I bet you couldn't even think of anything to do with it."

"I still have it!" Screaming, the voice said, "I'll give it to you, just let me out!"

"No chance," Jason said. "They'll just find it without you. Probably already have. You are a loser."

"She forced me! She forced me to! She got what she had coming!"

"What did she have coming?"

"She knew too much!"

"About what?"

"Everything! About everything!"

"Like what?"

"I told her everything!"

"Like what, I asked you!"

The deep voice said, "Let it go, Jase; it doesn't matter now."

"You're right," Jason said. "This idiot doesn't know anything. He's just looking for excuses before he dies."

"I know a lot."

"Like what, you pathetic little shit?"

"What about you, you loser? You and your little whore wife?"

Jason said, "What do you know about her?"

Smugly. "I know a lot."

The swirling water rose quickly to Jason's lower calves, and the wind and the whistling noise disappeared abruptly, and then resumed in the opposite direction. The low roar stayed constant.

"It's past the last air vent," Jason said.

"I know all about you, Jason Keltner."

"That makes one of us," Jason said. "So, tell me what you know about me, smart man."

"I know you can't even keep your best friend from fucking your wife."

After a moment, Jason said, "That's hardly classified information."

"I have power over you, 'Jase.'"

"You have your hand in your pants, little boy."

"I have power."

"You have delusions."

"I have more money than you've seen in your whole life!"

"Enjoy it for the next few minutes," Jason said.

"It's mine!"

"Right. Just like you killed Monica because she knew too much."

"She forced me! She made me tell her. She led me on. I had to do it. She made me do it. I had to kill her. She got what she had coming!"

Jason's ears popped, and the water rose faster, to his knees. A low singsong came from across the pipe, and Jason realized that it was a prayer. He tried to think of one, but didn't know any.

"They won't find it!" The voice was hysterical. The water rose to Jason's mid-thigh and the current pulled him off balance. He fell and breathed water.

"Where'd you hide it?" Jason asked.

Gasping in hysteria, the voice said, "They ... won't ... find it! I slipped it under the carpeting where the maids ... where no one never ... no one will ever find it!"

"Under the carpeting!" Jason shouted incredulously. "It's already gone, you idiot! Maids? What was it, a motel room? You incredible loser!" The water rose to his chest and lifted him from the pipe floor. He tread water. "Game over, my petite little kumquat; you fucking lose!"

The voice shrilled, "No! It's—" and was cut sharply off by the sound of inhaled water. Jason heard a frenzied splashing. After a gasp: "It'll still be there!"

"Help!" screamed the other voice.

"Hang on, Rick," Jason said. Floating, he couldn't gauge the rise of the water in the darkness until his head bumped gently against the upper curve of the concrete pipe. He could hear the others sputtering and thrashing as the overhead pipe surface pressed closer. He found the entry hatchway and banged on it and clawed at its sealed edges, and felt the other two sets of hands scrabbling beside his. The hatch mechanism was on the other side, outside.

The airspace got smaller. Jason was forced to turn his head sideways to breathe, and as he took in a lungful of the last of the air, the cold water rose past his eye and then past his nose and his other eye, and filled his inner ear.

The airspace disappeared.

Jason fought panic. The low roar became duller as water displaced the air in his ears. The screaming stopped. It was almost quiet.

47

A series of grinding creaks reverberated in the pipe. Jason aimed in the direction he thought was up and kicked his legs. He thought he felt air, and kicked twice more, and his head broke the surface of the water. He opened his eyes; there was dim light in the pipe.

Another head broke the surface several feet from him, but despite the slight lifting of darkness, he couldn't make out the features. The head wailed softly between violently shuddering breaths.

"Mr. Fluffy, I presume," Jason gasped.

There was a splash and loud breathing at the far end of the pipe, near the closed valve, and a deep, unsteady voice drawled, "Jason?"

"I'm okay. How are you?"

The drawl intensified to a burlesque. "I'm jes' okey-dokey, y'all! Can we'uns stop this goldurn drownin' now?"

"Hoo doggies," Jason said.

A last creak sounded and the entry hatch opened. Light streamed in, blinding Jason. He squinted against it and then closed his eyes.

"You're alive," Norton Platt said. "What a surprise."

"Turncoat," Jason said. "Lousy longhair commie pinko mercenary running dog."

"It's a living," Platt said. "Your pupils are dilated. Give it a little bit."

The sounds of hyperventilation came from where Jason had seen the first head break the surface. Still breathless, Jason said, "Get Mr. Fluffy out first."

Platt lowered something and there were a lot of splashes and then the hyperventilating sounds rose through the hatchway. Jason opened his eyes just enough to see without much discomfort and looked at Robert's serious face bobbing in the water next to him under wet bottle-blonde hair. A chain ladder hung down from the hatchway, and a faint buzz droned outside the hatch.

"Nice going, Rick," he said.

"Thanks," Robert said. He sounded insincere, as he always sounded to Jason after a performance.

The chain ladder was pulled up.

"Hey," Jason yelled weakly, "Let the ladder down." His voice didn't echo.

The ladder didn't come back down. "Hey," he called again, treading water. "Any time, you guys." He opened his eyes a little more. Through the open hatch, he could make out a spare latticework of bare two-by-fours and four-by-fours in front of a blue sky.

The slender figure that appeared in the hatchway was not Norton Platt.

"Bravo," Pascal said. "*Bravissimo*. Thank you for your efforts on my behalf."

Jason glanced at Robert.

"What do you mean," Robert said wearily.

"Goodbye, " Pascal said. He disappeared from the hatchway.

"Hey!" Jason yelled. "Hey, what's going on?"

When no answer came, he yelled again, "Somebody want to lower the ladder?"

"In a minute, Jason," Platt's voice called. "We're a little busy being detained at gunpoint right now."

"Was that Pascal?" Robert said to Jason.

"Yes."

"I think he's taking Mr. Fluffy away," Robert said a minute later.

"That's how it sounds."

Car doors opened and closed somewhere not too far away, and the engine started. Platt appeared in the hatchway as the sound of tires on dirt faded. "Watch out," he said, and pushed the chain ladder through the hatchway. It splashed into the water. Robert climbed out first, and Jason followed him up onto a rough plywood deck. The droning buzz he'd heard inside the pipe came from a large red gasoline generator that sat stolidly on the dirt a hundred feet from the deck. On the other side of the generator was an unfinished house with studs and no walls. Beyond that was a row of similarly skeletal houses. The white cargo truck was parked nearby on the dirt, next to Martin's CVCC and a large red tanker truck.

A flimsy-looking plywood shack had been erected at one corner of the deck, and a thick orange cable from the generator had been run over the dirt into it. A rudimentary door hung crookedly on hinges.

"He took him away?" Jason said.

Platt said, "Yes," and handed each of them a very large Care Bears beach towel. Platt had a walkie-talkie on his belt.

Jason looked down as he toweled himself. The hatchway was visible through a square hole in the rough deck. Two dozen cables of different weights and colors ran in an orderly fashion from inside the shack at the corner of the deck into the square hole, and then splayed out in different directions.

"How'd it go?" Jason asked.

"Fine, once we got him in there with you. We had a little complication when he took control of the valves from on-site instead of where we thought he'd be, but Vince got there pretty fast, knocked him out, and brought him here."

"And you decided to go ahead and dump him in the fake pipe instead of just taking him into custody, even though he'd changed the plan by being in the wrong place?"

"It was a judgment call. We had him, but I still wanted to know where he'd hidden the money. And though the confession isn't admissible in court, it's still good to have. And anyway," Platt grinned, "style counts. Why waste a great setup?"

Jason looked around for the Preacher. "Where's Reverend Billy?"

"He left with Mr. Pascal."

"It was nice of Pascal to let us borrow him." Jason finished toweling himself. "So you got it all?"

"Audio and video, which Mr. Pascal took at gunpoint. He's got a dupe. We still have the originals."

"Doesn't sound like a fair trade to me. We get to use his construction site and Reverend Billy, but he takes Mr. Fluffy and the tapes?"

The door to the enclosure swung open and Martin came out with a green canvas bag.

"Everybody okay?"

Robert said, "Yes."

"I'm fine," Jason said. "How are you?"

Martin beat one open hand rhythmically over his heart. "Man, I thought I was gonna have a heart attack a couple of times. It's good to see you guys in person."

"Yup," Jason said.

"Here's some dry clothes," Martin said, handing the bag to Jason.

Platt's walkie-talkie crackled and said in Leslie Bookman's voice, "All done, Norton. It looks good."

Platt detached the walkie-talkie from his belt and said,

"Okay, thanks," into it. He put it back on his belt and said, "Bookman's been out at the entrance to this housing tract. Pascal and Fluffy have been detained there by Detective Emily Johns, who incidentally sends her regards. Mr. Pascal will be out by suppertime, if you eat late. Mr. Fluffy will be transferred to the proper Federal types, who have been looking for him for a long time."

"Emily," Jason said.

Delahugh's head poked out of the little enclosure and he said, "Got it, Norton. Motel-Six in Redlands."

Platt smiled. "Good," he said. "Now we're done." To Jason, he said, "The money's been found. Now Mr. Pascal probably won't feel he has to kill you."

"It's Happy Day in Castaic," Jason said.

"Get changed," Platt said. "We have to load out."

It took three hours to pack up the sound and video equipment that was in the deck enclosure. Most of it went into blue padded racks that looked like the ones Platt had set up in the front room of the Manor. Then a crew of four women arrived with a flatbed truck and a crane. They pumped the water back into the red tanker truck from which it had originally come, and then hoisted the pipe with the crane. The pipe was twenty feet long, and dirt fell from it as it lifted. Platt detached a speaker array while the massive pipe hovered, twisting gently, over the ground. He loaded the speakers into his cargo van, and then detached a dozen contact microphones from the exterior of the pipe and stored them carefully in individual cases.

The crew secured the pipe to the flatbed and left. Delahugh and Leslie Bookman followed them out in the red tanker truck. Jason made a point of thanking them before they went, and Leslie Bookman smiled disconcertingly at him again.

"The whistling sound worked great," Jason said, as he

helped Platt load the last of the racks into the back of the white truck. The rack contained digital signal processing equipment that had created the echo effects inside the pipe. "I couldn't hear any equipment hiss at all."

"I heard some in the monitor mix," Platt said, "but it was masked well enough down in the pipe. Will you be fired for abandoning your route when they find your truck at the Foothill plant?"

"Nah. You have to murder a supervisor or steal a computer to get fired from Municipal. But I'm quitting anyway. That job's not right for me."

"That's what I thought," said Platt. "I'm glad to hear you're quitting. Line up something else first, though." He pulled the cargo door down.

"Good advice. I probably won't follow it."

Platt locked the cargo door with a padlock that hung from the hasp. "Need a ride?"

"Going toward Pasadena?"

"Sure."

"Sure."

In the cab of the white truck, headed South on I-5, Platt said, "Well, it worked. How do you feel?"

Jason said, "Monica's still dead."

"That's all?"

"I feel like that should be all."

"Is it?"

"No."

"What else?"

"A little incomplete." Jason tried unsuccessfully not to grin. "And maybe a little great."

A few minutes later, he said, "I have to ask again."

"Why I'm involved?"

"Yes."

"People have been looking for your Mr. Fluffy for a long time, for a lot of reasons."

"And that's the only reason you're involved?"

Platt pursed his lips. A mile later, he said, "Remember when you asked why I knew of Paul Reno?"

"Yeah."

"Remember what I said?"

"Something about keeping an eye out for new talent," Jason said.

Platt looked at him pointedly. "I found some," he said. "You did a good job. I may call you some time if something comes up that I could use you for."

Jason couldn't think of anything to say for a few minutes. Then he said, "So Monica wasn't your friend?"

"No."

"And you left that message in her MUSE mailbox just as what? Bait?"

"Yes."

"And I bit."

"Yes."

Jason said, "I guess I don't mind that. So, what are you? FBI?"

Platt smiled enigmatically.

"Oh, come on," Jason said. "Give it a rest."

Platt chuckled and said, "Okay. No, I'm not FBI. I ... freelance."

Jason said, "Oh."

"We should do a post-game wrap-up soon."

"Not yet, though," Jason said. He looked back at the road. "There's still something I need to finish."

48

It was Open Mike Night at the E-Bar, and Jason was sitting outside in the cool evening, at the table farthest from the stage, wondering how much farther he could move the table, when Paul came around the corner in his leather jacket and sat down.

"You must like this place a lot," Paul said.

"Thanks for coming."

Paul wasn't having it. "Is this an apology?"

"Not exactly."

"Then what?"

"I'm sure you've heard this and that lately."

"Yeah? And?"

"Let me get to it at my own speed."

Paul looked casually around the alley. "It's your dime."

"Things seem to have sorted themselves out. The Preacher's still preaching, so I assume he and Pascal worked something out. Probably the Preacher helping out at the fake pipeline earned some brownie points. I got my killer, and Norton Platt says he won't be seeing daylight for a long time. Turns out Fluffy's done a lot of lousy things to a lot of people."

"Is there a point to this?"

"Nobody still knows what Mr. Fluffy's real name is."

"So what? I'm not that interested in stuff I already know. What do you want?"

"So now I'm back to usual. Well, almost usual. My car still thinks it's a convertible, and I'm unemployed, and I hurt all over, and my piano's broken, but I'm basically back to normal."

Paul looked bored.

Jason said, "Except that there's one thing that never really got tied up."

"Oh yeah? What's that?"

"I still don't know who shot at Robert and me on the porch."

"Really."

"Yeah. Strangest thing. Nobody seems to want to take credit for it."

"Does this conversation go somewhere?"

"Oh, maybe not. It's just that it doesn't quite fit with everything else. I mean, first of all, it happened before my rear window got smashed, so it doesn't fit nicely in a logical crescendo, if you see what I mean. And then there's the fact that the shooter used a rifle."

"Why's that strange?"

"Say you want to shoot somebody from the street, and they're on a porch twenty, thirty feet away. What do you use?"

"Maybe a rifle. What's wrong with that?"

"A mediocre shooter would use a shotgun."

"Maybe he was a good shooter."

"A good shooter wouldn't have missed. Two big dumb stationary targets, thirty feet max, with a rifle, in plain sight."

"So?"

"So why would someone pick a weapon perfect for shooting accurately, drive up in front of the house, and miss? It's almost as though they weren't trying to hit us."

"Shooting at you and trying not to hit you."

"I know." Jason raised his hands. "I know. It sounds dumb. Bear with me here." He put his hands on the table. "It's almost as though somebody wanted to scare me away from danger."

"Who would do that?"

"Good question. Any ideas what the answer might be?"

"Nope."

Jason looked at him for a while. Paul gazed calmly back.

"Okay," Jason said, finally. "I figured it was dumb."

"Yeah," Paul said. "It sounds dumb to me, too. Anything else?"

"No."

"I mean, as long as we're not friends, we don't really have any reason to hang after we're done talking."

"You're right."

A little while later, Paul said, "This band sucks."

"They sure do," Jason said.